This book is dedicated to: -

Mark Richards -1953 – 2023. A friend greatly missed.

Grandad Webb - I'm not just cashiering anymore.

Grandad Davies - My little nib. Miss you every day.

# THE DISAPPEARANCE OF PETER MARKHAM

DONNA MORFETT

RAMPART BOOKS



ISBN 978-1-915778-33-8

# THE DISAPPEARANCE OF PETER MARKHAM

# 1

'Shut your snivelling—will you? You pathetic little man. You're doing my head in.'

It was a cold night, sharp on the breath. This had taken more courage than was thought. His cries, though, were spoiling what should have been a pleasure. Suddenly, this had become serious. No turning back now. That stage had passed. Methodically winding the duct tape around the man's wrists as he twisted and turned, came the reminder of why this had to be done. Strong, deft hands had trained for this. Taken him unaware and shoving him into the car was quickly followed by taping his feet. The shock, though, had done the trick. His expression when he was jumped was something to be captured in a picture. He did not know what was going on. At first, he thought this was a hoax designed by his wife, yet he was still uncertain if he should laugh until he saw the knife.

'What, what are you doing?' he cried, his eyes riveted with terror while his face seemed to say, *Oh God, please let this be a joke*. 'You can't,' he kept crying. 'Do you know who I am?'

He was manhandled as if he was nothing. 'Why don't

you answer me? Let me go, you arsehole.' The worst was he kept spitting, aiming for the face. But it didn't matter. The mind was saying in that steady rhythmic voice of a train. *I have him. At last, I have him.*

Face down, his hands were secured behind his back, squiggling, and still complaining.

"What have I done wrong? Why are you doing this to me?" Came back with no answer. Moving stealthily, everything had been practised—practised and practised. Secure now. The first stage was over, and it was a relief although the heartbeat was faster. Satisfied, standing, and looking down into the man's eyes and smirking because his teeth chattered through the cold, or was it fear? Hard to tell, but a line of sweat on his forehead was significant. *Yes, you should be scared, you bastard.*

'Let me go. If you don't, you will be in serious trouble.'

Came again with no answer. Kneeling into his spine, pulling his head up by his hair, the last piece of tape was slapped over it. Peace from the whining. His eyes, though, were trying to work out who his attacker was.

Although it felt like forever, the entire snatch and run had taken less than five minutes. Like an automaton, it had been practised to the smallest detail to get it right. For several months, without realising Peter Markham had been followed. Every bit of his routine and behaviour was noted. Learning where every CCTV camera was situated, which worked and which didn't, what car he drove, and where would be the best place to make the move. Everything had been expected to be in control.

That's why, on that late autumnal November evening, when Peter stepped out of the Indian restaurant waving goodbye to the staff was going to be his very last night of freedom.

Recently, the clocks had changed, making it pitch black.

The restaurant was on a country road with little exterior lighting. The rest of the car park was in darkness. Something like this wouldn't have worked in the summertime.

Peter had been drinking, not to excess. Strict about alcohol, but he liked a glass of red with his meals, especially after a long day of fighting suppliers and errant staff. Mellowed enough now not to pay strict attention to his surroundings, and in a cheerful mood—life had been good to him as he walked the swaggering walk of someone who had made it.

Unlocking his car, Peter had chucked his jacket into the passenger seat, already seeing himself in his bedroom, never believing for one moment that someone was waiting for him. Quick, dramatic—a shock. A strong and determined hand had passed over his mouth as he was danced to the passenger door: one push and he was in. He didn't know what was happening, spitting little sounds of surprise. Whoever was holding him was strong, resolved. The knife stripped him of any control. Oh yes, this went very well.

A suitable location where everything fell into place. Now success, and time to afford a breath. Everything worked according to plan. Time for a celebration, but not the type that Peter Markham was used to.

# 2

For the sins of the past, this was Peter Markham's atonement, stripping him naked and then positioning him spreadeagled working quickly almost without thought—this had become a crucifixion. Bang, bang, bang: nails were driven in by hate and revenge. How wonderful this was listening to his muffled screams as the nail hammered into his hands. Isn't this wonderful, Peter? 'Aren't you happy? If not, you are so ungrateful.'

But why was he complaining? He had greedily taken the Rohypnol-laced water. Oh well. The first nail through his hand awoke him, but Peter was still too groggy to fight. This work was bliss. But Peter needed to be fully awake for the rest of what was in store.

Nearly time to live out those fantasies.

Working systematically, Peter's clothes were put into a drum. There must be no fibre evidence for the police to find. Removing the white suit, the type worn by decorators, or ironically crime scene investigators, from the bag, and now double-gloved, next the hair was tucked in by a net. All precautions were taken not to leave trace evidence behind. Even the eyebrows were shaven, and the current ones were drawn on. It would look too obvious to cut off the eyelashes in case they fell as DNA evidence, but this was taking it a step too far for day-to-day appearance.

Already, Peter's clothes were in the drum. When everything was finished, the white suit and mask would follow before setting it alight. The only sound to be heard now was the sound of concentrated breathing.

The rest of the tools were carefully laid out so Peter could see them while his eyes went everywhere. Deliberately holding each one up to his eyeline for inspection before placing it down made for smiles, while watching his eyes widen as he guessed what was about to happen next. Those pitiful noises escaping from his duct-taped mouth were a stimulant to go on.

'Oh yes, my friend, we are here for some serious work. What to choose? Ah yes, the bolt cutters.' Holding them up again for his inspection before snapping the handles together, removing any doubt of what they could do. His face became horrified while his eyes were expressive. No person in their sane mind would do this to another.

Starting with his little finger on his left hand was quickly cut off at the first joint with a crunch. A surprise to both of them that this had actually been done. It was a dream or a nightmare, depending on whose perspective. Working around his left hand, the echo of his screams shivered through every cell in the body. Peter's body became rigid and straight, just like a board or as if he just electrocuted. Of course, it must be agony, but oh, such fun.

Could it get any worse? Yes, it could and will. Now Peter was trying to buck his hips, anything to escape the pain, an annoying interruption, but the job had to be finished. Clamping the cutters over each digit and closing them shut was practised on vegetables—especially carrots. Carrots were easy, fingers messy, but it gave a good idea of where they fell. These needed burning to make it difficult for identification. Once you got into a rhythm, it was easy.

Now for the next hand. Walking around his head, bending down, his right hand was grabbed. 'I'm afraid you won't be playing the piano again, Peter; we all have to give up something for the next stage.' Again, the tape moved in and out quickly as Peter tried to control his breathing; he knew already what was going to happen next. Fascinating how blood pumped out of the stumps. A good job he didn't know there was going to be another round of joint shortening.

Stepping over him, his eyes widened in anticipation as the gag was ripped off. He stared convincingly in horror.

'Who are you? Why are you doing this to me?' He wheezed, terrified. 'You must be mad.'

'You don't remember me, do you? Well, I am disappointed Peter. Very disappointed. It will become very clear to you soon. Don't worry. I have a few small jobs to do first. I'm sure you understand. I've been waiting a long time for this, since 2007, if that helps your memory.'

2007? What did that mean? Already, the second stage was in progress. A knife to make minor cuts into his flesh ready for the vinegar. The tang of the vinegar was strong and stung the eyes, but worth it, so wonderful to see the pain rippling across Peter's face when it caught another cut.

Smiling and pleased with what had been achieved, but that was enough for today for both of them. He mustn't pass out. There is always a remedy for everything. A high-energy bar was rammed into his mouth and then massaged his throat to swallow. Messy eater. After it was finished, another roll of duct tape slapped over his mouth.

In this bag of tricks was a recent purchase. Again, holding this out so Peter could see. He looked confused until the metal tool was turned on. Gas for a blowtorch. His eyes went wide when it was lit.

'No, please, for mercy's sake,' he cried; this was just about distinguishable. 'Please, I will give you anything. Please,' his tragic eyes sobbed.

'I don't enjoy doing this to you, Peter, but it's for your benefit; we don't want you getting infections.' The smell of burnt flesh filled the air from each cauterised stump. He bawled like a baby, shrieking and howling before passing out.

Collecting all the fingertips and singing while working, one should always be hygienic and tidy. Counting the pink distal phalanxes, these were tossed into the drum, pitter-patter, counting to make sure none were missed. Heave-ho, all the tools went into the boot of Peter's car before starting up. I hope his little wife hasn't panicked yet and reported him missing.

# 3

In a quiet office, DI Cora Snitton was absorbed in paperwork. Most of the staff were out on follow-ups or filling in final paperwork for their cases. A couple of the new staff, Darcey and Luke, graduate coppers, were working in the office. Cora had moved to major crimes in the last couple of months and was still finding her feet. It was a quiet day, but it would not remain that way for long.

PC Nicola Hunt took the call, confused at first why this office had been patched through. The woman at the end was crying incoherently, Cora could hear from where she sat. She was reading as well as listening to the conversation.

'Take your time. I have a problem understanding you. Please speak slowly.'

Nicola was patient and reassuring. There was probably a simple explanation for her husband's disappearance. Someone would visit to take details, but if her husband should turn up in the meantime, which is what usually happens, please let them know. Standard procedure for missing people.

Before Nicola spoke, Cora held up her hand. 'It's okay, I caught the gist. Give me the details.'

'Her husband had been to Lutterworth for a regular business trip and hadn't returned.' Nicola looked at her scribbled details. 'He takes the trip once a month and always keeps in regular contact with her throughout. He knows she panics. He was due back home before midday today. Usually, he rings her in the evening before travelling, and in the morning before leaving. She hasn't heard from him since yesterday lunchtime. I could barely understand her.'

Cora sighed. She hated these sorts of cases. They never end well. Often the man was up to no good and was seeing a bit on the side, and decided she was the better option. Instead of confronting the wife with the truth, he just chickened out and went AWOL.

'Thanks, Nicola, I'm curious. Why has this landed in major crime, and not mispers?'

'Yes, boss, I understand your curiosity. But you haven't heard who the missing man is. If I say, Peter Markham, does that explain it?'

Cora blew out a low whistle. 'Oh right. Him. The guy responsible for bringing commerce back into the town, improving the roads, and every charity you can think of. He's reported to be on the King's New Year's honours list. Is that the man?'

Nicola nodded.

'Darcey, you're with me.' Darcey looked up.

Cora collected her coat, phone, and car keys before leaving. Reaching the unmarked pool car, Cora stood by the driver's door and waited.

'Is everything okay, mam?'

'Had a call about a missing husband over on Mangrove Lane. The usual thing, wife distressed. PC Hunt took the call. I said I'd see what's what. Thought I'd take you with me in case she's emotional, which, if you didn't know, is not my forte.'

'A misper? Why are we going?'

'Does the name Peter Markham mean anything to you?'

She waited as the synapses flew around her brain to make the connection, then Darcey's eyes widened.

'Yes, that's why,' nodded Cora. 'We better get moving.'

Jumping into the car, Cora started the engine and waited as Darcey scrambled to fasten her seatbelt. Cora, for some reason, felt calmer now that Darcey was working with her. They had been working together for a couple of months, easy-going, and considerate, and Cora liked her. Usually, it was difficult to let her guard down with people, but there was something about Darcey that broke through her well-built barriers.

'Typical scenario. Husband visits his business in Lutterworth. He does the trip regularly. Leaves on a Monday; and returns on a Wednesday lunchtime, at the latest, unless there's something that needs his urgent attention, or there is a terrible accident and held up in traffic. It's now Thursday morning, and Mrs Markham has heard nothing, not even a text. Any ideas?' Cora glanced at Darcey.

'The first thing that springs to mind is another woman. Then there is suicide or can't take life anymore and runs off. Or something terrible has happened.'

'I agree.'

'A unique spin is, he's one of the wealthiest, most prominent entrepreneurs in the county, a man who can do anything and does.'

'Well done. With that information, any change to your theories?'

Darcey sat back and closed her eyes. Glancing at Darcey, Cora raised her eyebrow. This was different.

'Ok, so a rich entrepreneur still leads me to think he has

a woman on the side. However, when money comes into the equation, I'm thinking of jealousy, or someone trying to take revenge or mistreatment. I'm also thinking he's lost the money and doesn't want to admit it. Terrible investments, gambling addiction or whatever, possibly some kind of organised crime.'

'Your mind is certainly buzzing,' said Cora, impressed by Darcey. The young Detective Constable showed great logic and intuition. She thought before she spoke and didn't blurt out the first thing that came to mind. All qualities that would lead her to become a fantastic detective.

'Excellent Darcey. If this man is missing, then this could lead to something big. Anyway, we're here. It's that house just on the left, with the double mahogany door.'

# 4

The large, detached house was set well back from the street, with huge iron gates protecting a majestic driveway. High bushes led from each side of the gates to stretch around the sides of the property. A big, impressive estate which said success. A garden off to the side with thick hedges at least eight feet high, while a small BMW was parked in front of the house, which could be the wife's car.

The door was answered by a red-eyed, Mrs Markham. She had been expecting them.

'Mrs Yvonne Markham? You rang the station concerning your husband. May we come in?'

Not responding, she stepped aside for the officers to enter. Utter devastation. It was obvious Mrs Markham hadn't slept or changed her clothes for at least a day.

'Darcey, would you mind making Mrs Markham a cup of sweet tea, please?'

Nodding, Darcey left to find the kitchen.

The large drawing room was beautifully furnished, with so much space clutter had swept itself away. Chintzy curtains plunged the windows, adding the spectacular to a plain décor. Splashes of colour came in the form of prints and cushions. Two large comfortable, cream-coloured sofas coveted a large, heavy, and very ornate coffee table in an antique metallic and brown finish. While a couple of magazines waited to be glanced through. This was nice; this was luxury. Over the other side of the room, waited two comfortable armchairs hugging a television. It was easy to picture the couple together in the evening with their glass of wine. Very ordinary people in a luxurious house.

'Shall we sit?' suggested Cora, taking out her notebook. Obediently, Mrs Markham sat. 'I understand this is difficult, but I am going to have to ask you some questions, and I need you to answer fully and honestly. Do you understand, Mrs Markham?'

Staring at Cora, Yvonne mutely nodded.

'Right, Mrs Markham, I know this might sound like a stupid question, but since you reported the disappearance of your husband, has he been in contact, or turned up at all?'

'No, no, I haven't heard a thing.' She glanced at Cora before looking away. 'You can call me Yvonne.'

'Thank you, Yvonne. I need you to talk me through everything leading up to when your husband left the house. When you were expecting him home, any communication while he was away. Anything that seemed different or odd? Be as thorough as you can.'

The evidence of Mrs Markham being attractive was still there, shoulder-length dark hair, dyed now, brown eyes, and good cheekbones, probably about five-feet-five and slim.

But it was Yvonne's body language which spoke to Cora. Taut, anxious; she was trying to remember but also conceal. This woman kept her wedding vows, one of those old-fashioned women who worshipped their husband. His word was command.

'Peter woke early, on Monday. He always did when he

had to travel a long way. His alarm went off at six thirty. After his shower, he dresses always wearing a suit. He wants to portray the right image, you know, a gentleman; smart, dignified. Peter has standards.'

'Sorry to push you, but time is of the essence in a case like this.'

'Yes, sorry.' A sob escaped, begging to release a torrent; this really wasn't Cora's department. Where had Darcey gone?

'I'm sorry, you're right. While Peter showers, I come down to put on his coffee and make his porridge. I used to make him sandwiches for the car, but he told me that now, as he's older, he had to stop for the toilet, so he might as well grab a drink and something to eat at the service station. I chat while he eats; it's our normal routine, and then he leaves the house at seven. He likes to be on the road before the worst of the rush hour traffic begins.'

Cora nodded. So far, so good, but also dull.

'After Peter leaves, I usually go back to bed for a while and read or try to read, but it's impossible for me to go back to sleep after Peter leaves. It's the way I am. Nothing felt off or unusual. Peter was the same as he had been for our thirty years of marriage.'

Carrying a tray and three steaming mugs, Darcey entered. Despite not being keen to drink from other people's crockery, Cora was parched. Carefully placing the tray down, Darcey handed a mug to Mrs Markham, who wept quietly to herself. This was where Darcey was at her best. Hurrying to Yvonne Markham, she sat by her side.

'When your husband was away, did he keep in regular contact, Mrs Markham? Text, phone calls?' asked Darcey.

'Oh yes, you need to know that.'

They waited while she sipped; it was comforting to have

something hot. Darcey, forever patient, waited, urging but not pushing.

'He was wonderful in that way. He always messaged me when he stopped to let me know he'd arrived, understanding I'd be frantic, and call me every evening, and we would speak for half an hour, and then he'd fill me in on his day, and I'd let him know anything that had happened here. Not that there was ever much to tell, but that's just how it was for us.'

Once more, Yvonne's eyes filled with tears. On cue, Darcey squeezed Yvonne's hand.

'You're doing great, Yvonne. Shall we move along to the day he was supposed to come home? When did you realise something was wrong?'

Another sip of tea as Yvonne paused for a moment. 'He'd messaged me good morning, told me he had a quick meeting and was going to pop up the road to the next site, by Leicester. He was going to spend some time there before returning to the hotel in the evening. He usually ate out on the second night, sometimes entertaining his clients, or meeting up with old friends, as he used to live there. I heard no more from him after that first message, which must have been just before nine. I didn't become too concerned when I heard nothing at lunchtime. Sometimes he gets wrapped up in his work and forgets. I began worrying when I'd heard nothing by dinner time. When he missed his evening call, I was panicking.'

'Has this ever happened before, him not contacting you? How did he sound when you spoke to him the previous evening?' asked Darcey.

'He was fine, the same as always; he gave me no cause for concern. I mean, I wasn't expecting anything unusual, you know? But we've been together so long, I would know, wouldn't I? Do you think he's committed suicide or something? Is that why you keep asking me how he seemed? Oh my God, you do, don't you?'

'We must consider all possibilities and that's one of them,' replied Cora, firm and unemotional. 'There are lots of other situations, any of which could lead us to finding your husband. If we don't ask these questions, we have nothing to investigate. I need you to stay calm and think about anything that seemed different, anything at all.'

'That's the thing, detective. There was nothing, except for not staying in touch. When I hadn't heard from him Wednesday night, I rang the kids. Jake said he was expecting him to help with a job in his new flat, so he thought he might have heard from him to arrange it. Peter was good like that, you know, always dropping everything to help the kids.'

'Okay, so when did you know something was definitely wrong which made you decide to call us?' Darcey squeezed Yvonne's hand again.

'Peter always left his hotel around seven. He usually texts me to say he was on his way. Again, I heard nothing and was getting frantic. Even with a stop on the way home, he was never back later than two. When it got to five, I was certain something had happened. I'd been listening to the twenty-four-hour news to hear if there had been any terrible accidents on that awful M1, but there was nothing, nothing.'

As to be expected, Yvonne began sobbing again. Darcey hugged her tight.

'There, there,' Darcey said. 'Everything will be all right.'

'Mrs Markham, I have a few more questions. Then I'd like to have a quick look around, if you don't mind. Standard procedure. I will also need something of your husband, toothbrush, usually for his DNA, just for identification if necessary.'

Calamity struck again as Yvonne gasped, her brown eyes consumed with tragedy.

Cora couldn't cope with Yvonne's emotions. 'When a person goes missing, we must determine how vulnerable they are. Did your husband have any physical or other disabilities or impairments that would make him vulnerable?'

'No, no, nothing like that.'

Making a note, Cora continued. 'Thank you, and is there anywhere you think your husband may have gone to for a few days? Does he own any other properties or have any family he visits?'

'No, both his parents are dead. They died before we married; he was an only child. He doesn't have any friends. He works, you see.'

'Thank you. What is the registration of your husband's car?'

'It's PY30. It was a gift for our thirtieth wedding anniversary. Peter and Yvonne.'

'Thank you, now for the last couple of questions. Do you have a recent photo, and are there any diaries or electronic devices that might give us an idea of what your husband's movements would have been?'

'I have a photo on my phone. We were always taking silly selfies together, so there's one from a couple of days before he went to Lutterworth. Would you like me to message it to you?'

'Yes, please, if you would, I will leave my colleague here to sort that out. Any electronic devices or diaries?'

'Peter was very tech-savvy. I know there are no written diaries because he had all the latest gadgets. He kept everything on his phone or laptop, but he'd have taken both with him. I don't think he has anything else.' She looked vague.

Snapping her notebook shut, Cora stood, 'Thank you,

Mrs Markham. I'll get straight onto the office with his registration and have a quick look around. Then we'll get out of your hair.'

Glad to get away from the stifling atmosphere of an emotional woman, Cora was glad Darcey was there. Now to investigate if there were any signs of why Mr Markham had vanished. If their perfect marriage was so perfect, he would be home by now. But like most marriages, cracks may have appeared that Mrs Markham refused to see. Her cop's gut feeling was telling her this would not be an ordinary missing person's case.

# 5

Driving back to the service area in Peter's car. It felt peculiar and odd to be sitting in his luxury Mercedes, when only a couple of hours ago, he had been sitting here, unaware of a future running towards him. No car could be as clean as Peter's. No clutter in the glove compartment or lazy pieces of paper lying harmlessly on the floor. Recognising a fellow obsessive with secrets to keep, it was impossible to hate him more.

Getting out of the car, there was no need to repeat the procedure of the other day, already wearing the protective gear. The intention was not to leave any trace evidence in the car, even though it was going to be burned. You could never be too careful. Thankfully, the quiet back roads meant fewer cars passing. Getting closer, the stench of piss hit. He'd obviously not been able to hold himself any longer.

Quietly approaching Peter, hoping the footsteps didn't echo off the roof. Peter must have been on high alert because his head was moving, trying to locate where the noise was coming from. His chest began rising and falling as panic set in. At least he had survived the night, but he will wish he hadn't.

'Did you miss me?' now standing over him enjoying the power ripping the duct tape from his mouth. This too went into the drum. 'How are you doing today, Peter? Don't you remember who I am yet? I know this get-up doesn't help, but I hoped you'd remember, anyway.'

'What the fuck are you doing to me, you crazy bastard? Let me go this instant. I don't know who you are. I've done nothing wrong. People will look for me. I'm important.'

Laughter echoed around the cavernous space. He would not be beaten by fear.

'Oh Peter, Peter, Peter, you really think you're missed? Well, I'm happy to let you know no one is looking for you. You haven't even been reported missing.'

Last night switching on the telly, disappointment and anger grew seeing his mugshot on full screen. This was a surprise because he'd not been missing for twenty-four hours.

'Disappointed? Did you think your darling wife would miss you and go frantic with worry? Your beautiful daughter, Olivia, isn't it? Pregnant with your first grandchild. Weren't you supposed to be helping Jake with some DIY? Seems not, I'm afraid. Oh yes, I know all about you and your family, Peter.'

'You're lying. Just because no one cares for you, it doesn't mean everyone is the same. My family loves me. They'll be scared witless by now. So, fucking let me go, you arsehole. You touch a fucking hair on any of their heads, and I'll kill you.'

A smile. 'I need you to think about this carefully, Peter; you seem like a smart guy, so I'm sure you can grasp the simple concept. I have kidnapped you under the cover of darkness, secured you in a derelict, out-of-town location. I have not hidden my identity from you. Do you really think I am going to let you go, so you can tell the police and get me arrested? Does that seem likely, Peter?'

It suddenly struck home. His shocked reaction as the realisation hit him was that he would never get away with his life; death was staring down at him and the fears he had contained throughout the night broke—the tears flowed.

'Good boy, I thought you'd get it eventually. Don't worry, your family is safe. It's just you I'm interested in, although I think they might like to know what sort of man you are, and what you got up to and the pain and heartache you left behind.'

Getting out a bag of tricks from the boot of his car and laid them out slowly and carefully. No point tormenting him by holding them up today. He'd turned his head, not wanting to know the next horror. For the next session, a pair of pliers were selected. The noise attracted him. What was this nutter going to do next?

'Open wide, Peter, be a good boy now. I don't want to force you.'

'No, no. Haven't you done enough to me? What have I done to you? Please don't.'

Leaning over, Peter's hot spittle flew forcefully. A shock which needed punishment. Slapping him hard, a red hand-print filled his face. Dirty Bastard, so you still have a bit of fight left in you.

Raising the pliers up, they were firmly slapped into the other hand.

'That wasn't a smart move, Peter, not smart at all.' Wiping the saliva off, the pliers were raised and smashed down on Peter's nose, breaking it instantly. Blood erupted; his yell, though, allowed a block to be shoved into his mouth to keep it open. One by one, each tooth was yanked out. Easier than expected except for his screaming. With all his money, he had neglected his dental hygiene, naughty Peter.

Not as many teeth as had been removed as expected before he lost consciousness. The intention was to speak to him and jog his memory about what he had done. This was what it was all about. Well, it didn't matter because there was still plenty of time.

Returning to the warmth of the car, a book could be read while waiting for him to surface again. Torture wasn't as entertaining as expected.

# 6

Looking around the house while Darcey interviewed Yvonne was going to help. Cora was curious about this man, Peter Markham. Compared to his younger life in rented rooms, he now lived in a castle. This had happened in the last sixteen years. How did he manage it, coming from almost poverty to fortune?

Starting from the top of the house, Cora worked downwards, impressed by the staircase and the thickness of the carpet. But it was the photographs on the wall which caught her attention. Everyone a happy portrait of a smiling family in different settings: mountains, beaches, and countryside. The boy was the double of his father, inheriting his strong jawline and nose. But where his father was dark in colouring, his son was blonde-haired and paler. The girl was a beauty, tall even at a young age. She towered over her brother and her mother. Everything declared that this was a happy family, and without a doubt, Peter was a good husband and father.

On the left-hand side were three doors, and on the right, another two. The first room was the daughter's bedroom in pink. A big mirror to one side of the room with a bar. This little girl had everything she wanted, including the dreams of being a ballerina. The next room was the same, except the boy's fantasies were played out around a train set. The perfect family, but no family was ever that perfect. Without doubt, Peter was a good husband and father. So why had he gone missing?

The next room was the family bathroom. Of course, she shouldn't have expected anything else. A roll-top Victorian bath was something she had dreamed of, but it was the medicine cabinet she needed to check, frequently a give-away. Nothing here except the usual, and very expensive face cleansers and toners while the meds, touching them gently, belonged to Yvonne unless Peter travelled with his.

Poking her head around the corner, was Peter and Yvonne's bedroom, the large king-sized centred the room. She had to be careful about what she was doing, for it could be construed as snooping. If she found anything now, it would be inadmissible in a court of law.

What do people like the Markhams keep by their bedside before sleep? Cautiously pulling the drawer open revealed an empty drawer for Peter, but on Yvonne's side, the little chestnut drawer revealed a small Bible. Was Yvonne Catholic? Did she need to pray every night before she went to sleep? Picking up the Bible, she flicked through when it opened to a page where there was a small photograph of a newborn baby. Strange. Was it a boy, or a girl dressed in a lemon-yellow sleep suit? Turning the photo over, nothing was written on the back, but the passage next to the picture was strange and enigmatic.

*It is mine to avenge; I will repay. In due time their foot will slip; their day of disaster is near and their doom rushes upon them.* Cora looked at the header; Deuteronomy: Romans. 32:35.

How she would love to ask Mrs Markham what it meant.

Frowning, Cora opened the door to a walk-in wardrobe. A scene she could only dream of as clothes upon clothes ran on hangers along the wall. While on the other side, apart from taking her breath away, was Peter's. There must be fifty jackets or more, everyone in protective wrappings. Jumpers stacked on shelves arranged by colour. On the other side were rows of dresses and ball gowns, many with sparkles. This was paradise and something she could get used to, if only. A cornucopia of extravagance. Skirts, blouses, jeans, and formal trousers. Ah, Cora sighed, this was another life.

But as for Peter's clothes, what did they say about him? A mixture of shirts and trousers, a couple of jackets, a tux, and a grey suit with tails. Over the top, perhaps, but apart from that, nothing unusual. Nothing glaringly missing, no signs to say that Peter had been preparing to run away. Rifling through the closet, some painkillers, vitamins, and Sertraline, why hide them? The label said Yvonne Markham, 200mg a day. This was high, and she should know. It hadn't been so long ago she was on the same tablets. Severe depression or anxiety, so why was Yvonne on them? Something to follow up on, but nothing concrete, not yet.

Nothing screamed as being out of place, no copper's instinct shouted anything. So, into the last room. Back into the hallway to the last door. Would this be the room containing the clue she needed?

A mini gym, who would have thought that, and with all the modern equipment? Treadmill, rowing machine, weights, kettlebells, and things Cora wasn't sure she wanted to know about. The far wall was mirrored from floor to ceiling. Nothing out of place. Did they ever use it? Yvonne looked in great shape, so perhaps.

Getting to the bottom of the stairs, Cora took a proper look at the layout of the house. She hadn't noticed how large the house was before. Going left was a large, clutter-free entranceway.

The first door Cora came across was one of the most amazing rooms she'd ever seen, the sort of room she could only dream of—a study come library. The walls contained dark oak shelving; every inch filled with books. Stepping inside, Cora didn't realise she was holding her breath as she ran her hand along the spines. This one contained the classics and the next a lot of crime fiction, Ian Rankin, Val McDermid, Kathy Reichs, Stephen King, along with some lesser known as David Mark, Wes Markin, and Mark Tilbury.

Next up were biographies and autobiographies. Political leaders had an equal place amongst sports stars. Finally, there were reference books on a whole variety of subjects, from home and car maintenance to wars, history, geography, and politics. The books by Morgan Greene and Kate Bendelow had been well read. The marker of the man was what he was interested in. Looking at these closely, she moved further along the shelf until coming to the Satanic Verses and Mein Kampf. Food for thought.

Finally, Cora crossed to the focal point of the room where a large mahogany desk sat. It was beautiful and must be antique. A green baize mat on the top and a couple of little shelves. As with the rest of the house, it was immaculately tidy. No paperwork piled up here or stray coffee cups. Three small drawers on either side had paper, notebooks, and other stationery. The bottom two contained paperwork.

The next few rooms were the usual utility rooms, a conservatory, and a larger living room containing an enormous television. Next, a dining room with a table that could easily accommodate twelve. How many friends did the Markhams have or was this only for family?

Finally, stepping through to the large clean kitchen,

decorated in monochrome, black and white tiled floor, black island in the centre, and white cupboards with black fittings, was very impressive. The whole of her flat would fit in this one room alone. Yet, nothing stood out here, no secrets disturbed. Disappointed, it was time to return to the two women in the living room hoping Darcey had calmed Mrs Markham by now.

## 7

Darcey's kindness had worked as Mrs Markham's sobs were easing off. The best thing for her was to tell her, *we have found your husband*, and *he's on his way home*.

'What happens now officer, I always thought someone had to be missing for twenty-four hours before the police became involved?' Yvonne steeled herself bravely to ask Darcey.

'That's a common misconception, Yvonne. If someone is concerned, then they can report them within hours, especially if that person is vulnerable, like an elderly relative, or someone with a learning difficulty, for example. Finding them quickly is vital. Is there any reason you know why Peter may have disappeared? Was he having any difficulties with his health, or at work?'

'No,' Yvonne sighed. 'You know what men are like keeping everything locked away in here,' she pointed to her head, 'I like to think I'd have noticed if there were any marked changes, but there weren't, he was the same man he's always been, kind, concerned, loving.'

'Mrs Markham, I know it's easy for me to say, but it's still possible your husband will walk in the door at any moment, hungover and embarrassed at all the fuss he's caused. Stranger things have happened, believe me.'

'Thanks, I will keep that in mind, but that isn't my husband. He is very ordinary. He likes his routines, one glass of red in front of the telly of an evening, never two. His lunch and dinner at set times, always fish on a Friday. I couldn't get him to move away from that. I love my husband, but sometimes it would be nice if he did something impulsive. Are you married, detective?' Yvonne smiled at Darcey.

'No, Mrs Markham. I don't want to rush into anything, although I know my mum wants grandchildren. She drops it into the conversation as often as she can. My nan is worse. Before she's even in the door, she's asking if I've got someone yet.' And then her voice changed. She had a personal question to ask. 'What about your children, Yvonne? Are they both Peter's? Have there ever been any problems there?'

Flinching, Yvonne looked as if she'd been slapped. 'Yes, of course they are. What are you suggesting, officer, that I am some floozy getting pregnant by any man that crosses my path, and what do you mean, problems? No, of course, there aren't any problems. We are a happy family. The odd argument, naturally. We've given our children principles and love; Peter and I have done a good job with them. They love their father, Peter's always popping to Jake's apartment to help with DIY. And Olivia, she's daddy's girl. I find it highly offensive at what you're trying to imply.'

'I'm afraid these are questions that must be asked. I need as much information as you can give me to help explain why your husband hasn't returned. I can see you have a strong family unit.'

During her absence, Cora knew Darcey was still finding out those awkward questions. Looking at her watch, the time had arrived to make a call to the station to start the ball rolling on an investigation. Phone and bank records, CCTV, checking the car registration against traffic cameras, and interviewing witnesses needed to be done now.

'So, what happens next, detective? Is there anything I can do apart from sitting here and crying? I need to be doing something.'

'We need addresses, contact details, the names of hotels where Mr Markham stays for his other business. Anything you can think of would help.'

'Yes, I can do that.' Yvonne began with her phone. 'Here is a good list to start with. Look, here, this is Peter's principal business in Lutterworth. The people to speak are Raj and Mick. They run the place between them. Then this one's in Northampton. The person there is Frances. He usually stops off at Newport Pagnell services, so some of the staff there might recognise him. He's been doing that journey for so long, someone must.' Yvonne paused. 'Please be gentle with my daughter. She's pregnant and suffering horribly from morning sickness. She's so close to her dad; I don't want her worrying unnecessarily.'

'Thank you, Mrs Markham, I know this is a difficult time, but please don't give up hope. We will keep you updated as soon as we hear more. Here is my card. If you hear from your husband, let me know immediately.'

'Thank you so much for your time.' Yvonne seized Darcey's hands. 'I know you will do everything you can to return my husband.'

# 8

Cora remained quiet and thoughtful as they drove from the Markham residence. The photo of a baby hidden in the Bible struck her as unusual. It looked like it had been hidden away, but why?

'Did you get anything interesting from Mrs Markham?' asked Cora after a while.

'Not really boss, the usual you know: why are you here and not out looking for him? Everything was rosy; they had the perfect marriage. Children adored their father, they had no problems, and all that sort of thing. What do you think, boss? Do you think any marriage can be that perfect?'

'I dunno, Darcey, my parents divorced when I was young, and most of the people in my family are divorced. Some tried a second marriage, some successfully, some less so. My nan, for example, she'll have been married to her second husband for coming up to fifty years. They adore each other.'

'Aww, that's sweet. Are you close to your grandparent's, boss? You changed when you talked about your nan.'

'Yeah, I am. When my parents split, my mum had me, a seven-year-old, and my four-year-old sister. She had to work to survive, and the only way she could do that was to leave us with my grandparents. Sometimes we went to my eldest auntie, who by then was a single parent herself. Her eldest boys went with their dad, and her youngest two stayed with her. As we grew older, my nan used to take all the cousins away in her caravan during the school holidays. I swear Darcey, I've been to more places around the UK than I could tell you. I wish I'd paid more attention, but you know when you're a kid, you don't, do you?'

Looking away, Cora missed Darcey's smile. She surprised herself at how open she had been about her private life.

'My childhood differed from yours. Both parents were happily married. Six sibs. We never wanted for anything. We went on hols abroad every year. It was wicked. My grandparents passed away when I was too young to remember them. I'm the sixth of seven, so my parents were getting on by then.'

'You said six siblings; you have six siblings? Bloody hell, your house must have been insane.'

'Yep, it was a nut house all right, but it was awesome. Christmas was ace, and I wouldn't swap any of it for the world. Oh, and before you ask, four sisters, two brothers, and yep, my parents had a telly, but they always wanted a big family. They are great. We are only a year or so apart, so there's only just over eight years between the eldest and youngest.'

How different their lives had been, arguments and threats, an angry mother beating their dad, always suspecting that he was two-timing her until he walked out and never came back. What went wrong with her mother? They never heard from Dad again. These memories still haunted Cora.

---

Hurrying into the warmth of the police station, they went upstairs to see if there had been any developments. Missing persons were troublesome cases to manage, especially if, as Cora suspected, Peter Markham had gone off with another woman. He might be too embarrassed to show his face. It's a fallacy to believe that anyone had a perfect marriage.

Laughing, Darcey ran to the toilets again while Cora went to the open-plan office everyone shared. Her tidy desk was in the corner with only a photo of her dog, which showed the state of her emotional and family life. She hadn't spoken to her mother for coming up to eight months. The last time they'd spoken, Mum steered the conversation back to herself every time with her complaints about how badly she'd been treated with Cora as a daughter, the same old thing until Cora tired of it and rung off. Her sister had seen sense by escaping to Ghana with a guy she'd met at the gym during a personal training session. Cora hoped she was okay and safe, but they rarely spoke. As soon as Cora and her sister turned eighteen, their mother decided they were adults, and no longer needed a mother. This was why she was so independent and probably why she was still single; she struggled to let other people in, but that was another story for a rich therapist to unpick.

Before starting her search, DCI Felix Blackwell, her boss, needed updating on what she was working on, needing to know that she wasn't neglecting the other cases she was currently juggling. It seemed that as soon as you solved one case or moved it aside, three more appeared.

Walking to the far corner, through the glass partition, she saw him sitting hunched over his desk. Knocking, Cora waited.

'Come. Ah Cora, take a seat. What can I do for you?'

'Hi boss, just thought I'd let you know we've picked up a missing person's case. There doesn't seem much in it yet. I'm trying to decide on its relevance. We've already had a chat with Mr Peter Markham's wife. By the way, he's the one who opened the new library last year. You would have seen Peter Markham at every Dunstable charity function.'

New to the job, and in his early forties, Felix Blackwell was handsome. This was the word of every woman in the station, including Cora. She may be independent, but she wasn't blind. Felix sat up straighter as the name Peter Markham was mentioned. He knew as well as she did what it was like when so-called important people vanish. They could have a serious problem on their hands.

Eventually, he sighed. She knew of his recent promotion after impressing the chief at every stage of his career so far. To her knowledge, Felix Blackwell was one of the youngest coppers to be promoted to DCI, and he had a lot to prove, especially to the station's elder statesman. So far, he'd not had much grief, but it was early days. A lot of stress for a young Felix, Cora tried her best to get along with him by not making any ripples. She wasn't deaf to the whispers about her being difficult and aloof, as she also tried not to let it bother her. But it hurt, though she might look tough. This was not the case inside.

'Okay, Cora, thanks for letting me know. Keep me updated as it progresses. Let's hope he's just gone off with some bit on the side and returns with his tail between his legs; it would make our work so much easier.'

Keen to get cracking to impress, Cora pushed the chair back under the table. There were butterflies in her stomach while an uncomfortable blush pinched her cheeks. Felix Blackwell was so handsome.

'Thanks, boss will do. Oh, I found a photo of a newborn baby hidden in a Bible, alongside a weird passage about revenge. Not sure if there's any relevance to that. There were family portraits all over the house, happy ones, in groups, and some individually. It's a mystery,' she frowned. 'Why a photograph of a very young baby should be hidden. Any ideas?'

'Well, we will keep it to ourselves for the moment. Did Mrs Markham show you this picture?'

'Well, no,' Cora shrugged. 'But I wondered why in this day and age a woman like Mrs Markham would keep a Bible.'

'Tread cautiously, Cora, and don't rush things. We will find Peter Markham, but you can't go acting outside the rules. Do you understand?'

'Ok, thanks boss, I'll let you get on.'

She had been stupid, but police procedures always held one back instead of assisting. Felix, though, had made things clear. She had been told that she was too eager, and now she had just proved it.

---

Walking into the office, Cora clapped her hands to gain attention.

'Right, everyone. We have a prominent entrepreneur, Peter Markham, reported missing by his wife. He was supposed to be home by yesterday afternoon. Unusual for him; he always keeps in touch on his journey back from Lutterworth to his wife, a trip he makes once a month. Mrs Yvonne Markham hasn't heard from him since Wednesday morning. Any luck with the vehicle reg?'

A young PC stuck up her hand.

'Yes. Hayley, isn't it?'

'Yes ma'am. We caught the car on ANPR cameras travelling around the Lutterworth Town centre as recently as yesterday evening. No hits so far today.'

'Ok great, well done. Have hospitals, other stations etc been informed?'

Another voice in the room shouted, 'Yes, boss.'

'Have we readied the TV appeal, pictures posted on our social media, ambulances, taxis, and buses been informed?'

Another disembodied voice shouted, yes, boss.

'Fantastic job, everyone. Okay, so far concerning Yvonne Markham, nothing obvious came up when we chatted with her. She's devastated. And no way was that an act. Briefly. A happy marriage, two kids, first grandchild on the way. Both kids are his. Nothing Mrs Markham could think of that would cause him to wander off. We need to check his finances to see if he is concealing a mountain of debt. And his social life to find out if there's a hint of another woman. He took all his electronic devices with him, so we'll have to tackle through the mobile network provider to give us Mr Peter Markham's activity logs. The number is on the report. Dave, can you get onto that, please? I know that's your speciality.'

'On it, boss.' Dave shouted from the back of the room, his eyes already on the screen, face deep in concentration while his fingers flew over the keyboard.

'Peter Markham is not classed as vulnerable. We managed to collect his DNA, quite an arduous task as the man keeps himself impeccably clean. So, Darcey. I'll ask you to chase that down for me, please.'

Darcey nodded she'd heard.

'Okay, that's all for now. You know the drill. But don't forget—this isn't the only case in our caseload—so we can't devote all our time and attention to it. Updates at tomorrow's briefing.'

To begin with, Cora started with the old tried and

trusted Google and was pleased to see several results appearing about Peter Markham. Everything would help her get a measure of the man. With her chin in her hand, she began reading with fascination. Markham had been given several business awards over the years. Described as dynamic, he picked up struggling businesses and brought them under the umbrella of the Montgomery company. By selling parts off, he made the business more profitable, but sacrifices had to be made, and many people were laid off. Which didn't make him popular, mused Cora.

Scrolling down was another article. A young woman had been fired by Markham; she was trying to sue but was being blocked by the big guns at the Company. Clicking on the link: the woman, Miss Tracy Littlechild, felt she'd been unfairly treated during her time working for the company and was claiming unfair dismissal on the grounds of gender discrimination and mental health; they were trying to pay her off.

Okay, Ms Littlechild, let's see if I can find any details on you in case I need to speak to you later. This could be a lead, and the first sign of Mr Markham's halo slipping. Could this be anything to do with his disappearance? Probably not. Cora scratched her head.

A shadow passing her desk made her look up. The other young recruit, Luke, was standing, waiting for her attention. Smart and so far diligent. She noticed he and Darcey had hit it off well, bouncing quips off each other. She guessed they were of similar age and was glad to see members of her team getting along well.

'Yes, Luke, what is it? Have you found something?'

'I've tracked down the hotel Mr Markham stayed during his visits down south. It's the Old Palace Lodge. The manager there is Mrs Marge Smith. She is happy to speak to the police. Her duties are from early morning until late evening.'

'Great, thanks Luke, I'll grab Darcey, and we'll head on over there to question her and see if she can give us any clues as to the whereabouts of our missing man, and if he has any secrets. You know the sort of thing? While the cats away.' Snatching her coat, Cora missed Luke's look of disappointment. 'Great job, Luke, thanks. Can you see where we are with the media briefing? We'll need that to be done ASAP?' Cora said as an afterthought.

Nodding, but saying nothing in case his voice betrayed his disappointment. It was unfair that he was the one who found the hotel and contacted the manager. Why was Darcey going with the boss for questioning? He'd come through the same ranks as her and was just as qualified. What would he need to do to be recognised? He felt he was being left out. Not that he had a problem with Darcey.

Sulking and resentful, Luke went back to work. Yet, he was a professional, and if he had to work harder to be seen, then that's what he'd do. The boss had called in a long list of tasks while their work team was tiny. The hope was he'd be the one to find something that would locate Mr Markham.

# 9

Bored now, yet the adrenalin had fired up the system to go onto the next step. Was he ready? Or was he still pretending to be unconscious? Torture wasn't as much fun when the other person wasn't playing their part. And come to think of it, that life-altering sense of justice and revenge hadn't happened. Such a great disappointment. This man, Peter, again glancing in the rear-view mirror, had ruined the once good life and changed it forever. How can one have so much power over another? And yet, killing him was letting him off lightly. His wife and kids would suffer more, especially the pregnant daughter, yet it had to be done this way. It had gone too far to turn back.

Out of the car, stretching, arching every crick from sitting in one position for too long. Slamming the door hard created a ring of echoes in the underground disused car park. Time to exact the next part of the revenge.

Was he awake? If he wasn't, then a good boot in the side would wake him. Groaning, Peter tried to move away, but unfortunately for him, he was secured too tightly. Another boot in the side for good measure. Snivelling little weasel, he was more pitiful than ever, laying there, accepting whatever was thrown at him. After the initial swearing and spitting, Peter remained mute. His end was inevitable; tears rolling down the side of his face showed he had given up fighting.

'I think by now you've realised, Peter, that you are going to die. If you haven't, you're a lot more stupid than I gave you credit for seeing as I've told you at least twice. I know you'll be wondering who I am and why I'm doing this to you. So, I will tell you because it's time.'

The story began with when they'd first met, and what he'd done to suffer the torture. He listened, eyes growing wider as the details of the past were poured out.

'You see, that's how life works, Peter. It's about responsibility, what you did to me, I do to you. Don't you have something to say to me?'

If he said sorry, would that be enough to forgive him? Nice to think it would, but no, what Peter had done was impossible to forgive.

'So now you see, Peter, how you've ruined my life. I couldn't let you live and carry on with all your wealth and wonderful life while I still suffered. You're scum, Peter. So I will put you out of your misery shortly, but I have just one more job to do first.'

Trembling, waiting in fear, the inevitable was about to happen. Had he guessed the next step? Grinning, while walking over to the boot to return with the knife that had been brought specially for this moment. Unable to resist tormenting him further, this too was held up to Peter's eyeline while running a finger along the blade's edge ever so gently. No point getting careless now by leaving blood behind.

In short, quick breaths, like an outboard motor running out of fuel, Peter panted. Bending down, the duct tape was ripped quickly from his mouth. He didn't even scream, just sucked in air, hyperventilating. Instinctively knowing now what was going to be done, in horror, he shivered, watching, eyes following the hand of death going to his naked torso. He was so vulnerable, there was nothing he could do, his cock was grabbed with one hand, pulling it tight. It can't be happening. No. The knife—with no sign of hesitation—sliced his penis off. It came away as easily as a hot knife through cold butter.

The scream only took a moment, but seemed to emerge from the very depth of his soul. Echoing around the empty high ceilings to vanish into the afternoon mist. The blood spurted and dripped down the well-covered gloved hand holding it. Then it was held up for him to see. He witnessed his penis being tossed in with the clothing and the withered fingertips. The teeth had to be disposed of in another way. What was the point of it? Whoever God was, please forgive him.

The time had come to put this scumbag out of its misery. Would it be better to leave him here to bleed out and let the rats do the rest? Everything was done that needed to be done, but there was still a chance that Peter would be found and saved. Although the chance was slim, it was never zero. Using the same knife that had been used on his penis was now thrust straight into his stomach and sliced upwards. Death came calmly as his breaths grew shallower until it stopped. The light of horror died in his eyes. He was at peace now. Nothing more could be done to him.

Onto the next stage.

Pulling the knife out and cleaning it off, the all-in-one decorator's outfit was placed back in the boot. Sad to see the knife go, but there mustn't be any mementos. Along with all the other tools, this too would be thrown into the river. A strange feeling to know that at last Peter Markham was dead while stripping off to walk naked to the drum. The can of petrol was going to erase all other evidence.

Throwing everything in was followed by the process of looking for any more evidence. Everything achieved was followed by a great sense of peace. Peter was gone; there would be no more of him. Standing there after everything had been achieved was almost a spiritual moment. A sacrifice had been made, and now was the time to move on and start a new life as it should have been before. Soaking everything in the drum with petrol, a match flew up into a flame. After one last sweep around to ensure nothing was missed, it was tossed into the drum. Two seconds later came the whoosh. The heat hit with an impact and now everything was over. Again, the thought followed that Peter at last was dead. Time to walk away without looking back.

---

Time for the complete disposal. There was a field not too far away with access to the river unseen by CCTV for the next part of the disposal. Pulling Peter's car to a stop, the bag of clothes was put at a safe distance so these could be grabbed in a minute.

Removing the other petrol can from the boot, the front and back seats were soaked as was the boot even flicking some on the roof. Taking up the empty petrol can and placing it onto the back seat, along with the hairnet and gloves. Seizing the box of matches and lighting another, the one small flame was chucked into the car. An ecstasy of exhilaration for when the fire caught this time, it sounded like a bomb had gone off.

Wonderful to be standing watching the fire angels leaping from what used to be the roof. The job was finished, and everything had been achieved. Would Peter have been upset to see his flashy car with the three-pointed star on the grill burning? Should the car have been burnt before the final assault, to let Peter see how his life had been torn from him? But the car had been needed to transport him to his resting place. Oh well, you can't have everything. He was dead; there was no need to think about him anymore. Time to get dressed, and to carry on with the rest of life.

The chill suddenly seeped through her waiting bones, reminding of how mortal and small we are as the sun fell deep beyond the horizon. The wind was bringing in damp air across from the nearby river, numbing fingers and toes. Justice had been looked for and served. Dressed, and picking up the backpack, the straps tied over the shoulders. A job well done while the silent figure walked towards the town centre. The new camera had not been noticed. This had been the only witness.

# 10

Cora found Darcey at her desk. How did the young woman find anything amongst the clutter?

'Luke has found the hotel our missing man stayed in. We'll pop down there and have a chat with the staff to see if we can learn anything new.'

'Okay, boss. Surprised you're not taking Luke, as he was the one to find the info.'

'Thought this needed a woman's touch, that's all.'

It was the way Darcey looked at her, puzzled, that made her wonder if she had made a mistake by not taking Luke. Even Felix had told her this was a team. Something to ponder about another time. For now, she needed to focus. This case had been frustrating from the moment Peter Markham was reported missing. Yvonne was not just any wife and mother; Cora couldn't help feeling that she was putting on an act. On the surface, they were the perfect family, so why was there a photograph hidden in Yvonne's Bible?

As it was Peter Markham, news spread like wildfire. A press conference for the missing man was held last night and a specialist hotline was set up for any sightings—the police needed help. As the phones began ringing, the cranks and nut jobs were spinning their usual tales of alien abduction and who knows what else. There had been no legitimate sightings yet, so Cora was happy to leave it with the team while Darcey and she went to question the hotel staff.

'C'mon then, let's go. We've got a bit of a drive ahead.' Taking her jacket and keys, Cora sped out of the office, leaving Darcey to hurry at a jog.

'Where are we going exactly?' Darcey asked as she slid into the passenger seat of the standard-issue Vauxhall Astra police car.

'Lutterworth,' Cora replied, 'before we go, do you need the loo?'

'No, just been. Thanks for asking.'

'Good,' smiled Cora. 'I don't fancy stopping on such a short drive, and I already know that any drive with you proves to be highly likely.'

It pleased her that Darcey dissolved into a fit of giggles. Cora didn't know anyone who needed so many bathroom breaks.

Releasing the handbrake. They drove slowly out of the car park.

'It's a small market town in Leicestershire, junction 20, so not too far.'

'Boss, does the DCI know we are off on a road trip?' Darcey stopped giggling.

'No Darcey, not yet. I will call him on the way.'

---

The pair fell into companionable silence until they were well along the M1; Darcey breaking the silence, intrigued by the woman who was her boss.

'Boss, if you don't mind me asking, why did you decide

to join the police? It's not one of those professions you want to do unless you have a good reason.'

Cora took a moment and then a deep breath.

'There is a story behind why I joined the force, but it's not one I am prepared to share with you yet. I haven't shared it with anyone, so nothing personal.' This was not a satisfactory answer for Darcey. 'How about you Darcey—why did you join up?'

'That's easy, boss. Family. Dad, grandad, a couple of uncles, and two of my older siblings are in the police force. I never really wanted to do anything else. I was always fascinated by the forensics side of things. Something I'll look at in the future, but for now I'm loving it.'

Again, they fell into comfortable silence, although Cora was never sure why confident, carefree kids should follow their family into the police. Were they expected to? Yet, there was nothing in Darcey's demeanour or tone of voice that suggested she was anything but genuinely thrilled with her decision.

Cora, though, was strongly regretting one of hers. Why on earth had she signed up for that competition, and even more strangely, how had she won? Now she was being sent on to the next round of the new comedian's awards, being held in Brighton in a week's time. This was her secret life away from the police.

---

The miles flew by as the blur of trees and hills and mountains made this ride indistinct from any other motorway drive. Glancing at Darcey, her phone was constantly beeping and every time she looked, it was to find Darcey's deft fingers flicking over at incredible speed, replying to whatever witty missive she'd received from her friends. Then she rummaged in her bag and found a bag of crisps. Inwardly, Cora cringed. There was nothing she hated more than the sound of people eating. It made her unnaturally angry, but she knew she had to bite her tongue and say nothing, without seeming like a total nutter. If Darcey noticed her boss's tension as she munched her way through the bag of Wotsits, she showed no sign of it.

As they reached Northampton, then Rugby, they were close and time to give Darcey a nudge. Her quick snack had been a brief interlude between messages. She never kept still, and neither did the weather as the heavens opened to make this part of the journey treacherous. Traffic was backing up and red lights as far as the eye could see.

'We're almost there; do you have any thoughts about how we should tackle this?'

'Not until we get there, boss. I like to get a feel for people first. Once we speak to the manager, we'll know whether it's worth pushing further.'

'Great answer, but we still need a plan. Obviously, we need to speak to the hotel manager, the front desk receptionist and anyone else you can think of?'

'Food boss, boys, and their food. He'd have to eat at some point. Something might have been overheard if he ate there, or anywhere else he ate, which might give us something to go on.'

'Good call. Yes, boys and their food, I've noticed that too.'

The dark grey skies stayed solemn above the small town as they came off the motorway, causing both women to go quiet. Looking out of the window, they watched the houses, shops, pretty buildings painted white or other pastel colours flying past. It looked clean and although winter had killed off most plants, there were still some planters with the odd, colourful foliage. The sat nav took them past a McDonald's and a bunch of traffic lights. Once they saw an old-looking church ahead, they would be close, for the hotel was directly across from it.

# 11

Pulling up to the Old Palace Lodge hotel, Darcey whistled, 'He must be doing all right for himself. This ain't no Premier Inn.'

'No, it isn't,' Cora laughed. 'Apparently, Henry the Eighth stayed here. C'mon, let's go and see what we can find.'

Pulling her coat more tightly around her, a gust of icy wind caught Cora unaware while waiting for Darcey to catch up. Entering the lobby and flashing their warrant cards, the concierge opened the doors for them.

The building itself was old and impressive. Dark wood panelling on the bottom half of the walls, gold wallpaper on the top while scattered bright-coloured chairs stood around, and a large pink sofa dominated the main area by the bar. A traditional large fireplace sent out welcomed heat into the room. While lit sconces adorned the walls, and a few small coffee tables were dotted about.

Crossing to the reception desk, Cora was grateful the place was empty as she held her warrant card to the young man sitting there.

'Is your manager around?'

Upon seeing their warrant cards, the young man hurriedly picked up the phone to ring through.

'Hi Marge, a couple of police officers out here at the front want to speak to the manager. Okay, okay, sure.' He then looked at Cora. 'The hotel manager is just finishing up with what she's doing and will be out shortly. Why don't you take a seat while you wait? Would you like some tea or coffee?'

'Nothing for me, thank you. Darcey?'

'A coffee, white with two sugars,' Darcey looked at Cora. Yes, she had a sweet tooth. Eyeing the room, they went and sat on the big pink sofa by the fire. It was deliciously comfortable and warm.

'Did you catch the guilty look flashing over his face when we held up our cards, boss?'

'I did. I wondered if you caught it. Lucky for him, we aren't interested in whatever petty crime he has committed, but he needs to tell his face to look less guilty that's if he wants to carry on.'

This tickled Darcey and she laughed at the levity from her boss, who didn't make jokes often, but when she did, they were brilliant.

Pleased for the banter, but before she could comment further, an imposing woman, who must have been over six feet tall, came in their direction. Severe looking with her hair scraped back into a high ponytail, not one strand loose. Her matching skirt and jacket suit were not off the peg. Slim, but curvy in the right places with a friendly face.

As she approached the two women on the sofa, she gave a disarming and genuinely warm smile and held out her hand for them, putting both women immediately at ease.

'Marge, Marge Smith, Duty Manager of the Old Palace Lodge.'

'Marge, I'm Detective Inspector Cora Snitton, and this is

Detective Constable Darcey Clarke. We are here about the disappearance of Peter Markham.'

'Of course, please follow me. We can use my office. I'm not sure how I can help, but I will do all I can.'

Following the woman, she led them into a room hidden behind the reception desk.

---

The manager invited them to sit down while she took her place behind a large oak desk. The office was small, but not claustrophobic. A bookcase against the right-hand wall contained lots of folders; previous accounts assumed Cora. A couple of photo frames of a smiling family with a couple of gappy-toothed kids, one standing with Mickey Mouse, another in front of a waterfall.

'My kids,' Marge noticed Cora looking. 'Ricky's twenty-five now and works in construction, and Autumn is a nurse. Vinny's the youngest. I loved those days when they were sweet and relied on me, but I have my first grandchild due this year. Do you have children?'

'No, neither of us yet,' replied Cora. 'You have a beautiful family, and congratulations on the grandchild. Is Marge your real name, if you don't mind me asking?'

'How intuitive, but no, it's not. There was an employee a few years back now who had nicknames for everyone, some inventive, some not, some based on their initials, some about a feeling. For whatever reason, she always called me Marge. She never said why, she just said I seemed like a Marge. She said it so often that the rest of the staff picked it up, even some of the regular guests, so it's stuck with me ever since, even though she left a long time ago. My real name is Carol.'

Cora didn't comment. 'Now, about the guest, Peter

Markham, whose disappearance we're investigating. Are you able to go over what happened the last day he stayed here?'

'Well, Peter was a regular. Quite distinctive, with his smart suits and short grey hair. He was well known amongst all the staff as being friendly. He remembered each one of our names, even those who were new. He would call them by name the next time he visited, which was usually once a month, from Monday to Wednesday. I know he lives somewhere down south, Dunstable I think, but he came from around here originally, yet he had no accent. He began working for a company before becoming a partner. We had drinks together a few times. He is what we call a talker. Though after a couple too many, he likes to brag. I can see that this would upset others, but not me; I like that sudden rags-to-riches story. He told me he had been lucky in business. He had that business acumen; lucky fingers also, I never knew what he meant, and then suddenly, he was rich; it doesn't make me jealous. Anyhow, he would spend a few days visiting the various sites. I found him quite private, although he did gush about his family and how much he missed them.'

Just as Cora went to speak, Darcey cut in. 'And the day he went missing, did you notice anything different about him? Did he seem on edge? Say anything out of the ordinary?'

Cora was surprised her junior colleague had interrupted. She must have spotted something that gave her reason to. Sitting back, Cora took this opportunity to watch what Marge was messaging with her body. Nonverbal communication was vital in comedy and came in handy for police work.

'Now, let me try to remember.'

'That's okay, Marge,' Cora cut in. 'We understand, but this is important, so please, whatever you can remember, it might be the clue we need.'

'The day he went missing, umm? He had gone out at his normal time around 8 am. He's a man with regular habits. Cheese on toast with brown sauce, never anything else for breakfast. He would always joke about it and always smiling. Oh yes, he also waved when he went off for the day. It was his habit to come back to change clothes. Usually, he goes to the local restaurant, just off the A4303. I believe he knew the owners from when he lived here before.'

'Thanks, Marge. Do you know the name of this restaurant?'

'The Maharaja. It's on its own on one side of the road; there's a Harvester on the opposite side. I know he ate in both, but he tended to favour the Maharaja.'

'I need to ask what happened to his belongings?'

'We left everything as it was, even when he didn't return from his meal, but when we saw the news that he was missing. I rang the helpline and was told to leave everything as it was.'

'Thank you, Marge, you've been most helpful. What about his car? When he left that day, did he drive?'

'I honestly can't say. His car has one of those personal plates. PY30 is a number not to forget. I remember asking him about it. He said his wife got it as an anniversary gift. He loved it.'

'Good, thank you. Now I need to question whoever it was at the front desk that night, then we'll be on our way.'

'Yes, of course. Just a moment. You can use this office while I cover. I'll make sure you aren't disturbed.'

'Thanks, Marge, you've been very helpful. I appreciate you taking the time to speak to us today.'

‘What does PY30 mean, boss?’ asked Darcey, doing her large eye effect when Marge left.

‘I thought you would have worked out that, Darcey. Peter, Yvonne celebrating 30 years of marriage.’

# 12

Helen Carlisle wandered slowly along the high street on her way to work. She was early and doing the closing shift, so she didn't have to start until midday. Buying a paper from the local newsagent after exchanging the usual pleasantries. She was in a good mood and enjoyed her job most of the time. A social person, she loved chatting with people, so the off-chain coffee shop suited her.

'How's it looking Ivy? Everyone on their best behaviour today?'

Ivy was one of those coffee-shop characters, a people watcher still interested in life even in her late eighties.

'Aye, lassie, you know how it is, everyone looks shifty to me these days.'

'Can't argue with that, Ivy, I don't know what it is. Seems worse since COVID-19. How is your knee? While I think about it, have you heard about that missing guy? He used to come here occasionally.'

'Yeah, I heard. He's a wrong'un, always said that. You mark my words, I'm telling you now that whatever happened, he deserved it. My knee, that's all right, dear, it's still there. I might have to contact that tasty surgeon again, though. Someone dashing and handsome who wouldn't kill me off.'

Helen loved the random statements Ivy came out with. They always caught her off guard.

'Ivy, what are you like? Isn't he in his sixties, balding and a bit portly?'

'What's wrong with that luvvy? Isn't that chap of yours a bit on the bigger side? I'm not dead yet lass, these eyes still see as clear as what yours do, and I can tell you that man is something else. It's all in the eyes.'

Helen chuckled. She knew Ivy liked the men. 'You realise he's probably gay? If you happen to see him, look for a wedding ring, or knowing you, you'd probably just ask him outright.'

On hearing the door open, Helen saw Claire behind her, wearing a polite smile. 'Will you two keep it down, you're scaring off the trade.'

'Better get going Ivy, don't wanna get into trouble. Now remember if you see any handsome chaps walking along, and with your dodgy knees—don't go doing yourself a mischief.'

Before Ivy could respond, Helen walked inside to the warmth.

# 13

'I'm sorry for that,' apologised Helen as she reached the counter. Claire was a laid-back woman and a great colleague and friend. They worked well as a team, and Helen respected her immensely.

At barely five feet tall, Helen towered above Claire Birkin. Slender and elegant, she always had her short, curly hair tied back. Her deep brown eyes were accentuated by light make-up. For a woman in her late thirties, she looked great.

Back to work. Helen put her handbag away and retrieved her black apron. Someone had left a newspaper; customers always like to read with their drink. She went to take it, but in her haste, the falling paper fell open. It was then she spotted the headline:

*Prominent businessman Peter Markham, missing...*

It continued.

*Peter's wife contacted the Police after he failed to return home from a visit to his business in Lutterworth. The couple were due to have dinner with a local peer. Rumours were circulating, suggesting Mr Markham was likely to be on the next honours list for an OBE.*

*His family is becoming increasingly concerned about his welfare saying, it is completely out of character for him not to keep in contact...*

The media were making a big fuss about Peter Markham if only they knew what he was really like hiding behind the shadows of charities.

# 14

Stepping out of the office ahead of the manager, Cora and Darcey hadn't noticed that Marge had taken a swig from her hidden bottle. In silence, quickly licking her lips, Marge introduced them to the receptionist. So far, it was looking like a pointless visit.

The nervous receptionist sat in the boss's chair, his eyes catching both of them in turn. Darcey took a smaller chair just off to the side while Cora remained standing, resting her bum on the edge of the desk, arms crossed, eyes not moving from him. Darcey had taken out her notebook, leaving Cora to question him.

'Why are you so nervous? You look like you've seen a ghost; you've not stopped fidgeting since you sat down. It's driving me crazy; can't you sit still?'

Almost immediately, he stopped moving, except for his knee tapping. Cora smiled to calm him down. Chatting to the police could be daunting, but her instincts told her this was more than nerves but actual fear.

'What's your name, young man?'

'John.'

'John, what?'

'Kirkham, John Kirkham.'

Steadily, Darcey noted it, ready to check his record as soon as they got back to the car.

'Okay, thanks John, and your age? I'd take a guess, but I'm always miles off, especially when they are younger than me. Do you see Darcey here? I wouldn't have pegged her for being no more than nineteen. But I won't embarrass her by revealing her true age; it's not something you ask a woman, John.'

The knee bobbing was slowing down. The theory worked that by asking simple questions such as name and age, he would relax. His infernal movement was driving her crazy.

'I'm just twenty-two. My birthday was last weekend.'

'Ah, twenty-two, what an age. I remember being your age, partying, drinking, and having a great time. Some of the best years of my life. I hope you're doing the same.'

This elicited no response. It could be a loaded question, and John was too scared to answer for fear of implicating himself in something illegal. How hard it was to be young. Better get on with the questioning.

'Are you aware why we are here, John?'

'The missing guy, I guess,' mumbled John, barely audible.

'That's right John. If you could speak up a bit, please, you aren't in any trouble. We just want to establish what happened the last time Peter Markham was here, and if it will give us any clues as to why he has gone missing.'

No response, but a nod, and something nearing eye contact. Greasy hair, and baggy clothes. He might even be handsome if he scrubbed up a bit. Lovely eyes though, and if he smiled, it would change the whole look of his face. What had life done to him to cause him to look so hopeless and forlorn?

'Okay, John, if you could just tell us in as much detail as you can remember about the last time you saw Peter Markham, nothing is irrelevant or silly. Any little detail could be vital, so please, miss nothing out.'

A flash of something crossed his face. Guilt maybe or it could have been a reflex, these little things intrigued Cora. Taking a deep breath, John looked at her square in the eyes.

'Mr Markham came here about once a month. I was quite new at the time, and he was nice to me. He remembered my name and referred to me by it every time, which made me feel kind of special. I thought he was a proper gent, you know. After a while, though, he changed. Not physically or anything like that, but he seemed, how can you say? Jumpy. Then one day my opinion of him reversed completely. He asked me to guide a hooker he'd just ordered up to his hotel room. Strange thing was, he always went on about his family, and how much he loved and missed them, but here he was, wanting an escort. It was common knowledge amongst the other staff, and the old receptionist before I started here, that this was the usual arrangement.'

Could this be the same man, Peter Markham, that John was talking about? This was a surprise after what they had been led to believe by Yvonne Markham, but Cora kept her face expressionless.

'Okay, thanks for that, John, for being so forthcoming. Just a couple of follow-up questions if you don't mind, then we'll let you get on with your day. First, how often, during Peter's visits, did he ask for an escort—every night of his stay or—'

'Yes, detective. He must have had some kind of sex addiction or something.'

Darcey noted this down and ringed it.

'Thanks, John. Final questions. What websites did he use? Do you know any of them specifically? Was there anything about his stay when he went missing that seemed out of the ordinary? And anything about his demeanour or behaviour that looking back on made you think something was bothering him?'

'It was punternet.com I think, and a couple others. I can write them down for you. But no, apart from that, he seemed the same as he always did.'

Time to shake hands. John did pretty well in helping their investigation. Turning to leave, Cora had some parting advice.

'Oh, by the way, if you're smoking weed, or whatever illegal thing you're up to, we were all young once, John. If you make your face look less guilty, it will probably help.'

Suppressing a smirk, Cora was trying her best not to burst into laughter as they left the hotel. If John's jaw could get any lower, it would have hit the floor.

'DI Snitton, did I just hear you tell a young man how to evade criminal action?'

'Who me, DC Clarke? The officer who carries the rule book around with her?'

But the time to share a little levity was thwarted when Cora felt her phone vibrate in her pocket.

Answering it, she listened as they gave her the pertinent information and thanked the caller before hanging up.

# 15

Harrison text his mates. They were due to scope out a new venue for their latest Live Action Role Play, commonly known as LARP, in the community. They had first found out about these events as a result of an online Dungeons and Dragons community, where they'd chatted and made a team, and become friends as a result.

Landon and Jaden were brothers. Kit was a bit of a free spirit who Harrison had a huge crush on. Their friend, John Kirkham, was older than the rest and the hotel receptionist at The Old Palace Lodge. John was the first to bring up the idea of the LARP and asked if his friends were into Zombie role-play.

Of course, none of them had tried it, but they were certainly willing to give it a go. They didn't have much to do other than play their online games or Xbox. The more John told them about it, the more intrigued they became. You don't have to wait to roll the dice or ask permission from the dungeon master. You could go and act out whatever scenario you'd planned. There was a wide variety of costumes and weapons available, or you could design your own. It sounded ideal.

John explained the idea he had, as there weren't many LARP events in the local area and told them about an abandoned shopping centre which would be perfect. That's how Harrison found himself at the edge of the decrepit building, alongside Kit. He assumed the brothers were grounded again, as they usually were. John was at work but had given them the What3Words' location, so they'd know they were in the right place.

'Well, it's certainly old, and abandoned,' whistled Harrison, 'and super creepy, like something is menacing. Feels like there should be music playing. Ow, what was that for?'

'You were sounding like a knob,' laughed Kit. 'Lucky I only punched your arm and didn't knock you out.'

'Oh yeah, I feel so thankful. Shall we get on, I don't really wanna be here when it gets dark. Not that I'm afraid of the dark?'

Kit motioned, pulling a zip across her lips, which made him laugh. He was totally in love with her and found everything she did cute, funny, or both. Not that Kit was aware. Well, he didn't think she was, anyway.

Looking at the area, it was huge. There was what used to be an entranceway, he was sure he remembered his foster parents talking about Christmas markets and fairground rides from the old days. He wouldn't know; he was never lucky enough to go there before it was finally sold off and left to rot. His early foster parents didn't believe in treating their charges like children, or often humans. Dreadful memories of a past he didn't wish to visit again. The pigeons swooping in made him laugh as they hoped to find a scrap of something edible.

Some kind of statue, maybe even a former fountain, was the central point while the plant life had taken over and was trying to reclaim the mall. All the concrete barriers and paving were chipped and cracked with weeds poking through.

Kit led the way, carefully picking her way across the rubbish. Discarded cans, tyres, crisp packets, and other food detritus, along with a couple of mattresses, sleeping bags, bike frames and the ever-present shopping trolley, minus its wheels. Kit was going to the corner of the building where there was a gap, boarding had been placed to protect intruders from the smashed windows.

Harrison barged in front; he would not let a girl enter a dangerous building first. He gripped the old chipboard to yank it hard, but it wasn't necessary as rain and time had rotted to crumble in his hands. He stumbled back slightly, the extra unnecessary force nearly sending him backwards, but Kit was close enough to stop him.

There was a hole big enough to allow the two to enter. Peering inside, Harrison took the initiative and stepped into the old building. Kit eagerly followed. Despite being early in the day, the first thing they noticed was the gloom. Neither of them had thought to bring torches, but they both had their phones.

Waving their phones around, trying to take in the details from the torch made this world appear strange and spooky. It was apparent that many people had been there before and taken everything they wanted. The shops were hit by a hurricane of thieves and neglect. Weird to walk through a world of the dead. Kit picked out a doll, dirty with an eye hanging down, causing her to shudder. She continued to look around and saw newspapers, creased and brown, curled up at the edges, empty takeaway containers, with who knew what still congealed inside. Harrison jumped as his phone swept across a mannequin before he realised it wasn't real and glad that Kit wasn't looking his way. He stepped over some discarded screws, bunches of cardboard and plastic, but saw nothing else of interest except the mannequin. This would take a good photo. Sizing this up with his mobile, he sent it to John, '*This gonna be any use to you?*' Not expecting a reply, for at least for a couple of hours.

'You seen anything good yet?' Shouted Harrison.

'No, nothing, just a creepy, eyeless doll, and loads of crap. You?'

'Nah, it's just rubbish. S'pose we'll need to make sure it's safe if we wanna role play here. There's a mannequin. I sent a pic of it to John, along with some others, to see what he reckons.'

'Hopefully, John thinks it's worth it. This place is a tip,' said Kit.

'True. Though we haven't gone all the way yet; I don't know what else is waiting for us further in.'

'Why does John get to make all the decisions anyway, who made him boss?' Kit asked.

'He's the LARP equivalent of dungeon master, while we're still little warriors.'

'Of course, I suppose that makes sense. I guess coz he's so old.'

Harrison smirked 'He's not that old. Jeez, he's only like five years older than us. Look, here, there's a door. I wonder where that goes?'

'Only one way to find out. Shall we push and see?' asked Kit, her voice beginning to echo.

Pushing the door open, ignoring the squealing rusty hinges, Kit made her way carefully down the concrete stairs as a blast of cold air met them.

'Wait up, Kit, you don't know who, or what, is down here. Hang on. What's that noise?'

'Sounds like buzzing to me. Intense buzzing. I've never heard a noise like that before. Like loads of bees or something. Sod the noise, what's that smell?' Kit shouted over her shoulder, making her way down the stairs. Harrison followed quickly behind, concerned she should step into danger.

Just as he was about to step off the last step, he heard the loudest, most piercing scream he'd heard in his life raising all the goose-pimples on his arms.

'What is it? Are you okay?'

He ran to Kit's voice and almost tripped over her. They were standing in something thick and gooey, and gripping onto each other's arms to prevent them from falling into whatever it was.

'Are you okay? What is that?' asked Harrison.

'I don't know. I can't tell if it's an animal or what?'

'I don't think so. It's too big. Shall we go closer? Unless you're scared?' asked Harrison.

'I'm no chicken. Come on, let's go poke it.'

*Oh God.*

'I'm sure we shouldn't go touching that stuff, Kit.'

'It smells dreadful. I don't think I'll ever get rid of that smell from my mind.'

Inching towards the mass, flashing their mobiles, they suddenly realised this was no animal.

'Harrison? It looks human.'

'Yes, I think it is.'

'There are thousands of flies and maggots crawling all over its face.'

Mesmerised, they couldn't take their eyes off the moving carnage. It looked more like rotting meat than it did human.

'I think we've seen enough. No need to poke it?'

Holding her hand over her mouth, so she didn't throw up, Kit stood morbidly fascinated.

'I think we should go back and call the police,' urged Harrison, still staring at the corpse.

‘Yes, let’s do that,’ Kit was trying to shake herself free from the living feast.

They ran as fast as they could without saying another word. Mouths struck dumb, still seeing the thriving mass of human remains. They had made it all the way through. Then finally, Kit let go and brought up the contents from her stomach.

Dialling 999, Harrison couldn’t stop shaking.

‘Hello, police please, I think we’ve found a dead body.’

# 16

Rushing to the car, Cora put on her coat, pulling her hat down over her ears, braving the wall of cold. She knew the way to the old shopping centre, a place where she spent much of her childhood. Hanging out with her mates, and just kidding around. No need to use the siren. From the description, the victim had to be very dead.

'Where we off to, boss?' asked Darcey.

'A body has been found at the old shopping centre; you know the one on the edge of town. It was supposed to be making way for a football ground or a cinemaplex.'

'Do you think it could be our missing man, boss?'

'Did you think I would dash off quickly if it wasn't?'

'Good point, sorry, wasn't thinking. So much information to take in today, not sure what to believe by what we've been told so far. It feels like everyone has been open and yet hiding something.'

'I know what you mean. I was thinking the same thing myself. Once we reach the scene, it might become clearer.'

'Do you have any idea what we are going to find when we get there, boss? Did they give you any clue on the phone?'

'No, you know what they're like, although apparently, some kid called it in. Just told the operator about the body before dropping the phone. The fact that he was sobbing in the background made her think it wasn't a prank.'

From ahead, flashing blue lights told them they had arrived at the scene already, a few uniforms and an ambulance. The coroner's van and forensics hadn't arrived yet, but they wouldn't be far away. Forensics didn't like people trampling over their scene. This was Cora's chance to have a look first. Stopping at the outer cordon, she recognised the uniform keeping the log.

'All right Fran, you pulled the short straw today, huh?'

The young, uniformed officer grimaced and held out the clipboard for the boss to sign in, before noting the time.

'All your kit is just over there. It seems the body is underneath the building on the old service road. DCI Blackwater is there.'

Cora and Darcey entered under the scene of crime tape that Fran was holding up. Already quite a few people milling around the outside wondering why they were up here if the body was below. While Darcey seemed to be somewhere else entirely. This was her first actual murder scene, and despite all the training and practice runs, nothing prepared anyone for the reality. Perhaps she was scared that she was going to do something wrong and mess it up, Cora guessed. She wouldn't let her do that, remembering the fear only too well.

But Darcey had strength of character about her, and not only that, she also listened. She had a professional approach in situations like these. Cora was happy to guide the young detective through all the protocols to ensure she got as much from her first crime scene as she could.

Once Cora and Darcey had donned the stiflingly hot scene suits, covered their shoes, and put on their gloves and mask before joining the gathering of people. Cora held out a tub of VapoRub to her young colleague.

'What's with the VapoRub?' Darcey looked at the jar and then Cora.

'This is your first murder, isn't it—your first dead body?'

'Yes.'

'Take some then,' ordered Cora, taking a small amount, she lifted her mask to put some under each nostril.

'It helps. Although it doesn't entirely mask the smell, but helps dilute it. This guy has been here for a week at least and it's not going to be pretty, although the cold weather may have slowed things down.'

Nodding, Darcey copied her boss.

'Are you ready? From what I gather, this is a nasty one. I just want a quick look before Forensics turns up. They hate people trampling their scenes. Then we'll talk to the kid who called it in. But we will need to wait until his parents arrive.'

'Okay boss, let's go.'

She was right, there was a slight quiver in Darcey's voice. Her hand trembled as she swiped the VapoRub under her nose. She was glad though, for if Darcey was too confident then she was more likely to mess up, it was necessary to have her on the ball. Fear tended to do that. If she was honest, Cora wasn't looking forward to seeing what was down there. By the look on some of the people's faces dotted around, she knew it was going to be a bad one.

The inner cordon was just on the edge of the building. The slight gap had been widened to allow adults through. Darcey was a step behind. The temperature dropped a few degrees once they were inside. Dark, although a spotlight had been brought inside to ensure none of the officers injured themselves. *Health and safety no matter what* Cora thought to herself.

Another spotlight was placed further along the old centre, so Cora went towards that. Bewildered, Darcey was looking around at the chaos, the broken glass, and the debris. She hadn't seen this place in its glory and could not imagine the grand place as it had once been. Nothing of its life grandeur was left behind, it had been completely stripped. A jungle of broken concrete, wildlife, birds, and bat droppings along with water had crept in for life never stayed stationary. Much of the floor was broken, which meant they should step carefully. Cora was grateful now that the spotlights were well placed.

As they reached what must have been the centre point, Cora and Darcey both stopped at the same time. 'What is that smell?' Darcey whispered.

'I assume the body is just underneath here. That smell Darcey is the smell of death. It's only going to get worse as we get closer. I hope you're ready. Once you've smelt it, you'll never forget it. It will remain with you forever clinging to your hair and your clothes, and you will even taste it. Are you sure you want to continue?'

Cora watched carefully for Darcey to wince, knowing this was what she had signed up for. She wouldn't wimp out at the first crime scene because, like herself, she also wanted to find out who this person was and why they had been abandoned in a disused shopping centre. In the end, Darcey simply nodded, afraid that if she spoke, her voice would betray her.

Every emotion passed across the young woman's face before it finally rested on determination. Cora knew that when she asked that question, Darcey wouldn't leave.

They saw the door at the end where the two kids had been, now propped open with lights strung down its length. Leading the way, Cora took each step slowly. It was getting colder while the smell increased. She also sensed the metallic tang of old blood she'd come to know so well.

When she got to the bottom, she stepped out of the way so Darcey could come out of the stairwell. This would allow them both to arrive at the scene together. She could hear the low hum of voices and see another spotlight had been set up just around the corner. Nodding in that direction, Darcey followed her prompt.

---

Standing by the body, DCI Blackwater had been present for about half an hour. As luck had it, he just happened to be passing when the call came in. Aware of the missing businessman, he hoped this would be him. He hated missing people, especially when they'd disappeared for a while. At least a body would provide answers by giving enough clues to determine how they'd died, and, more importantly, who'd killed them.

Felix Blackwater had grown up in an affluent household. He lived in one of the big houses. His mother was a solicitor, but his father was a butcher. Felix had helped his father in the school holidays and was not as affected as some of his colleagues were by the smells and sights of dead bodies.

This one, however, had got to him. Whoever killed this man had been angry and had savagely gone to town. Not that he was much of a man now, for what had made him a male had been removed and wasn't anywhere to be seen. There were a lot of cuts, and some looked like burns. His fingers were missing, and he suspected his teeth had also been extracted.

The spectacle of the man tied with his arms apart and his legs spreadeagled was enough. First impressions gave Felix no clue which of the many wounds had been the fatal one. The pathologist was going to have a job on their hands cataloguing all of those.

The photographer had nearly finished snapping from every angle. Apart from the body, there wasn't a lot else to see. Felix began looking about him. One of the first things he learned was never to focus on what was in front of him but to look in all directions, including up. This theory had come in handy before. Amazing how far blood and brains can fly, even when you have cleaned the floor and bleached it. Some pesky bits land in light fittings and on the top of picture frames.

As he looked, he saw his DI heading around the corner with one of the newer recruits in tow. It was unlike Cora to take to bring out a newbie, considering she was a bit of a lone wolf, and would only accept a partner once they'd been bedded in a bit. Although he hadn't discussed it with Cora, he also thought Darcey had something about her, a spark that showed a lot of promise. He thought this scene, her first murder, would be a great test to see what she was made of. If she handled this well, then she was going to be a fantastic addition to his team if they could keep hold of her.

'Hello Cora, it's a bit of a grim one, I'm afraid. They've really gone to town on him. So, you brought one of the newbies?'

Cora blushed and laughed; Darcey noticed. Looking into the face of her boss, he was a striking man, with chiselled features, a square jaw, and slight stubble that guys of a certain age seemed to favour these days, but no flecks of grey yet. She couldn't place his age; except he was older than her.

'Darcey Clarke, sir. Pleased to meet you.'

Felix laughed, liking her immediately. Cora smiled too. Hard to believe she was a bumbling nervous wreck when they first met and that she had totally embarrassed herself.

She went to shake his hand and stumbled to punch him in his most private area. As he'd doubled over in pain, he'd hit her head with his forehead. Not knowing how to react, they descended into laughter. Their relationship hadn't suffered as a result, although she got reminded of it often; but her stern stares and sarcastic responses soon stopped that. Having a sense of humour didn't mean she appreciated ridicule. It was then she asserted her authority.

'Pleased to meet you, Darcey, and glad to have you on the team. I hope Cora has been looking after you. She has quite a fearsome reputation.'

Cora raised her eyebrow, but Darcey knew better than to answer. This was a situation where there was no right answer.

'Ignore him. He likes to ingratiate the young ones with humour.' Cora took Darcey to the body. 'He's quite the lady's man.'

'He doesn't affect me, he's old enough to be my dad,' Darcey laughed.

'How old do you think he is? I don't think he's that old. Never mind, don't answer that. We have a job to do.'

As they stepped over to the body, both women let out a long breath. Cora had seen a lot of bodies since she'd been in this job, but this one was the worst. Not only had he been brutally tortured and mutilated, he'd also been here for a while and decay had set in.

Meanwhile, Felix had walked away and spotted an old oil drum that showed signs of being used. On top of the burnt ashes was the tiniest piece of fabric. He smiled; his intuition hadn't let him down. It could be nothing, or it could be the clue they needed.

# 17

Walking around the body, bound so tightly and spreadeagled, the victim would have been in pain, although comfort was not an issue with the person who did this. The knots weren't standard either. They were tied in such a way they couldn't be loosened to escape.

Looking more closely at the rope, it was the standard blue colour. The sort of rope available in DIY stores across the country. Damn, oh well, better look for something else. It was quite a clean scene, not a lot of rubbish, considering this was a disused area. She'd expected to see the remnants of homeless people and animals, suggesting the space had been cleaned to get rid of evidence.

Cora recorded the overall scene.

The man had been stripped naked. *Where had his clothes gone? Was he brought here naked, or was he stripped and his clothes disposed of?* And neither did he have any identifying features, no tattoos, or piercings. When he was taken to the morgue and autopsied, they might find more out about him then. The issue of his missing fingers and teeth would be a problem to slow them down, but once DNA was taken, they'd know. Although Cora thought she already knew who it was. The number of injuries on the body was staggering. A few bruises and general abrasions, as well as his missing manhood. It made Cora shudder that whoever it was had put that much thought into killing him. *The bastard.* The cause of death may have been the gash in his stomach. Some of his intestines were hanging out, what was left of them. Insects had descended and got to work.

A few hardy flies remained. They didn't want to be deprived of their tasty meal. Neither did the maggots she could see writhing around in the various open areas.

Cora was careful where she stepped, even though stepping plates had been placed around the body. From what she'd seen so far, the killer had been very careful.

'Nasty one this,' another voice also looking on.

The tiny woman, barely five feet tall and slim, looked up. Still new to the job, she came with great references from some of the most respected SOCOs in the country where she did her training. She had a reputation for having the sharpest eyes.

'Oh, hiya Cora, didn't see you there. Everyone looks the same in these damn scene suits. I'm thinking of getting one in bright pink.'

Cora smiled, knowing how much Selphie loved pink. When stressed, she also made jokes. It was her way of dealing with a difficult scene.

'I'll take a purple one if you find a supplier. White isn't my colour.' Cora considered the body again. 'I know you can't tell us much for now, but is there even a kernel we can take away with us?'

'You know me, Cora, until he's on the table, I really don't like to say. I can only tell you that the wound in the stomach was the cause of death. All the other wounds were pre-mortem and cauterised to slow or stop him from bleeding out. That's some clever killer you got there. As to the time of death, don't even think of asking. With the cold down here, and the wounds, I couldn't even begin to guess. There are still maggots present, but even that isn't helpful on this occasion.'

'I understand Selphie. You know I had to ask. Anyway, who's doing the postmortem?'

'Darren Walker, I think.'

'Okay, cool. Er... I'm interested. Do they give you a step so you can see into the body when you observe?'

Selphie stepped back from what she was doing, spun around, and stretched up to look Cora in the eye. Pausing a beat, she then burst into laughter, so much so tears were streaming down her cheeks.

'You cheeky cow, and actually, yes, as it happens, they do. Now bugger off and get away from my crime scene before you contaminate it.'

Still chuckling to herself, Cora walked away. She'd known Selphie since university. They'd crossed courses a few times and formed a firm friendship almost straight away. Some of Selphie's fellow students found her a little odd and too blunt for their liking, but it never bothered Cora. Quickly she realised Selphie had a wicked sense of humour, not too dissimilar to her own. She was thrilled when she moved back to their force area.

---

At that moment Felix shouted, 'Cora, over here!'

Stepping off the plates, Cora took the long way around to get to Felix. She was close enough to breathe in his aftershave, although it was slightly tainted by the smell of Vicks. Yet he still smelt wonderful. What was she doing, acting like a silly schoolgirl when this case was serious? Standing over a container, Felix peered into an oil drum.

'Did I hear the imitable Selphie Ho laughing?'

'You did boss, I keep telling you she's great with a wicked sense of humour. I just asked if she needed a step to do the postmortem.'

Felix looked horrified 'Tell me you didn't?' Felix was mortified. As long as he lived, he would never understand women. 'Anyway, look at what I've spotted,' said Felix, directing her eyes. 'There's been a fire in here recently, and judging by this tiny piece of fabric, whoever it was had been trying to destroy the evidence.'

'Great catch Sir. What made you look over here?'

'The fact he has no clothing and there were no signs of them. I thought I would have a look around to see if there were any signs of disposal. I caught the slightest hint of a bonfire, and as a result, found this.'

Impressive, Cora hadn't spotted the burning above the nauseating smell of decay.

'Wow, remarkable, Sir. Let's hope it's the key to unlock the case. What did you think about the victim?'

'First thoughts. That someone hated him that much because of how they went to town on him. Cutting off his junk, probably while he was still alive. It made me wonder if it was a woman because of the level of brutality. But some of those cuts are deep, and he's no lightweight to drag and tie so tightly. This leads me to think it was a man.'

'I agree. What about the location, I'm guessing they didn't want to be caught and weren't expecting some kids to come here, let alone to venture underneath the building?'

'Absolutely. By the time they found the poor guy, he could have been skeletonised and potentially not found until someone earmarked it for redevelopment. Hopefully, the fact he's been found now is a good omen for the rest of the case.'

But law enforcement didn't work by hope.

'Okay boss, I'm gonna question the kids with Darcey.'

'What?' Felix looked surprised. 'Did I just hear you refer to a recruit by her first name? Usually, you hate newbies, and tell everyone you don't want to be lumbered with them.'

'DC Clarke has something about her, that essential spark which yet remains to be seen. But I think she's a good'un.'

Felix nodded while Cora shouted to Darcey, both were eager to return to the fresh air.

---

Squeezing back through the small gap, they blinked to find themselves back in the light of day. Shedding their scene suits, they added them to the collection ready for examination later.

'Are you okay?' Cora asked. Darcey's restraint and courage had impressed her.

Taking another deep breath, she responded. 'Yes.'

*But was she okay? That was horrific. That poor man. Who would do that to another human being? How on earth were they supposed to take anything away from that to find who had done it?*

'I think so. I can't believe how much damage was done to that man. How can someone be that evil?'

'That's a question even after all these years I don't have an answer to. All we can do is take what we have and investigate. Find the person or persons responsible and bring them to justice. So, putting your investigator's hat on, what were your impressions?'

A test question to see how closely the young recruit chimed with herself and Felix, and whether her instincts about this young detective were proven right.

'Very violent. Lots of anger. I would say it would either

take a man or two people to get him there and tie him up. Removal of clothes to humiliate, and his private parts, well that suggests a woman, maybe. But the strength needed, I'm not sure. Removing teeth and fingers might just be for torture, or it might mean they are forensically aware, which is never good. Question. How did he get there? How did the killer get there and get away again?'

'Good. I agree with you about the humiliation of being stripped naked. But yes, you're right. The rest is pretty much what Felix and I concluded. I considered them also to be forensically aware, certainly making our lives more difficult. Good job Darcey.'

Darcey blushed; she wasn't used to being praised but appreciated it. She was mostly just glad that she hadn't seen her breakfast again or embarrassed herself in front of her boss or the DCI. 'Thank you, boss. Just doing my job.'

'Okay, let's speak to the two teenagers, and find out what on earth they were doing wandering around an abandoned shopping centre discovering dead bodies.'

---

The two youngsters looked up, sensing they were being scrutinised. The boy looked like he'd been sick down his front.

'Hey, I hear you two found our man down there?' Cora started walking towards them. 'I need to ask you a few questions, okay? Then you can go home and get cleaned up.'

Two forlorn faces who this morning had been young suddenly felt themselves to be old. Even though she'd been told they were between fourteen to sixteen, they still looked so young.

'That's right, Miss,' replied Harrison. 'I know we weren't supposed to be there. We heard something funny.

I've learnt my lesson. Are you going to tell my foster parents?'

'We have. They are on their way to collect you.'

The thought of his foster parents finding out was more upsetting to him than the dead man on the service road. The sound of tyres and doors slamming as two people came rushing over to engulf their son in their arms, overjoyed to find him safe. Kit sat there with eyes downcast, waiting. Guardians needed to be there because the kids were underage.

'Would you be responsible for Kit as well?' asked Cora. 'We are having problems getting hold of her parents, and time is important.'

'I understand,' said Esther, Harrison's guardian. She had her arm around the boy, glad to have him safe.

'Good.' Cora's attention was directed to Harrison and Kit. 'I want to know why you were in the abandoned shopping centre when it's plainly off-limits and dangerous.'

'We were looking for a new place for our latest Live Action Role Play scenario,' started Kit. 'Our friend John Kirkham told us about this place. He's the head of our local faction. He's at work. And as we had nothing better to do, we thought we'd check it out, and take some photos to send him.'

'Okay, thanks,' responded Cora. 'Now, can you walk me through exactly what happened? Every step you took, everything you touched, it's very important you miss nothing out.'

'We went in through a boarded area that had already been pulled away.' This time, Harrison took over. 'We looked around the first shop, kicked a few bits on the floor. There was a creepy mannequin and a doll with its eyes falling out. I took a bunch of photos and sent them to John, and then we just kept walking till we saw the door at the end. We heard a noise, so thought we would check it out.

We touched nothing near the body or go near it. Then we ran.'

All this came out in one long breath, as quickly as Harrison could get it out of him.

'Thanks, Harrison. Do you have anything to add to that, Kit?' asked Cora. She had her mouth sealed closed and was now looking slightly green again. 'Okay, we will leave it at that.'

'We'll need you both to come to the station as soon as possible to make an officially signed statement,' said Darcey, looking at Graeme and Esther. 'We want to make absolutely sure you touched nothing when you were down on the service road.'

Both children vigorously shook their heads.

'No, Miss,' said Kit weakly. 'I just wanted to run from the smell and everything.'

'I want to thank you for reporting the body. It's made our job easier. We need to find the person responsible to get justice for this man and his family.' Cora said, looking at the parents again. 'Can you arrange for them to come to the station within the next twenty-four hours to complete the statements?'

'It's best you keep an eye on them,' added Darcey. 'They might be in shock. Get them checked out if you're concerned at any point.'

Unkind to witness two children joining adulthood in such a hard way as both women watched the teens walk to the Chilton's car.

'I was surprised at how well the children handled themselves,' said Darcey, watching the car drive away.

'Brave kids,' said Cora, feeling queerly emotional. 'Did you pick up about their friend John Kirkham? I was wondering if it was the same John Kirkham who we interviewed at the hotel. What are the chances of that?'

'I wondered why the name sounded familiar. I was going to check my notes when we were back at the station.'

'C'mon then, let's go back to the office. There's nothing more we can do here. We'll have to wait and let SOCO do their thing. In the meantime, we need to figure out if this is our missing man, and if so, why he's here, trussed up like a prize turkey in an abandoned shopping centre service area with his dick removed.'

Darcey was done for, all emotions drained from her soul. This had been a horrendous journey and something she didn't want to repeat. But she was a member of the law, and if she wanted to remain, she would have to face scenes like this again, perhaps not now, but in the future. Cora waited until Darcey got in and buckled up. Starting the engine, deep in thought, they drove off.

## 18

Darcey, Cora, and Felix arrived back at the station, each thinking over what they'd seen; it was one of the worst crime scenes any of them had attended.

Forensics were scouring around for any tiny clues that would help them, but so far, it was a clean scene. The scrap of fabric Felix had found could prove vital if it had any DNA on it, which was unlikely after being burnt. If not, then at least for inclusion or exclusion purposes later.

Cora waited as Felix held the door open for his two colleagues to enter the busy incident room. As he did, he held Cora back.

'You'll be deputy SIO on this Cora, get the team together. Use uniforms to fill in the gaps. You know how tight budgets are.'

'Yes boss,' but Cora was furious. 'It's all about budgets. Sod the poor souls who must bury what's left of their loved ones after they've been carved up. As long as we catch the murderer in the most cost-efficient way, everyone wins, right?'

'You know I hate it as much as you do Cora, I am trying to provide you with what you need to do for your jobs while dealing with the people above telling me I'm spending too much. Just do what you can okay, and no going off on your own. Keep me updated, then I won't breathe down your neck. I trust you.'

'Sorry about that sir, but we are constantly doing our jobs with one hand tied behind our back. Soon it will be both hands and blindfolded. You know I give it my all, as everyone else does. But that guy—wow, that was some powerful rage unleashed.'

'Yes, it was. I would also like you to be mindful that you are working with a team. Be careful not to show favouritism.' After giving her a meaningful look, Felix walked away.

What did he mean by that? Cora was fixed on the spot for a few seconds. *She was fair to every member of the team, wasn't she? That's the second time he's mentioned teamwork recently*. Taking a deep breath, she opened the double doors and went in after rounding up the small team. The upstairs room had been readied while they were at the scene. Cora told Darcey, Luke, Dave, Beverlee, and a few uniforms to be there for a briefing in ten minutes.

Gathering what they needed, Cora went straight there, feeling prepared. The interactive whiteboard was set up, as were a couple of old-fashioned whiteboards. These were handy for notes. Already, the crime scene photos were pinned up, as was an image of the missing businessman. It hadn't been confirmed yet that the body was that of Peter Markham. That would come in the next day or so once Selphie and the pathologist had completed their part. Time of death was the vital piece of information now.

Glad that she'd gathered Peter's toothbrush from his belongings at the Old Palace Lodge extracting his DNA would certainly make identification a lot quicker. The other thing Cora requested from admin was to search for any other missing persons that might match the description of the murder victim.

Shuffling, muted voices were heard as the team came along the hallway. A quick look in her notebook confirmed what she'd learnt so far today. It had been a long day of questioning different people, but not gaining much. Darcey and herself had gone back to the hotel to have a word with a red-faced John Kirkham. He didn't deny the relationship with Harrison and Kit. His struggling eyes confirmed that the derelict shopping centre was his idea for roleplay; and that he had asked his young friends to check out. Darcey and Cora exchanged glances on their way back to their car.

'I don't know about you, but I believed him,' suggested Cora.

'Me too, by the terrified look on his face.'

There was a lot more re-interviewing now a body had been discovered. She was getting the distinct feeling there were some who knew more than they were prepared to share.

Darcey arrived first. Having been with her at the scene, it was less for her to finish and hand over since they had worked together. Tired, Darcey still looked keen. Her eyes shone brightly sitting at the front, saying nothing but waiting with her notebook open.

Luke followed closely behind. Like Darcey, he also showed great potential, but if they wanted to move up the ranks, it often meant losing them to somewhere else. One leg crossed over the other with a notebook balanced on one knee, Luke looked at Cora for reassurance. She nodded and smiled. His floppy blonde hair gave him a boyish look. Not a tall man. In his teenage years, he had suffered horribly from acne.

Compared to Darcey, who had grey-blue eyes that gave her a slightly icy look and a more severe appearance. Her hair cut short, not quite a pixie cut, but not a bob either. It was ice white, blonde and in another lifetime perhaps these two could have been siblings, so remarkable was the similarity in their appearance. The shape of their eyes and noses were almost identical. The telltale signs of piercings had been sacrificed by Darcey for the job. Still a huge number of piercings in her ears, including a daith piercing, and who knows what other bits. Occasionally, Cora caught glimpses of tattoos. Still a bit of a wild girl; she'd have to remember to ask about those one day. It was something she'd been considering, but perhaps when she retired.

Bounding in next was Dave. Slightly older, more her age, not that she'd ever asked. He always behaved like a child overdosed on sugar. He was their nerd, their Digital Forensics and mystery guy. She knew nothing about him, nor did he give anything away about himself. She didn't even know how long he'd been with the police or what he'd done before or why he'd joined and remained here in Luton when he had the capabilities to do much more. Once this case was over, she'd find out.

Dave never quite looked fully put together, like his uniform, he was always off-kilter, although Cora could never put her finger on why. The buttons were done up correctly, and his shirt was ironed but looked wonky. If it wasn't for his slightly receding hairline, Cora would have guessed he was no older than twenty-five, but despite him shaving close to his head, the advancement backwards was impossible to hide. In addition, Dave grew a beard, which was always neat, and meticulously trimmed, but showed flecks of grey. Popular amongst the team, he never had a bad word for anyone. Always smiling with a reputation as a joker. When he got stuck on something, he was diligent and thorough.

Finally, Beverlee ambled in, the eldest of the team. Shy and reserved and slightly chubby, now out of breath after tackling the stairs. The lift must be out of order again. She saw Darcey, Dave and Luke sitting together, why Beverlee placed herself as far away from them as she was able was an enigma. Keeping her head down, hoping her long lank brown hair would cover her face to make her invisible. But behind that hair was a lovely smile and the most stunning blue eyes Cora had ever seen. The woman clearly had confidence issues, but the longer she hid behind her hair and stayed back, the less chance she'd have of moving up.

Cora knew little about how Beverlee worked, when she'd joined, Beverlee had been seconded to another team. Only recently, she'd re-joined major crimes, and so far she'd heard nothing but praise for her. Hearing her plonk heavily into the chair, Cora knew she was settled. After a quick look around to see the uniforms had joined; it was time to begin.

'Thanks, everyone, I'll try to be quick as it's getting late. I'm sure you all know by now a body was discovered over in the old out-of-town shopping centre by two young teens. The level of violence inflicted on the man was extreme. Post-mortem hasn't been carried out yet, but he was subjected to many minor cuts and burning, which amounted to horrendous torture. Cause of death, as far as the pathologist could tell, was from the large slash to his abdomen, severe enough for his guts to spill out, but Selphie couldn't be certain because of the number of uncommon injuries, however,' Cora sighed. 'So far, she could not give an accurate time of death, what with the cold weather and colder temperatures in the service road, decomposition would have been delayed.'

One of the team went to put their hand up to ask a question, but Cora held hers up in a wait-a-minute gesture.

'First job is to identify the victim. It could be our missing man, Mr Peter Markham, but it could be some poor sod we don't know about yet, so let's not jump to conclusions, okay? Questions?'

'What are the likelihoods of this not being Mr Markham?'

'A great question. Sorry, I don't know what your name is.'

'It's Paul, ma'am.'

'Thanks, Paul. I would venture a guess of slim to non-existent. The question stands—why would anyone want to wreak such havoc on another human being? Until we find out who it is for now, it could be anyone. We have a toothbrush from the Markham home, so we've rushed this for DNA. Guess who gets to check out any other mispers?' Cora looked at Paul.

Grinning, Paul nodded his acceptance of the assigned task.

'We won't know any more until we get more information, so that's what we need to do. So let's get gathering as much as we can. I'm sure I don't need to remind you, CCTV, bank details, social media, all the usual stuff.' Cora glanced at the clock. 'It's late, so another hour and then we'll wrap up before an early start tomorrow. We want this closed as quickly as we can, so this will be intense for as long as it takes.'

'Jobs are assigned on the board. It's now Operation Fraction. Dave, are you okay to keep HOLMES 2 updated? I will be the deputy SIO, answerable to DCI Blackwell. I need to update him regularly. He will arrange a press conference with the media in the morning. Thankfully, with the location, they hadn't got a sniff yet, but you know what they're like.'

Looking for affirmative nods from her team, what Cora saw was eagerness to get the job done. This was what she was looking for, hungry appetites to find their murderer.

'Thanks, everyone. I would like to remind those who

haven't worked with me before. This is a democracy, we work together. There are no stupid questions; so, don't be afraid to speak up. That's all. Off you go.'

Chairs scraped, coats rustled, phones bleeped, and voices chattered as they left for their respective assigned tasks. Cora stood and looked at the photograph of the victim's battered body and wondered who was behind it. Who could be that angry to inflict that number of injuries on a man?

---

Thoughtfully sitting for a while, going through what they had so far, but first, she needed to allocate the resources before deciding what must be done next. Updating HOLMES2 with actions from the little they'd learned had also to be done. Another essential was to check out Mr Markham's employees to find if there was anything there. At some point, his children would also have to be spoken to.

Time to write down her thoughts in her investigator's notebook. Things like what happened to Mr Markham. Where did he go? Where was his car last seen? Did anyone spot it? Where is it now? ANPR needed to be consulted. Finances? Was Peter Markham struggling? Anything, absolutely anything that stands out? Blackmail? Gambling? Other women, was his wife hiding something? The photo of the newborn baby. What the hell was that about, and was it relevant? This family had secrets, but could she be overreacting? The way that man died, how could you not react to this hate?

Leaning back in her chair, Cora raised her hands above her head to stretch. A sigh, and some deep breathing. She would not find out any of the answers to these questions tonight. She had some jokes to write, and some yoga to do. Being a police officer, it's necessary to be fit.

Just as she was ready to leave, the phone rang. It was late. Should she allow it to ring? To call this late in the day was bound to be important.

'DI Cora Snitton.'

'Hi Cora, it's Selphie, you're working late.'

'I was about to leave; you just caught me. I hope this means you have some good news for me.'

'Well, I have news, whether it's good for you, I do not know, but I think we can safely say the man on my morgue table is that of Peter Markham. There's an old break in his tibia that matched his medical records. I will wait for DNA to confirm, but I am as confident as I can be right now that he's one and the same.'

'Brilliant. Thanks, Selphie, you're a diamond. Are you still up for that meal at the weekend, and watching my latest comedy set?'

'You betcha. Can't wait to see what jokes you come out with next. By the way, it's your turn to pay, so I'm thinking we should try out that new, and expensive, restaurant that's just opened.'

Cora laughed down the phone. 'Cheeky mare, you'll get a Spoons special, and lump it, lady.'

Selphie laughed in return. 'Tight cow, fine, I'll text you. See you.'

There was no point in saying goodbye. Selphie had already hung up. Typical Selphie, as Cora continued to put her coat and scarf on, ready to brave the cold. At least she could crack on with the case now, knowing for sure who the victim was. Was it good news? No, she didn't think so either.

# 19

As Cora and Felix discussed the case, they knew they'd need to get someone to deliver the news to Mrs Markham that her husband was dead. She will need a family liaison officer; this was essential.

Not being good with overly emotional people, Cora was sending Luke and Darcey dressing it up as part of their good experience and training course.

'I need you to go to Mrs Markham and tell her that her husband has been found. Handle it gently and answer her questions as best you can. I know it will be tough. She deserves the truth, but not the gory details. She'll have to identify the body or get someone else to. Usually, it's best the partner does, as it also provides closure. We'll be providing a Family Liaison Officer to give support and answer to questions when she thinks of them, so don't worry too much about what you say, as the FLO will pick up on anything else.'

'When do you want us to skedaddle, boss?' asked Luke.

'Now. It needs to be done before she even gets a whiff from the media.'

'Okay, boss. I'm driving this time.' Luke said, walking off

to grab a set of keys for one of the pool cars before Darcey could argue. Chasing after him, shouting his name, throwing in the odd curse words to emphasise her point, but he didn't break stride or react. They were like two kids fighting between themselves. Cora smiled. Felix returning to his office was also smiling. Their enthusiasm and youth brought light relief to a very grim episode.

---

At the Astra, Luke slid into the driver's seat and moved the chair back to accommodate his lanky legs. He was laughing as he waited for Darcey to climb in, still furious.

'You okay there? You seem a bit peeved, chickadee.'

'Just shut up and drive, will you? Do you even know where you're going?'

'Yes thanks, I had about half an hour to plug the address into the sat nav before your dinky legs finally got you here. Have you been for a wee? Didn't you get the job in the Willy Wonka factory?'

Darcey slapped his arm, not with any force, as Luke put the car in reverse. It was quiet on the roads, although they seemed to get stopped at every traffic light along the way.

'What do you think about this case, Luke?'

'I don't really know, my lovely. It seems there aren't many clues, and the more we find, the less we know. I've not spoken to as many people as you mano a mano, so I'm only going on what everyone else has written down, which is—well—yeah.'

Was that a hint of envy in Luke's tone? Not anger exactly, but she knew he was annoyed at being left out of the prime bits of the case because she would have been.

'I know what you mean. I can't even guess who killed that man. That was harsh, man. Crikey, those injuries.

Going out and questioning people isn't as exciting as I thought it would be. You're trying to listen to what people are saying and detect a lie, whilst also trying to spot minute changes in their body language. Plus, Cora's the boss; I'm just baggage.'

Was Luke reassured by her words? She couldn't really tell, but he smiled back at her, anyway.

'You, my sweet, are NEVER baggage.'

She leaned back in the chair and sighed.

'Do you remember what we were taught, ABC, Assume nothing, Believe no one, Challenge everything?'

'Yeah, of course, one of the first things we were taught. Why?'

'I suppose it's the challenging everything bit. So, we say we can't trust everything we've been told so far. Why on earth do we challenge and question further?'

Luke was quiet for a moment, flicking through the various bits of information they'd gathered so far. Not even a hint of a suspect, although it was still early days.

'I suppose it's the witnesses; they are the porky-pie tellers, right? People lie, and especially to the police.'

'Okay, so why would anyone kill Peter Markham—that's the question, isn't it?'

'Money, revenge, or love.' Darcey began pushing each finger down. 'One, Peter was wealthy. He lived in the fancy part of town. He stayed in a posh hotel and drove a posh car. So, we look at his wife to see if there were any new life insurance policies taken out. Follow the money and see who benefits financially from his death.'

'So, it's revenge, darling. We need to dig and find Mr Markham's skeletons. He must have some. That's when we need those pesky witnesses to start telling the truth. I reckon at least one is hiding something. What could he have done though, he seemed very vanilla. Snoooooooozzzzeee.'

'Vanilla?' laughed Darcey. 'Who uses the term vanilla? How old are you, fifty?'

'Well, he's not as clean cut as he seemed.' Luke stopped at the traffic lights. 'He hired escorts when he stayed in that hotel. I guess you never got around to checking HOLMES2 before we were called out to the scene, but apparently, this was what he was doing, requesting escorts. How ick is that? If his wife doesn't know, which I didn't get the impression she did, the man should be ashamed of himself. He's nearly a grandfather. Urgh. I can't think of anything more to make someone that angry. When he went missing, his record was checked and found clean. So, whatever it was, the sly sod hadn't been caught for it.'

They drove in silence for a couple of minutes.

'Man, the male of the species can be vile,' started Luke. 'You have someone like me, obviously wonderful, then someone like him, outwardly vanilla, inwardly a snake which is insulting to snakes. Thankfully, I've not met any like that so far! Also, nope, I can't think of anything. Perhaps it's obvious, and when we find out, we will wonder how we missed it, but for now, I have no clue.'

'Me either,' said Darcey. 'Which leaves love, and here we are. Oh look, Sharon is there already, that's good.'

Exiting the car, Luke and Darcey knocked on the door; Sharon had already spotted the unmarked car and hurried to stand with them. When Yvonne opened the door, she knew instantly.

'No, no, no, no, no, it can't be—' she held up her hands before collapsing.

Must be the worst news a wife could ever have to face as Luke and Darcey raised her to her feet.

'I'm going to make you a cup of tea, Yvonne, all right?'

Unsteady on her feet, they took Mrs Markham into the house and sat her down. Luke and Darcey looked at each other. Who was going to validate the news to her? Darcey would.

'Mrs Markham, Yvonne, I am sorry to tell you we received confirmation; the body discovered is that of your husband, Peter. I'm so sorry.'

Staring at them frantically, wanting someone to deny it was no good. Only tears were her comfort. What were they supposed to do next? They glanced at each other helplessly. And then Sharon returned with the tea.

'How do you know? How can you be so sure it's my husband?' Mrs Markham began grasping at straws. 'Surely it could still be a mistake?' Her desperate eyes pleaded, yes.

'The postmortem has been carried out; the pathologist has matched an old break in Peter's leg to one in his childhood. We are still waiting for DNA results, but we are as certain as we can be. We'll need someone to identify him officially. Your son will do if you don't feel you're able to, although sometimes we find it helps to see the body. You don't have to decide right away. You can let Sharon know, and she will pass it on. Sharon is your Family Liaison Officer. She will stick around and answer any questions you have in the coming days. She's a lovely lady, so please make use of her. I know everything will feel overwhelming right now, but Sharon has experience, and will be as forthcoming.'

Yvonne sat mute while Darcey watched her carefully. She wasn't sure if she'd taken anything in she'd been told. Reaching over to the bereft woman, Darcey put her hand on Yvonne's arm to look her in the eye.

'I'm afraid to tell you we believe your husband's death wasn't accidental. We have reason to believe he was murdered. Believe me, Yvonne, I want whoever did this behind bars as much as you do. We both do.'

She's gone into shock, thought Luke, she had that

faraway look of someone lost. They didn't want to leave her like that, but Sharon was there.

'We'll be off now,' said Darcey gently, her hand still on Yvonne's arm. 'We need to get back to the station and get to work. Unless you have questions for us before we leave?'

'Just catch them, detectives,' said Yvonne in an unrecognisable guttural voice 'Catch whoever took my husband from me.'

## 20

Pulling her coat tightly around her as she walked, Amanda descended the steps, hesitant to go out of the accountancy office. It was even more bitter cold after sitting in artificial heating for the last three hours. She wasn't going far, yet it felt like the temperature had dropped since this morning, hope it didn't mean snow. There were a lot of crooks in the finance world, and the biggest ones were the insurance dealers themselves.

Only a few doors down on the opposite side of the road was her favourite coffee shop. Apart from being handy, it wasn't a big chain, which was something Amanda preferred with more of a personal feel. On the times she went, it was never busy. Another bonus was that Amanda had become friends with one of the women who worked there. They hadn't socialised yet, but it seemed impossible as they'd already friended each other on social media and gone as far as exchanging phone numbers.

Walking past the currently abandoned outside seating, Amanda wondered if that horrible old woman was there. Something about her she didn't like. It was the way she looked at her, like she knew something about her that spooked Amanda. Quiet now inside, despite the cold weather, the holy month of Ramadan had sent many of the regulars straight home until they were allowed to break their fast. This was the best time to sit at her favourite table and chat with Helen until she was called off to serve a customer.

Someone had left a copy of today's newspaper on the table. The headline ran about the body found in an abandoned shopping centre. An icy shiver ran down her spine just as Helen brought her special coffee over. Helen had something to tell, which looked urgent. Pulling out the chair opposite, Helen sat down.

'Wonder who they found.' Helen had seen the headlines. 'The press is staying tight-lipped so far. I wouldn't be surprised if it's that businessman?'

'Aye, impossible to say, but I suppose there's nah other prominent people missing at the moment, so who else would it be to make the front pages?'

'Yeah, you're right. I'm sure plenty of people die every day but barely get a mention. I served that bloke in here a few times. He gave me the creeps; his eyes lingered a little too long if you know what I mean?'

'He came in here?'

'Sure, why not? Don't I pour the best coffee?' Laughed Helen. 'I think he had a rendezvous with someone because he kept on looking at his watch. Small world, isn't it?'

'Yes,' mused Amanda.

Strange, because the missing businessman was a regular visitor to the accountancy company's offices as well. Horrible man. She couldn't stand him either. Not that he had time for someone as lowly as her. Walking in straight through reception and into the boss's office, not caring if she was busy. She, though, concentrated on the screen in front of her and pretended she couldn't see him when he walked past. He never stopped, never said hello or goodbye, and for that at least, Amanda was grateful.

'Ay chick, I can't stand him either. I suppose no one deserves to be murdered, though.'

Between them, they quickly scanned the article in case they'd missed any salacious detail, but nothing else was gleaned.

Wishing to change the subject, Amanda reverted to her failsafe topic, the handsome regular customer who had caught Helen's eye recently. His name was Jack, recently divorced with a son.

'Anyway, Mrs, what's happening with Jack—have you seen him recently?'

'Well, yeah, I have as it so happens.' Helen tried not to look coy. 'About an hour before you got here, he came in. As it was so quiet, I was forced to stand there and talk to him. Iqra is in a bit later, there was only me here, and well, he, er, he gave me his phone number and asked if I wanted to go out for a drink sometime, so I said yes.'

'Really? Well, I am shocked,' laughed Amanda.

'I said yes before I could stop myself; it was too late to take it back. What am I going to do now? I can't go out with him; he'll realise I am a loser.'

This was a conversation they'd had many times before, more since the lovely Jack had arrived on the scene.

'Helen, chick, for goodness' sake, how many times do I have to tell you, you're amazing? But you already know this.'

'You're too kind to me, lovely. You always are, but the truth is, I work in a pokey little coffee shop in a nothing town. What do I have to offer someone like Jack?'

'I'm not even dignifying that with an answer, woman. However, I've never known a man who needs so much coffee. Every time I come in, he's here or just left. Another thing, you have become a lot gigglier and smiling non-stop.

It's right canny. So, no more pulling yourself to pieces, and let me know when the big day is so I can get a hat.'

'Never you mind woman, and don't you have a job to get back to?'

Checking her watch, Amanda couldn't believe her lunch hour had passed that quickly, but Helen was right, time to return to the office.

Just as she was going out the door, two police officers came in looking serious. Could this be something to do with the missing businessman? She wished she had more time to eavesdrop on their inquiry. She would ask Helen the next time she visited.

# 21

Still laughing when the two police officers entered, Helen was looking forward to messaging Jack. It had been a long time since she'd been on a date, and she was miles away wondering if things had changed much until one officer cleared his throat to get her attention.

'Excuse me, are you the owner here?' asked the taller of the two.

'I'm the manager. I oversee the day-to-day running. The owner leaves me to it, so I rarely see him. My name is Helen Carlisle, how can I help you?'

'Do you mind if we have a quick chat?' inquired the other.

'Of course not. Let me just lock the front door so we won't be disturbed.'

Turning the sign to closed and twisting the lock on a quiet day wouldn't be a problem, as there hadn't been many customers that day.

'Where are my manners—would either of you like coffee?'

'We won't thank you,' said the taller officer. 'I've had so

much coffee this morning. I don't think I could drink another drop.'

'I'm PC Hayley Bibbey and this is PC Carrie Weston. We're looking into the disappearance of Peter Markham, and our investigations have brought us to this coffee shop. We just have a few questions.'

'Not sure how much I'll be able to tell you. I saw he was missing, of course, but I can't say I remember him that well.'

'Is this the man you've seen come in here?' asked Hayley, producing a photo of him.

'Yes, that's him, he didn't stand out. He was polite enough. Can I ask? How did you know he came to this café?'

'You'll be surprised what people notice? Did he ever come in with anyone else?'

'He always came in alone. Sometimes, he left with someone, but usually not. I didn't like his attitude. If I could have, I wouldn't serve him, but the man was a customer. Is it true that whoever it was went to town on him?'

'This is an investigation, mam. Is there anything that has happened, anything that seemed odd or out of character recently, that might give us a clue why he disappeared, or what would have led to his death?' asked Carrie.

'It could be the smallest thing or something that wouldn't have seemed unusual but could be vital to us,' added Hayley.

Pausing to reflect, Helen thought back to her few interactions with the man. 'As I said, he was just a customer.' But then she thought about him; narcissistic, oozed confidence, money, and a certain amount of arrogance. Not someone she had a lot of time for. 'No,' she shrugged. 'As far as I was concerned, he was just a nobody. I'm sure his family love him.' she watched them taking down notes.

'Anything else you can think of?'

'Sorry, no, there is nothing. The woman who just left will know more. I think she works with him, or he pops into where she works.'

'Do you know her name?'

'Funny you should ask. I only know her as Amanda.'

# 22

Kayleigh Buckley was the Forensic Pathologist on duty when the body of Peter Markham came in. Being a newbie; Darcey had drawn the short straw and was made to attend the postmortem. Not being too squeamish, she wasn't too worried about it. After smelling a dead body, it couldn't be much worse seeing the postmortem, *she hoped.*

Strange how life goes on after a horrendous murder. Sitting there waiting to be called in, Darcey thought about hate; someone hated Peter Markham enough to torture him before killing him. Constantly she wondered what was going on in the mind of this person. What did Peter Markham do to deserve such malice?

The hospital was on the edge of the town, but close enough to the major transport links, making it a hub for all the worst incidents in a thirty-mile radius. Connected to the local university, and as a result, was recently given a massive cash injection. A modern and bright-looking building on the outside inspired hope for the future. New buildings were popping up to accommodate all the facilities they needed while the morgue was located, as all morgues were as far away from the living as they could manage. Despite the exterior of the building looking bright and cheerful, the morgue was down in the basement, so bodies could be transported without being seen. There were four suites, one set aside for the worst bodies. Darcey had heard a lot about those. Beware *the floaters* were something she recalled being told on her first day and dreaded having to witness one of those.

The receptionist was expecting her and told her she was to head to Suite Three, where everything would be provided. Signing in, Darcey took a deep breath to steady herself before making her way along the hallway to Post-mortem Suite Three. It was like returning to school.

Already gowned, Kayleigh stood waiting with the body on the table. An assistant was taking photographs, and another was getting ready to remove any evidence that was found to secure it correctly.

Getting herself properly attired, Darcey remembered the tip about VapoRub and came prepared.

'Nice to meet you, you're a new here, aren't you? I'm Kayleigh, head pathologist.'

'Nice to meet you, Kayleigh. I'm Darcey. Yes, I'm new to the team—got the short straw, or so they think at the station. They sniggered when the boss sent me here, but I find it fascinating. My degree is in forensics.'

'Well, it's nice to meet you, Darcey. If you feel you're going to puke, try to hold it in until you're out of shot of my body, and if you faint do it that way,' she pointed towards the back changing room.

Giving a wry smile, Darcey was confident that neither of those tips would be needed. She certainly hoped not, because she would never live it down. Poor Lukey still got teased, and that was several months ago.

'So, Kayleigh, what have we got then?' Darcey approached the table.

Kayleigh smiled. She liked it when they were keen and when they asked questions. This recruit looked strong with no tinge of green.

'The guy was naked when he was found, and there isn't much to collect before we open him up. We'll scrape his nails and brush through his hair.'

Kayleigh began cataloguing all the injuries, which took some time because there were so many. One of the major ones was the removal of the penis, and the other obvious one was the large gash in his stomach.

What Darcey wasn't prepared for was the sheer number of other injuries present. There were cuts, scrapes, and bruises all pre-mortem; this man, Peter, had suffered before he died. Kayleigh took her time noting each injury and its location before moving on. She spoke loud and slowly enabling Darcey to keep up.

'This guy suffered before he died.' Kayleigh said, looking at Darcey, 'It's one of the worst collections of injuries I've seen in a long while.'

Darcey nodded.

'Okay, it's time to get a look inside, see what's going on in there,' said Kayleigh.

She cut the long Y incision around the already large hole that had been sliced into his abdomen.

'Organs look healthy, heart-healthy, no signs of narrowing arteries or disease. Liver is fatty; Mr Markham liked a drink. We'll check his stomach contents shortly if there's enough left.'

The postmortem progressed with nothing else surprising. The only part Darcey had to look away from was the removal of the vitreous humour from the eyes. That was too much.

'We'll take his brain out now, and then we're almost done until we get results back from tox,' Kayleigh said.

'What have we here? Early signs of ageing, I reckon he'd have developed Alzheimer's. Nothing else stands out. Do you know who this man is?'

'We think so, just waiting for confirmation, but it looks like it's the missing businessman.'

Looking thoughtful for a moment, Kayleigh went back to her notes.

'Well, I think I have all I need. My initial observation is that the gash to the abdomen killed him. The knife was inserted low and sliced in an upward arc, judging by the depth. I will take extra measurements, so you have more to go on in terms of type and size. My report will be with you as soon as I can manage it. I know that boss of yours will breathe down my neck wanting it yesterday.'

'Thanks, Doc, I appreciate you being patient and thorough in explaining what you were doing. It was fascinating, although I feel I shouldn't say that since the guy was a son, dad, and husband. Soon to be grandad.'

'Nothing wrong with being fascinated by science. Just be careful who you say that in front of. I am glad you found it interesting. It makes my job easier. The victim's widow will be less thrilled, I imagine.'

'Yes, I imagine too,' Darcey couldn't help but chuckle. She liked this woman. 'Don't worry, I'm not that naïve. Thanks again Doc, I will tell the boss you're rushing the report. It might give you longer before she's on at you.'

Smiling, Kayleigh offered no response but headed off to the changing room, leaving the techs to sort everything out and replace the body in the chiller.

Following a step behind, Darcey removed her scene suit and everything else, placing it in the bin where she'd seen Kayleigh throw hers. Gathering her belongings, she looked forward to getting back into the bright natural light.

———

Now the missing man had been found, the case would be upgraded to murder and the joint force team would throw everything they could into solving it.

So much time had passed while she had been hidden away in the cold underground room. The rush hour traffic had finished; it took her twenty-eight minutes to get back to base. Parking the pool car and locking it, she jogged up the front steps.

'Hi Lorraine, how is everything—nice and quiet I hope?'

'All calm at the moment, love, but you know how it can change in a flash.' Lorraine smiled.

'I do, Lorraine, only too well. Better crack on. Think the boss is waiting for me; I don't want to get on her bad side.'

'You'd do well not to, lovey, that's a fact. Though she seems like a pussycat to me. She always says hi, much like yourself.'

Entering the main door, Darcey took the stairs with excitement. A man's body had been picked through and yet she felt on a high. Two weeks ago, Peter would be carrying on with his life, ignorant of what was going to happen to him. What was it like to meet your death in the form of terrible revenge? The idea made her shudder.

Getting to the last set of stairs, already the increase in noise level, the hum of lots of voices, the buzz of phones ringing, pops and clicks and whistles and beeps. The sounds of a busy working incident room coming together to solve this crime. Teamwork was suddenly rather wonderful. Smiling, she took the last few steps slowly before entering the madness.

Cora immediately saw her and beckoned her over.

'How'd it go at the post-mortem? Kayleigh has already been on the phone to say you weren't sick and didn't faint.'

Shrugging off her coat, Darcey thoughtfully removed her scarf and rubbed her hands together to restore some warmth.

'It was interesting. But I don't think we know much more than we did until tox comes back. Cause of death was the slash to the stomach.'

'I thought that would be the case. I will be interested to know if he was fully aware during the ordeal or if he was at least drugged.'

'I hope he was. The pathologist said it was one of the worst sets of injuries she'd seen for a while. It would save one's mind to believe he was out of his head when she took him to pieces, but somehow, I don't think he was. How does she do it, seeing the worst of what humanity can do to each other and yet be so clinical?'

Cora grimaced; she knew only too well. Police officers rarely fared much better with their feelings, especially with the ones involving kids.

'Thanks, Darcey. Good job. Let's wait for the report. We need to get cracking to find out what happened to this guy, and why he ended up there. The wife should ID him, but I'm not sure if she's up to that. So, we need to check in with the Family Liaison Officer. How did Yvonne Markham react when you and Luke broke the news?'

'As you'd expect, boss, numb. Like she went off somewhere else. Then demanded we find who killed her husband. We left soon after, as there wasn't any point, especially as Sharon was already there.'

'Not an easy job. How did Luke cope with it?'

Darcey's face lit up. There was more to a great friendship with the young man than she was letting on. Cora raised an eyebrow. Speculating romance isn't always a good idea between police officers.

'Oh, he was great boss. Calm, no emotion. By the way, he

mentioned not being taken along to interviews and stuff. He wasn't grumpy or nasty but made a point of mentioning it, so I think he's miffed.'

'For God's sake. That's the third time in as many days I've been told not to forget this is a team effort. Like I ever could. That will be all DC Clarke.'

Moving to her computer, Cora deliberately turned her back on the DC. She wasn't angry with her, but she would have to apologise for her outburst later. Annoyed at herself, Cora wanted to do well and show she could lead, but she was failing at the very basic essence. Staring back at the computer, Cora read what they already had on the case. When she turned back, she saw Darcey still sitting there.

'A couple of PCs popped into the coffee shop down the road from the business. The manager said the victim liked to leer at young women.'

Cora went back to looking at what they had. An uncomfortable silence settled between them.

There was nothing more she could do now but concentrate on the case. She wanted to go back and question the hotel manager, believing she was holding back on her. Looking at the picture of Peter Markham's still missing car: where had that ended up? The details of the company he worked for and the businesses he visited. Boxes needed to be ticked and people questioned. The kids needed to be interviewed thoroughly, and the wife needed to be spoken to again. What was missing? The answer was in there somewhere—Cora was sure of it.

# 23

Approaching her building, Amanda had the usual apprehension, although she never knew why. A standard one-bedroom flat in the town centre in a block of a hundred flats, with laundry services on the bottom floor. They were fairly new, so weren't ruined by graffiti or the nauseating smells that often accompanied the stairwells. The smell of fresh paint still won out but was already beginning to fade with each week passing.

Despite the long day on her feet, the extra exercise was important. Remnants of her childhood eating disorder had not quite vanished. Reaching the fifth floor, Amanda leant against the shiny white painted door that led to her sanctuary. By the time the movement sensor automatic lights came on in the hallway, Amanda had managed to get her key in the lock and open the door. Casually kicking her shoes off to add to the small pile that had built up. Her bag got cast aside onto the small sideboard. Walking through the narrow-carpeted hallway, Amanda waited until she was in the small sitting room before turning on the lamp.

It was going to be a long night. She would just curl up in her favourite, and only chair, and try to read by the lamplight until she was tired enough for bed. With any luck, she'd manage to sleep tonight. Some dreams she'd been having lately had woken her with a start, her heart pounding hard and covered in sweat. What was causing them, she did not know, and could never remember them when she awoke.

Grabbing a glass of water, she placed it on the small side table and went into her bedroom to change into her night-clothes. It had been a strange week. Picking up her book, her thoughts travelled back to the coffee shop. She smiled, believing her friend might have finally found happiness. Helen was completely smitten with Jack. She hadn't meant to assume she would be a bridesmaid if they ever got married, but Helen hadn't even paused. Just teasing her about having to wear a green dress.

The problem with life was change, something that she couldn't cope with. For her, change meant losing friends and although she was pleased that Helen had found someone she cared for, for herself, it meant a loss. Still pretty and had been told she was clever, but if you don't have the personality to go with it, what was the point? Okay, so Helen said she had a lack of self-worth, but hers was even greater. Perhaps that was why she was losing her temper with the clients. She had better watch herself because she could lose her job.

# 24

Cora went to work early. Her night had been bad, worrying too much about the case. It was getting to her. Perhaps she was expecting too much of herself. This morning, she'd planned to see one of the business owners and take someone other than Darcey. Favouritism was frowned upon. She wasn't sure what it was about Darcey that had caught her eye apart from being comfortable with her. *Remember, this was teamwork,* kept echoing through her mind.

Still dark, winter was drawing on quicker now, making the world overcast. It took little to bring Cora down, and doubt was always stalking her, but that was her problem. Quiet streets for another half an hour before the onslaught of stressed and angry drivers. There was nothing Cora hated more than sitting in traffic, twiddling her thumbs, and listening to the same three songs on the radio. She could do a thousand and one other things instead of stopping and starting and then sitting patiently, waiting. She must crack this case. She must not fail. The pressure was immense.

Pulling into the police station car park, Cora put her car out of the way, under a floodlight. She couldn't be in any safer place, yet was anywhere safe these days?

'Morning Nikki—no Lorraine today?'

Nikki looked up from whatever it was she was reading and smiled at the woman who had just spoken to her. Nikki was new and hadn't learnt everyone's names, so she wasn't sure exactly how to respond.

'Morning ma'am, no, not today.'

Nodding, Cora continued to the door that led into the office. It was quiet. Even the night staff had little they could get on with except for CCTV footage to go through, and that was it.

The DCI wasn't in yet, but it wouldn't be long before he was. When there was a big case, Felix spent more hours there than anyone, causing her to wonder if she should take that next step up. He never seemed to get away from the office and always had to justify their actions to his boss; the buck stopped with him. Also, Felix had to consider costs all the time, frustrating Cora immensely. Their hands were tied due to whatever was most cost-effective. It felt like they were policing with one hand tied behind their back—often both.

Promotion to the major crimes team was something Cora was proud of. If she stayed at this level, she'd be happy, for in her late thirties it seemed to be a good place to be, especially when she remembered her mistake. How she hated herself and her gullibility from her first case. That poor woman: clothes torn, blood on her thighs and trickling down from her lip where she'd been hit. The hospital had taken all the evidence, and then because she'd missed one signature, as a young PSCO, the case fell apart. It was all her fault; she could never forgive herself for that. Move on, her therapist told her, but aren't lessons to be learnt.

Chucking her bag under her desk, Cora checked to see if any messages had been left since last night. Nothing important. A message from the boss for an update. Composing herself as her computer booted up, she needed to check out the two business owners while the office was empty. Googling Mr Montgomery, Cora read his biography on how he had made his money; starting with almost nothing, this man had a vision to get rich. Beginning with a market stall, he graduated to a small shop by specialising in local farmed produce. He had been clever and moved with the times, catching on to the new fads and making sure he had the market cornered before anyone else could muscle in.

As the business grew, Mr Montgomery realised he was going to need extra financial help. This is where things got interesting. The other men weren't his choice, but money was money, and he took what he could get. So where did Peter Markham fit in? Although the Internet didn't say, reading through the lines, Mr Montgomery used these people promising them partnerships which never materialised. Was there some hyped-up blackmail going on? The result was the financiers pulled out and the court case against Mr Montgomery was effectively a pay-off job. Mr Riley's daughter Lisa stayed on, though. What promises had Mr Montgomery made to her?

Time to look up Lisa Riley. Not much on her. Either she'd kept her head down, preferring to stay out of the limelight, or simply had achieved little. At thirty-nine, she was a rich kid turned tame—if that was possible. Certainly, a difference in lifestyle. Was it possible for a pampered daughter to buckle down to work? We all need money. But why did she stay working for the company?

A good idea to check Companies House next and examine their accounts. As Cora expected, the profits had fallen in the last ten years. That was common for some businesses as a sign of the times, especially with the increase in paying out big dividends and forgetting to invest back into the business. Fascinating. By now, Peter Markham was making his presence as the next rising star. Could he be using the same technique on Mr Montgomery—blackmail? The rise to the top was slippery. But Lisa Riley was no shrinking violet either. Put one and one together and suddenly there are a possible six people who would take great pleasure in murdering Peter Markham. Why then was Mr Mongomery still alive? Did he get to Markham before Markham got to him?

Must speak to the accountant, Cora added to the growing list, underling accountant three times; they often knew more about the business than anyone else. The accountants were the ones paying out the dividends. What they felt about the outgoings and incomings of finances would be valuable and a vital piece of evidence. Was she thinking blackmail? There had been more going on in Peter Markham's life than the slender covering of charities.

Hearing the door go, Cora was surprised to see Luke. 'Good morning, Luke, you're in early.'

'Oh my God, boss, I wasn't expecting anyone to be here. You scared the life out of me.'

'Guess I had the same idea as you and wanted to get an early start, but I'm the boss, Luke. Why are you here?'

Waiting as Luke took off the layers he wore to fight against the cold. A wisp of a boy; strong winds would carry him away. Were there weights in his shoes? Well, you must have a sense of humour at this time in the morning. Remember not to embarrass him though or lose her tough reputation. She'd already let her guard down a few times with Darcey by being too friendly her behaviour could lose respect.

'I like to get in and get settled early ma'am, I live right on the edge of town and the traffic can be awful. I can't be late, so I would rather be early.'

'Very commendable, Luke, very commendable indeed. Are you working on anything now?'

'Nothing that can't wait, ma'am.'

'I have been looking at Peter Markham and his relationship with Montgomery. I want you to do some checking on him and Lisa Riley. It's an area we haven't touched yet, finances.'

Smiling as Luke nodded, he walked off and sat silently and sensitively in his chair. A little smile lifted the corner of his lips. Part of the reason he was in early, as she suspected, was this chair. The youngsters fought over it, although Cora had no idea why. Luke immediately started logging in and typing at warp speed. His fingers flew across the keyboard.

Realising she was staring, Cora went and sat back behind her desk and took a sip of her coffee. So engrossed in her search, she hadn't noticed it had gone cold. One of the first things she learnt on joining the major crimes team was never to waste coffee and get used to drinking it cold. She downed what was left and got a refill.

'Luke. What do you make of this murder?'

'Sorry boss?' he looked up confused.

'On the surface, a happily married man with a family who adores him,' began Cora. 'Okay, so he's promiscuous, but as I see it, his wife doesn't mind or adores him so much that to her, he can do no wrong. But this has been bothering me. He returns home as the loving husband and father to become this other man. Is that so wrong? I mean, to have this other life. As far as I can see, he has done no harm.'

'I know what you mean,' said Luke carefully. 'Each of us has other lives just to survive the mundane. Yet, I couldn't do what he did, personally, because, to me, love is special—those wedding vow things are for a reason when you make them to yourself. But someone out there hated him enough to take him to pieces. Boss, do you believe in karma?'

'I've never really thought about it.'

'Well, I do. Someone out there has taken back what they

believed was owed them. My thoughts are that this murder was probably a one-off. Whoever did this got it out of their system and will do nothing like this again. A model citizen, you could say, someone you would meet on the street and wouldn't even know you had just passed a killer.'

'You believe this person will never kill again?'

'Why not?'

'Because I don't believe the world works like that. Something else will upset this person, and the only way to deal with them is the inevitable. They are happy until someone else comes along and upsets them. Killing becomes a habit, a way of dealing with their problems. They may tell themselves that it is a one-off—'

'You could be right. For me, the shock is knowing there is actually a member of the human race who could commit a crime like this. This was a horrendous murder. I still shudder when I think about it. However, I don't believe it will be long before we find out who it is.'

'I hope you're right, Luke,' Cora muttered to herself.

Her mind wandered back to the case again, thinking of what they could tackle for now. Chasing up forensics from the scene, the killer had left them nothing. Apart from that bit of fabric, the DCI found. Would the fabric prove to be significant? At this stage, it was all just a guessing game.

Just as she finished her coffee, the rest of the team filed in. Darcey first. Holding up her cup in question, Cora didn't want to be the sort of boss everyone feared. She was happy to make hot drinks for the team. Smiling, Darcey nodded, so Cora put some more instant in another mug with hot water. Unable to remember how her junior colleague took it, a splash of milk Cora hoped that was acceptable.

'Bit chilly this morning, were you?' Cora laughed. Darcey was struggling to remove her coat. She had a massive hoody on underneath. 'Here, take this. That should warm you up.'

'Absolutely freezing, boss. Had to defrost the car as well. The stupid thing was frozen outside and in. As if one or the other wasn't bad enough. I thought the inside windscreen was supposed to be protected from the elements. I hate this time of year. Hate it.'

'I hear you. It's awful. But nothing we can do about it—just be grateful you aren't a uniform still patrolling the streets. Mind you, if someone were to offer me a six-month secondment to a case in the Bahamas, I reckon I might do myself a mischief trying to snap their hand off for it.'

The smells of damp and wood smoke mingled with the coffee as everyone went to the kitchen to warm themselves from their commute. Chairs scraped, coats ruffled, keyboards clacked, and shouts rang out over the heads of those seated. The continuing success of the local Luton Town football team and their victory over Wigan in the FA Cup last night was a popular conversation this morning. Promotion to the Premier League was on everyone's mind. In a small room, the number of people felt more, the temperature was cosy even early in the day. The building had a steady temperature, that although stifling and suffocating in summer, allowed a comfortable warmth now.

The chatter was gradually increasing as everyone caught up on their nights. It was Friday, so they were planning their weekends, or sharing details. Cora allowed this while they got settled. At times like this, she felt like a primary school teacher waiting for hyperactive kids to settle.

Eventually, the noise level decreased. Clapping her hands, Cora walked to the front.

'Okay, attention everyone. Nothing much has happened overnight, but there are a few avenues we are looking into.

The CCTV is still being viewed, but I've moved Luke to look at finances. Beverlee, can you pick that up, please?'

Beverlee nodded.

'Where are we with social media for the missing man, and his family, any clues there?'

'Found out he went into business late in life,' Dave stood to answer. 'Peter Markham was a mature student at Nottingham Uni. I found some pictures of a leaving party. We are tracing anyone to find out who knew what sort of man he was back then. Yvonne Markham and her kids don't use social media. Olivia uses Instagram, but hers is all baby stuff.'

'Thanks, and who's next, Philip?'

'Thanks, ma'am, no signs of the car yet, but we have reports of a burnt-out shell in a field near the old shopping centre where the body was found. Forensics have been on the car overnight, but there isn't much left. Whoever burnt it did a thorough job, that's for sure. A new nature camera had been put up, as it's not the first car fire there. The farmer was getting sick of ruined crops. The footage should be with us this morning.'

'Thanks, Phillip, keep me updated on that, will you?'

'Luke and I are heading off to question the staff of the Company,' began Cora. 'Darcey, can you return to the hotel and finish questioning their staff? Take a uniform with you. I am still uncertain about John Kirkham.'

If Darcey was at all inconvenienced, Cora saw no sign of it. Luke was shocked, and scared, much to Cora's wicked amusement.

'Anyone got anything else—Any questions?' she looked at their unresponsive faces. 'No, right, then what are you all waiting for? We have a killer to find. Other jobs are on the board, Dave, HOLMES2?'

Almost immediately, a buzz began. Chattering voices

and tapping of keys. Cora checked Dave had heard, knowing he would do it without being asked. Grabbing her coat, Cora indicated to Luke to do the same.

'You ready?'

'Yes ma'am. Where are we going?'

'Just into Dunstable. That's where the main office is located.'

Holding the door open for the boss, he let her lead the way to the pool car park. Cora took the driver's seat, while Luke's wild eyes flickered over her briefly—hating women drivers. His mum was the worst driver in the world, erratic, and to his mind, dangerous. He never knew a woman who didn't drive with her mouth.

'Do you know why I'm so keen to speak to the accountant?' Cora asked.

'No ma'am, I don't.'

'Just boss please Luke, ma'am, makes me feel like the queen or my old English teacher. Who do you think speaks to all the staff, be they the owner or the cleaner and pays the wages and authorises travel or expenses? The accountants. They will have an insight into all the people they interact with.'

'That's genius, ma'am, sorry, boss. I'd never have guessed that,' smiled Luke, 'but you're right.'

'Top tip for the future, Luke. If you want real information about a company, speak to the cleaner or the accountant. They see and hear everything and have nothing to lose. They're a mine of information, and many a case has been pushed forward by speaking to these people. A good tip for you is to speak to everyone in the building, reception, cleaners, and learn their names. If you ever need a favour, they will help you enormously.' Cora winked as she said this and smiled.

'Thanks, boss, noted.' Luke grinned back. He could see

why Darcey enjoyed spending time with the boss. She was full of useful advice, and not necessarily about work.

In companionable silence, Luke wondered why he had been brought along. Everyone noticed that Darcey always accompanied Cora. He couldn't deny that he had been jealous of Darcey. After all, they were at the same level.

The crazy rush hour traffic had eased, which was part of the reason Cora had left a bit later. The New Road, as it was still called, even though it had been there since she was born, was clear now. The B&Q roundabout was always clogged with idiots not able to wait a second, often blocking the way for everyone. Bad weather never helped; this road was notorious for flooding. It always amazed Cora how poorly people drove in hazardous road conditions. The fields around the area meant fog was thicker and lasted longer, enveloping and suffocating the car as they crawled along. Without the fog, red kites circled overhead, looking for roadkill; big, beautiful birds soaring the skies, something she loved seeing.

'What do you think the plan of action should be when we get there?' As with Darcey, Cora wanted to see what young Luke was about.

'Well, you said they know everything, but we must go gently, not throwing out intrusive questions off the bat. We need to find out if there are any hidden secrets, without them realising they are telling us.'

'Any idea how we will go about it?'

Luke shrugged and grinned.

'Don't worry, that was a bit of a trick question. I don't either—we'll see what happens when we get there.'

Turning left at the Tesco roundabout, Cora drove slowly along Luton Road; the old Supertyres had been knocked down. When did they do that and why? It's where she had her car, MOT. What were they going to put in its place? Can't anyone stop for a moment?

Creeping into the centre, past the impressive Priory Church, built in 1132. Something to do with Augustine's monks and Henry the Eighth. These people lived in another world as well as another century; what would they think of modern society? Reaching the crossroads, infamous in the town's history, had now become a traffic snag. The traffic lights were no better than the old double roundabouts. Their destination was just to the left now, according to the sat nav. This part of town was full of large old buildings, once magnificent, but now fading and crumbling. Most had been re-purposed into dentists and nurseries. Suddenly, they were there. Pulling into the long driveway, Cora parked in one of the few spaces available. Luke expressively pinked up for next to the oppressive building was a seedy little strip club. If it wasn't obvious from the dancing women outside, the bright pink paint was the giveaway.

'Frequented that club there have you, Luke?' Cora couldn't resist.

'Only for stag do's, ma'am. You know what it's like, you just have to go along with what everyone else wants.'

'I was young once too, Luke. I have been to many hen dos. I know how it works. Don't worry. I won't judge.'

He guessed she was teasing by her smile.

The office was behind the main building. A tinny voice asked when Cora pressed a buzzer.

'Yes, can I help?'

'Bedfordshire Police, we need to speak to everyone about the disappearance of Peter Markham.'

The door was opened by a tall thin woman who beckoned them in. Her grey hair was held back in a stiff perm and not a hair out of place. Wearing an A-line skirt, white blouse and cardigan, Cora already had an opinion about the woman before she spoke, a meticulous lady who lived for the job.

As they walked through a very narrow and dark hallway, they came out into a spacious office containing three desks. Two were occupied, and the last desk was empty. The door to the side had a placard with the name Peter Markham.

'This is us. I'm Victoria. That's Rebecca in the far corner, and over there is Wendy. Rebecca is the company secretary, and Wendy is the Personnel and HR manager. And I am the management accountant and payroll.'

'Nice to meet you Victoria, I'm DI Cora Snitton and this is DC Luke Marshall. As you know, we are looking into the disappearance of your colleague Peter Markham. I'm afraid he is no longer a missing person. The body of Peter was found yesterday morning; his identity was confirmed by his wife. Because of the injuries to his body, this is now a murder investigation.'

'Murder, did you say?' On the nearest table, and looking pale, was Victoria.

'Yes, I'm afraid so.'

Wendy suddenly stood and ran out of a door into the back. They heard vomiting hitting the toilet bowl, while Rebecca sat stony-faced and unmoved. Cora decided to keep a closer eye on her. She wasn't sure if it was shock or underlying tension. People act differently to hearing bad news.

'I just need to ask a few general questions, if you don't mind?' Cora asked when Wendy returned from the bathroom.

"First of all, do you know if Mr Markham had any enemies? Anyone who would want to hurt him?"

'I can't believe Peter's dead,' said Rebecca, looking pale. 'He was such a lovely, gentle man. Why would anyone possibly want to hurt him?'

'Exactly, he was always kind and patient and quick to

help if we needed anything.' Wendy added, her cheeks flushed with a sudden anger.

'There must be some people who he had cross words with,' frowned Cora. 'He can't have got on with everyone all the time.' She looked at Victoria.

'There was the odd supplier which he had to be firm with, especially having to discipline them. Bad blood will be spilt,' said Wendy. Now she'd recovered from the shock. It seemed she had become the spokesperson for the group.

'And were there any disgruntled employees? Any that thought they were wrongly let go. Any tribunals or anything of that sort?'

'No officer,' said Wendy, suddenly impassioned with virtue. 'Nothing. We are very fair with our employees, a lot of procedures are in place to cover most eventualities. Flexible working, extra holiday days, company sick pay, and mental health accommodations. All appreciated by the staff, and if there is something else they need, they can suggest it to us, and we will discuss it at the monthly board meetings. The meetings are always open, and anyone can contribute. There is no *I'm the boss and you must do as I say, and you aren't entitled to an opinion.*'

Impressed by Wendy's loyal speech, came the question of how truthful was it? All the staff were loyal, but like the Markham family, it felt she had gone over the top.

'When I looked on Google search, I found a woman by the name of Tracy Littlechild, who'd taken the company to a tribunal for unfair dismissal on the grounds of gender discrimination and mental health.'

Wendy stiffened while the other two looked smug. Ah, some dirt, Cora thought.

'Yes, well, her case was dismissed. If you'd done your research properly, detective, you would find she had no proof. Her vicious allegations were thrown out.'

The expressions on Rebecca's and Victoria's faces spoke of a different version of this story, Cora observed quietly.

'Luke, can you take Wendy over to the main building and see if any of the key staff have anything more to add, please?'

If Wendy was at all put out by what Cora was trying to do, she showed no sign of it.

There was tension between these women, separating them might bring some answers while Wendy was out of the way.

'Okay, I have the feeling there is more to the story of the dismissed woman. If there is anything else you can think of, even the smallest thing could prove helpful.'

Rebecca was reluctant to speak. Her eyes kept darting to the door, but Victoria had no such qualms.

'Tracy was treated like crap while she worked here, detective. She was taken advantage of, overworked, and underpaid. Mr Markham, for some reason, despised her. I overheard the end of an argument in which it sounded like she had threatened him. Not long after, Tracy went off sick for ages, with anxiety and depression. Some rumours were going around about thieving. Tracy denied it and took it to a tribunal. The reason the case was dropped was because the Company said they had proof. She was too scared to take it any further. It was disgusting the way she was treated.'

'Thanks, Victoria and what about you, Rebecca—do you agree with that version of events?'

'I don't think she was treated as badly as Victoria made out. But yes, she was threatened if she carried on.'

'Wendy's reaction to his death was quite extreme. Was she particularly close to Peter?'

Finding more confidence, Victoria again was the first to cut in.

'That's the thing, detective. She couldn't stand him. She

sucked up to him while he was here, but as soon as his back was turned, she was slagging him off to anyone who listened. She was particularly close to Lisa Riley. They always seemed to whisper together.'

Her instincts were right. Cora needed Wendy out of the way to get these women to open up. Rebecca's silence was probably just a sign of a respectable woman, something to mull over later.

'Okay, thank you, ladies. You've been very useful. I will leave my card, so, if there is anything else you can think will be helpful, then please don't hesitate to get in touch. I will leave you to your day.'

Cora sat in the car waiting for Luke. When the door opened, she smiled as he shuddered and took his seat.

'Well, we didn't learn much there, except for the strange and uncomfortable atmosphere present when Wendy was there.'

'I'm glad you thought so. She didn't seem to be upset over the murder. Have you learnt anything at all?'

'Only that none of the employees liked Wendy,' began Luke. 'They looked petrified when she walked in. She didn't speak to me; she didn't even try to fill the silence but made it very clear she wasn't happy about having to cooperate. Do you think she was sleeping with him, boss?'

'That's entirely possible. Stranger things have happened. The big motives for murder are revenge, love, and money. Yet, I can't see any of them going to the lengths of the injuries inflicted on that body.'

Luke nodded, remembering the crime scene photos.

# 25

Already it was dark when Cora inserted her card to open the door to the stairs leading to the first floor where her office was. This was a new building built especially for Luton because of the high volume of crimes. The proper base was located between Bedfordshire, Cambridgeshire, and Hertfordshire. This office was eco-friendly, bright, and airy, and Cora hated it. A lot of the local stations had been closed, but those old buildings had character and history, with stories to tell. These new buildings were too cold and clinical, like a morgue.

Cora's eager eyes were set on advancement. She knew she had a fight on her hands to work her way through a system designed for men, especially those present in senior roles. This case was new, and if she gained ground then hopefully, she might be looked on favourably when it came to promotion. One benefit was more pay, and who could turn down money?

No point daydreaming as she went through the double doors into the office. It was early, so not many civilian staff were in. The phones and hubbub of a full office were still muted which is exactly what she was hoping for, time to think about the scene and what needed to be done. The DCI was a good boss, and she wanted to impress him for if she wanted promotion, his good word would be vital.

Pulling out her investigator's notebook, she wrote a few questions: *Who was the victim? Why the shopping centre? Was he supposed to be found? What had he done to make someone so angry? Male or female killer? How did they jump him, or did he know his killer well? Was he drugged? Injuries pre or post-mortem? Business problems? Gambling? Owed money? Affair? Jealousy?*

Still so many unanswered questions. They needed one break and like dominos, the rest of the answers would tumble. That was the idea. As with all murder cases, the victims' lives, as well as those close to them, had to be unpicked until every secret was out. A murder leads to all sorts of chaos in its wake. If the victim is the pimple on top of this abscess, then whoever else is involved is the ingredients to the poison. No one is completely innocent in a crime.

Her sympathies, though, were always for the family and friends. One of the first cases she worked on was where a man was killed in a hit-and-run. Cora had uncovered his secret gambling addiction. He left a debt-saddled wife trying to grieve for the husband she thought she knew, along with the humiliation.

Now was not the time to ruminate on the past. Looking down at her list of questions, she saw Darcey standing in the doorway bearing coffee. There were many reasons she had taken a shine to this young detective and bringing coffee and pastry unasked for didn't hurt at all.

'Caramel latte with soya milk?'

'Of course, boss. From Costa, I know that's your favourite. I passed one on the way back from questioning and thought I'd grab one. That coffee machine is awful; it has no right calling what it produces, coffee.'

'You're an angel,' Cora took the proffered drink. 'No, you're right there. I don't know what abomination that thing spits out, but it should be found guilty of contravening the Trade Descriptions Act.'

Darcey nearly snorted out the sip of coffee she'd just taken and started coughing, catching her breath, and giggling.

The next stop was Peter Markham's colleague and business owner. Start at the top and work downwards. Mr Montgomery was still the big boss, but now he was in his late eighties. He had been awarded an MBE about ten years ago for his services to charity and had taken a step back from the running of the business. There was a son from a previous marriage. Was he in the competition? Another source of conflict? Cora wondered. Right, Mr Barnaby Montgomery MBE. Let's see what you have to say.

Lisa Riley, though, was still heavily involved with the business, according to the latest accounts at least. Picking up the phone, Cora dialled Mr Montgomery's number. It rang out. She tried again, but it still went unanswered. No answering machine either. She made a note to herself to get one of the admins to keep trying.

Replacing the handset, Cora found the number for Lisa Riley. The lady herself answered on the second ring.

'Hi, I'm looking to speak to a Ms Riley, Ms Lisa Riley?'

'Speaking.'

'Hello, Ms Riley, this is DI Cora Snitton from Bedfordshire Police. I am investigating the disappearance and murder of Peter Markham. I would like to come and ask you a few questions. When would be the most convenient time for you?'

'Oh, yes, hello detective, I wondered when you'd want to speak to me. Wendy let me know you'd been by the office. I will come down to the station if that's easier for you?'

'You don't have to do that, Ms Riley, but we are keen to speak to everybody as soon as we can.'

'Okay, I will be there first thing tomorrow morning, 9 am. Would that suit?'

'Yes, that's fine, thank you, Ms Riley.'

'See you tomorrow, detective, bye.'

Cora huffed. She was well and truly dealt with. Ms Riley was a lady who knew her mind; Cora shrugged. Checking the number of Mr Montgomery, she was ready to try him again. This time, he answered, sounding breathless. After telling him why she was calling, he was surprised or was he being vague? She hated it when people pulled this number.

'Hello, detective. Yes, strange business that. Very strange. I will make time to speak to you. I would like the mystery solved so his poor wife can have some answers.'

'I appreciate that, Mr Montgomery. Would tomorrow morning be convenient?'

'I will clear my diary, detective. I imagine the interview wouldn't take long. What time will you be arriving?'

'I have a meeting at 9 am, so would eleven suit you, sir?'

One of his employers had been murdered, and he didn't appear to care.

'Thank you, detective. I will see you tomorrow at 11.'

Still holding the phone, Cora felt like she'd just been reprimanded, and wasn't sure why.

'What's up, boss? You look perplexed.' Darcey had caught Cora's expression and laughed.

'Oh nothing,' Cora returned the phone. 'I've just spoken to Mr Montgomery. I didn't like how he dismissed me. Anyway, tomorrow, we'll be seeing him. I have a feeling if we aren't there at eleven on the dot, we will be refused entry. The other, Ms Riley, is coming here at nine.'

'Right, okay. Who is Mr Montgomery exactly?'

'The owner of Warleggan Foods and Haulage Services.

The Company our missing Peter Markham worked for. It should have been owned by two people; Mr Montgomery is one; Lisa Riley was nodded to be the other. Montgomery is in his late eighties with an MBE for services to charity. He's mostly stepped back from the business. He has a disputed son, so I guess he's looking to pass it down to him, although I could be wrong.'

Unfortunately for Darcey, her boss had caught her smile. 'I'm glad you find it funny Darcey. I will make sure you take the lead when questioning him. See how funny you find it then.'

'No problem, boss. What sort of trouble can a man in his eighties possibly cause?'

'You'd be surprised.' Cora looked through her notes. 'Ms Riley should have inherited from her father. What she inherited has to be determined. I should imagine there is a great deal of backstabbing behind closed doors. I'll get Luke to do some more research into all of them and see if there are any skeletons hiding away that we need to know about. There has to be a good reason for Mr Markham to have been brutally murdered in this way, and money is one of the biggest motives.'

'That's right, boss. Love, revenge and money.'

'Often, Darcey, but never narrow your focus. Especially with murder. I have seen enough to realise that it's never that simple. Time we went home, ready for an early start tomorrow.'

'Yes, boss. Have a good evening.' Darcey was looking forward to drinks with her friends.

'You too, Darcey. don't go drinking too much in Jaks. I need you on top form tomorrow.'

'Wouldn't dream of it, boss. See you in the morning, bright, early, and bushy tailed.'

After making certain her desk was tidy, Cora also left.

Tonight she was looking forward to nestling up with her dog, Nibbles, on her sofa while taking another look over her script for Saturday night. She had always been told she was funny, a bit of a comedian, and realised she enjoyed making people laugh. When turning thirty came the time to stop dreaming and start doing. After winning the first heat of the competition for amateur comedians, and once she overcame the shock; she was hooked. Time to practise for the next round.

Being a lover of research, Cora looked up everything she could about comedy, and what made people laugh and what was needed, as well as the sort of avenues for beginners. She wrote some jokes and tried to figure out the sort of jokes she liked to tell. Looking deeper, she had not realised there was such a wide variety of humour. Making people laugh wasn't that simple. What made someone laugh could make someone else angry.

This weekend was Cora's first open mike night, on the south coast, somewhere near Brighton, and as far away from Bedfordshire as she could manage. The reason for this was not wanting to bump into any of her colleagues. No chance they would ever let her live it down; she would be the butt of jokes for years to come. No pun intended. If they knew, they would come along and heckle, and she was nervous enough already.

Thinking about the open mike night had turned Cora's stomach queasy. She had intended to stop off and grab some fish and chips on the way home, usually her favourite. The chip shop was on her route. Usually, the smell drove her crazy, but not tonight. What was in the fridge might be more appropriate and some wine would be better.

The sharp wind stung her face as icy rain pelted down. What a horrible evening. Wasn't there supposed to be global warming? It's getting colder these days, not warmer. *My God, woman, you sound like an eighty-year-old.*

Finally reaching the newly built estate, Cora parked her car in her allocated space, grateful it was near the door to her block and that it was right under a streetlight. Living on the third floor, especially after a long day at work, the climb was not what she needed, but it was home and, more importantly, affordable.

Slowly managing the last few steps, Cora opened the front door to feel the kind hands of warmth. This was why she enjoyed leaving Mrs Cate to look after Nibbles while she was at work. Her flat was always warm, sometimes too warm, but Cora was grateful she had someone to sit with her dog while she was away.

'Oh, hi love, you just got in?'

'Yes, Mrs Cate. Long day at work. Going to be a long winter if it carries on like this.'

'I dare say, love, not like we had in my day; we don't get the snow like we used to. That's one thing I'm grateful for, especially at my age. I like to keep a little of my independence. They'll be carting me off to the home if I break something before I can blink.'

'Yes, I fear you're right. Good job you're fit and sprightly. Don't know what I'd do without you across the way. So don't go getting any ideas when it's icy. I am happy to pop down the shop and grab a paper or whatever you need.'

'I know, love, thank you. I will be careful, don't you worry. I couldn't let Nibbles down. Look at him sleeping there enjoying the life of Riley.'

Fussing with her dog's ears, Nibbles moved his head around in appreciation but stayed on Mrs Cate's lap.

'Dinner Nibbles, you coming? I'm sure Isobelle would like her lap back.'

At the mention of dinner, Nibbles pricked up his ears,

stood and stretched, yawned, and finally jumped down. Going towards the kitchen, he stood by his empty food bowl and barked.

'Ha, ha, little sod, I better go feed him. He's not silly, is he? I should have known better than to mention food before his bowl was filled.'

Waiting and watching carefully as Mrs Cate eased to her feet to pick up her coat from the back of the chair. Why on earth she wore her coat just to cross the hallway was completely unfathomable?

'Yes, you go dear, and get that little man fed. I'll be off now, to catch up Eastenders before I turn in.'

'Thanks again, Mrs Cate. We have a big case on, so will you be okay for the foreseeable?'

'Of course, love; you know me. I love looking after the little scamp and he's great company, even when he's farting and snoring.'

'Yes, his farts are legendary for sure,' laughed Cora. 'I am looking forward to relaxing on the sofa as well, but I imagine this one is going to want to drag me out in the cold so he can sniff every blade of grass before doing his business.'

'Rather you than me, lovey. Right, I'll be leaving you.'

'Thanks again. I owe you one.'

Nibbles, wondering where his food was, began barking, making his impatience known. 'Ha, ha, better go feed his royal highness. Are you okay to see yourself out?'

'Don't be daft love, of course. Go on, be away with yah, go get that little belly fed before he wakes the entire building.'

Smiling with concern, Cora watched her neighbour navigate her way around the tightly packed furniture until she reached the door. Once she'd opened her door, Cora left for the kitchen, so Mrs Cate didn't notice she'd been watching. She wasn't sure if Isobelle was looking frailer these days; she wasn't even sure how old she was. Originally from Indonesia, she was tiny, but she defied the ageing process and didn't look a day over fifty, but most probably she was at least eighty.

Opening a sachet, Cora emptied it into Nibbles' bowl. A glass of wine for her, which she downed in two gulps and refilled. That would be her limit for tonight. She would drink this one slower.

---

Mrs Cate stepped out of the door, closing it quietly behind her. She knew Cora was watching but didn't mind. She had a lot of affection for the young woman who worked so hard to keep everyone safe. Ambitious and stubborn, her hope for Cora was that she would find future happiness, a spirited young woman whom she admired. Not that it was any of her business, and she wouldn't poke her nose into it either, but when she only lived across the way, it was difficult not to notice the comings and goings. Never had she seen Cora bring any young man or woman, she thought wryly, to visit her, let alone stay the night.

Just as the door clicked, Mrs Cate looked up. Was that a shadow in the corner further down the corridor? No, this was her imagination yet... was there someone up there lurking and waiting? Why would anyone stand there in the cold and dark hallway, for no reason? Continuing the last few steps to her front door, unlocking, she went in, securing the chain behind her. Feeling spooked, something was not right. If someone was standing there, she certainly wasn't going to risk finding out.

---

The man stood stock still and held his breath. He didn't think he'd been seen, but the old woman had sensed him it wasn't her who he was interested in. However, he knew the flat the woman had come from was now alone. He couldn't tell if the old woman had locked the door, or if Cora had locked it behind her, but that was of little consequence to him. He could pick any lock in seconds. The mass-produced ones used in these new builds were no challenge. Waiting for the sounds inside the old woman's flat to quieten and leaving a few more minutes, he moved. Now was the time. Pushing away from the wall, he quietly stepped towards Cora's door.

---

Sitting on her lovely purple fabric sofa after plumping up the cushions, Cora leaned back. Her own home: amazing to decorate it how she had always wanted. Simplicity was what Cora was aiming for. Bookcases lined one wall. Not quite the home library she'd dreamt of as a child, but close enough. The room was warm and cosy. A fake fireplace on the main wall gave the illusion of a fire.

Finally able to relax, Nibbles had had his fill of food and a couple of cubes of cheese. This was a guilt treat, for abandoning him all day. Not that he was alone. He loved Mrs Cate as much as her, or even more. Nibbles was a reflex purchase after splitting up with her last boyfriend. And then before she knew it, she'd been accepted into the police and was promoted up through the ranks. Everything moved quickly after that. It was a good job she'd connected with Isobelle from the beginning and Nibbles made it clear she was a good person by snuggling up to her legs. Right now, he was cuddled up beside her, rolled over on his back for a belly rub. Slowly sliding her hand over his wiry fur while sipping her wine, Cora just drowsed, too tired to read her script for her open mike night. The stress of the day kept invading her thoughts. So many unanswered questions. On paper, this man had the perfect life. A wife who adored him, the hotel staff said he always spoke about his family. Yet undercurrents kept pushing to the surface. A lot was being concealed, including the Old Palace Lodge manager. Now she was an odd one. Had she been in a relationship with Peter Markham, or did she know something but was covering it up? Then there was Mr Montgomery; Peter Markham could be into blackmail here? Everyone was keeping secrets.

A knock hit softly on the door. Anticipating that Mrs Cate had forgotten something, readily Cora opened her door. It wasn't until Nibbles started going ballistic that she realised it was a stranger. The stranger stepping from the shadows was no stranger at all, but no more welcomed for it.

# 26

'Daniel, what the fuck are you doing here? How did you find where I lived? I told you I wanted nothing more to do with you. Didn't you get the message when I moved halfway across the country? You have no right to be here.'

As she spoke, Daniel edged his way inside and walked Cora backwards until they were in her living room.

'Shush, woman. I am not here to win your heart again. Can't you shut that bloody dog up for a minute—I can barely hear myself think?'

It was five years ago when she thought she had seen the last of him, closing their door for the very last time. She wasn't hiding from him because he was violent or drunk. He was a man who was going nowhere. So, when the opportunity came for promotion. She was left with a decision about what she wanted in life. To be domesticated or a career

'I'll tell him to be quiet when you tell me why you're here.'

Daniel had been the man she was prepared to spend her life with. When he proposed, she said yes. And then everything went wrong. Before she knew it, they were arguing more than they were talking.

Sitting down in the same armchair that Mrs Cates had vacated not ten minutes before, he looked about. 'You still a cop?'

'Yes, a Detective Inspector. I can call the station right now and get you hauled off unless you tell me what the fuck you are doing in my flat. I will not ask again.'

'All right, all right. Cool yer boots woman. Glad to see that temper of yours hasn't chilled.' The evil stare stopped him in his tracks, as well as did the threat. 'Okay, well, I think you're going to be fascinated by what I have to say. If I am right, I believe I might have some interesting information concerning the case you're working on.'

'How could you possibly know what cases I'm working on?'

He was sitting in her flat, making himself comfortable and smirking—how dare he.

'A prominent businessman has been murdered in your area. You've just told me you've been promoted to Detective Inspector. There can't be many people they would trust with this case.'

'Okay, so let's say hypothetically I am. I still don't understand why you're here, except perhaps to congratulate me.'

That annoying smile again, the one she used to love, now got her rag; she had moved on without him since then.

'Still got that dry sense of humour,' he stopped. 'Oh well, never mind. Listen to what I have to tell you, Cora. I work for the Haulage company, and I got to know Peter quite well. He was my boss, once upon a time. We used to socialise, and boy, did he like a drink. We had quite a few drunken nights out; he's quite chatty when he's drunk.'

Pacing around her small living room, Cora knew Daniel had her. He could see the sparkle in her eyes, that hungry look all coppers get. How the five years of memories came flooding back. She'd loved him deeply for a while, and couldn't get enough of him. But he was a man stuck in his comfort zone, whereas she wanted more out of life. It was then her career took priority. As soon as she finished training, the job came first; he didn't even come second. She wasn't surprised when he started seeing other women. It wasn't excusable, but she wasn't entirely without blame either.

'Go on then, you got me. I am on the case. Anything you could give us that will help will be appreciated.'

'I have one condition.'

Sighing now, she knew this was coming; Daniel was never selfless, there was always a catch.

'I don't want to start things up again. We went our separate ways for a reason. Mostly because you couldn't keep it in your pants.'

Daniel suddenly laughed; a deep belly laugh, striking Cora dumb. That wasn't the reaction she was expecting.

'Don't flatter yourself, Cora. Some copper you are. Didn't you see the ring on my finger?' He held up his hand and waggled his finger. A solid gold band sat on his ring finger. 'I'm married now. Do you remember that fit girl from the pub who worked behind the bar most weekends? Long blonde hair and legs up to her armpits.'

'The last tart you cheated on, yeah, that rings a bell.'

'Well, she had an older sister who was nothing like her. One night when I was trying to sneak out after some banging sex when I saw her sister, Phoebe, sitting on the bar stool in the kitchen wearing p.js and looking shy and reserved, she offered me coffee and we got talking. It turned out we had loads in common; last June we got married. Our first child is due in the New Year.'

'Congratulations Daniel, that's brilliant news. I'm so happy for you.' but Cora was shocked. Daniel never seemed the type of guy to settle down, let alone get married and have kids. This woman must be special.

'Thanks, I wanted to invite you to the wedding, but I couldn't find you. You just disappeared, no forwarding address. What I wanted to ask was whether you would come round and meet my wife. It would mean a lot to me.'

He wanted her to meet his wife. She blinked. I don't think so. Was he nuts? This was one of the many reasons she left him in the first place—his unreliability. Yet this was bizarre. Who asks their ex-girlfriend to meet their wife?

Narrowing her eyes, she looked for those telltale signs of lies. Nothing, he must be telling the truth.

'Okay, it's a deal. You understand I won't be free for a while; the case I'm on is major.'

'Yes, I understand. I know how it is. Now would you like that information or not? I don't know how useful it will be, but it might give you a kick start with what you have already.'

'You know I turn nothing down, which might be useful.'

It was a few seconds before he spoke, searching for the best words. Would the information he provided be the breaking of the case? You can never tell with Daniel.

'When we went out drinking once, Peter started drinking heavily. He was urging me to do the same. He was a likeable man; I liked him. You would never have thought he was married by the way he talked. Aye, aye, I thought, this is the real Peter here. He began talking about his youth and then his exploits. He was encouraging me to talk about my conquests. I said that I couldn't see him being unfaithful to his wife and that he was a pussycat, which, for some reason, upset him. It was then that he started bragging about the women he had. I said I didn't believe it; it was then he told me he had taken it too far with a woman. Something about a red mist came over him. He couldn't stop even if he'd wanted to. He raped her.'

# 27

May 2007

The final year of their studies had been stressful. With their dissertations submitted, and the final exams taken, the students at Nottingham University could finally let their hair down, and they did with a party of all parties.

As a mature student, Peter Markham had struggled more than he expected. Married with a young family and turned twenty-seven, he wanted more out of life than just a man running around after others to make them rich; his wife, Yvonne, fully supported him as she, too, wanted more. Both agreed that returning to education for a Business and Management degree was the best way to go. Trying to fit in though when he was so much older frustrated him, giving him feelings that he had jumped too quickly into married life.

When Peter arrived at the student accommodation that last late afternoon, bodies were everywhere, in various states of drunkenness. Some slouched on the sofa, others passed out or were asleep. Some swayed to music, some just swayed. Music blasted from massive speakers. The heavy bass line made his head vibrate while the song was indefinable. What struck him the most was how wasted everyone was.

Plastic cups covered every flat surface, left where they were last put. Empty beer cans created a small pile in a corner. The room smelt of stale beer and tobacco smoke while one young lad was trying to add to it, but kept forgetting to release the can. Peter found everything amusing. They were so young and stupid.

Picking his way through the debris, he found the drinks table and took a beer. Tonight, he was going to allow himself to be young for once, and drink was the quickest way to it. Several cans down on an empty stomach affected his responsibilities; they were gone. Tonight, he was free. After being passed a couple of shots, he downed them as well. The *thump, thump* of the music became less intense. Getting into the groove, Peter for once was enjoying himself and dancing with some of the other late arrivals. He was on the highway to being drunk. Snatching a couple of beers to take away with him, Peter drank steadily. Moving around the gathered kids, chatting to some he recognised, and passing the time. He was that single young man again.

An hour later, knackered, he sat down and chill for a while. The sofa had cleared of bodies, cans, and discarded clothing, so he could sit unencumbered.

After a while, he had the feeling of being watched. When he looked to see whose eyes were on him, he nearly did a double take. Sitting on the same sofa was one of the most beautiful women he'd ever seen with the most incredible emerald-green eyes. Matched with long, dark brown, wavy hair and a shapely body. She was perfect. She noticed him checking her out, shuffled closer, and whispered in his ear, 'You like what you see?'

Peter shook his head, trying to clear it, but as she moved closer to him, her skirt, which was already short, had ridden up more. Her top was miniscule, and low cut, and her large breasts were making a valiant attempt at freedom.

'Ermm,' he coughed. 'Sorry, I didn't mean to stare. Just a bit drunk, you know, although you are very beautiful.'

Transfixed by the girl's smile, she reached out and rested her hand gently on his thigh. His body reacted as blood rushed from his head. All thoughts of his wife and young children had disappeared. Shifting as he became more uncomfortable while the girl's hand moved higher still, he could feel his cheeks burning.

'Yes, I saw you staring at my tits. They aren't usually called beautiful, though. Sorry, I'm drunk too.'

Peter's face went redder. He didn't realise he had been so obvious.

'Oh gosh, I'm so sorry. I didn't mean to stare, but that top is very skimpy.'

She laughed, pleased.

Most of the time, he kept to himself, but even so, he recognised her from one of his classes. Not that he didn't want to mix with the others, but some students weren't there to learn, while he wanted to get as much out of the experience as he could. For a family man, he tried to dress appropriately, always wearing smart straight-legged jeans and a V-neck jumper with a shirt underneath. Boots or shoes, never trainers. He'd only spotted her because she was one of the few people who ever volunteered answers in lectures. Despite her breathtaking beauty, she was smart as well, and her answers were insightful and relevant.

Looking away from her chest, he realised her hand was still on his inner thigh. It had been a while since anyone had flirted with him. Yvonne was home with two young children and hadn't been interested in sex since the second had been born. She was exhausted nearly all the time now. He didn't mind and tried to help with the kids. He loved being a husband and a dad, but he missed the intimacy.

Looking down at her hand, he wondered what she was going to do. Was she just resting it there, not realising because she was drunk? Or was she coming on to him? He responded in kind and rested his hand on her naked thigh, feeling her warmth and the softness of her skin.

Leaning over, he kissed her with passion, leaving nothing to the imagination. Now he was making his intentions very clear. She responded in kind. At least he thought she did. But he was surprised when the woman took his hand from her thigh and removed her own from his. Looking into her face questioningly, he couldn't make out what he saw. Was she scared or excited?

Nonplussed, Peter moved his hand slowly up her leg, up her tight, flat belly, finally up her side at least to get a feel of those magnificent breasts, round and firm. He rubbed his fingers over where he thought her nipples were and was rewarded when they became visible through her top. Confused, her hands were slapping at his, trying to push him away. She was leaning away from his touch.

'What's wrong—I thought you were coming onto me?'

'I don't know, I was—I am so drunk.'

Peter stared when her head lolled back against the rear of the sofa for a minute, but smiled when she sat up straight again and looked at him.

He stood and wobbled; he was a lot more drunk than he realised; what was in those shots? His head was fuzzy, and the room was spinning slightly, but now he was also horny. The light touch on his thigh had ignited a fire in him.

Going to grab the woman's arm to help her up, she

dodged it and crossed her arms in front of her. He tried again, and she slapped his arm away. For some reason he saw red, this woman wanted him, everything about her told him so. But now it didn't matter because he wanted her, so he grabbed her arm roughly, pulled her up off the sofa with one goal in mind. They entered the hallway; he was looking for an empty room. She was half-walking, half-conscious as he dragged her, both bumping off the walls in their unsteady state. A lot of others had either passed out drunk or tired, but some had the same idea as various screams and grunts emanated from the closed doorways.

Fully aroused, he was getting frustrated; he turned and shoved the woman hard against the wall, his erection obvious as he pushed his body into hers. He didn't notice when she winced as he kissed her, and annoyed now that she kept turning her head. She shuddered when he ran his hands up the inside of her top, wanting to get a hold of those huge breasts. Especially when he realised she wasn't wearing a bra. Rubbing her nipple between his fingers, even though her hands were constantly tearing his hands away, he didn't stop. If he'd looked up, he'd have seen the tears streaming down her face. And when she started screaming, this also annoyed him. He wanted her and he would have her. Thrusting his entire body weight against her, he held his hand over her mouth.

'Shut the fuck up, bitch. You can't lead me on, then change your mind. I'm going to fuck you, and I'm going to enjoy it. So shut up.'

All other sounds vanished; the only noise Peter could hear was the blood rushing in his ears. Horny and angry; the stupid bitch had come on to him and then started screaming as soon as he touched her. As they reached the end of the hallway, there was a fire door that led outside.

The late evening was still warm, and the rush of heat smacked Peter in the face. Directing the woman through, he saw the small courtyard with student accommodation located all around. Grateful it was quiet; most students were in their rooms or out partying elsewhere. There was a small area in the middle with trees and bushes. Benches were placed around it, creating a barrier should anyone be looking from their windows.

Pushing her hard against the wall again, Peter forcefully kissed her and lifted off her top to get a proper look at those breasts. He slapped her as she went to grab his hands to pull them away, but she was too drunk.

As Peter moved, he hooked his fingers in her skirt and pulled it down. She slapped his hands away again. This made him furious. He slapped her hard around the face this time, so hard he left a red mark. He avoided her attacks as she got angry and fought him off, trying to knee him in the groin and punch him, but he was too strong for her. He pinned her arms down and continued to swerve her attempts to knee him. Finally, she was too weak to carry on, so Peter took her stillness as acquiescence and carried on.

He pulled her skirt down, which started her whimpering.

'No, no, no, please no, don't do this.'

He spat in her face. 'Shut the fuck up bitch, no one is coming to help you, and I'm not going to stop, so you may as well quit the whining.'

Ignoring her, Peter pushed her tiny pants aside and shoved his fingers up her frigid pussy. Pleased when she gasped, believing she was enjoying it. But she was begging.

'Please, don't do this, I'm sorry, I don't want to, I changed my mind, I'm scared, it hurts. Please stop now, let me go. I won't say anything, please.'

But Peter was in a zone where he didn't hear her. Roughly moving his fingers in and out of her. And then annoyed when she kept trying to clamp her thighs together. He wedged his hands between them and forced them open. He was a lot stronger, and she didn't have any hope of stopping him from getting what he wanted. Unzipping his trousers, he gasped. Finally, he yanked her skirt and pants down in one move. Releasing his throbbing cock from his tight jeans was such a relief.

He grabbed his cock and stroked it a few times, making sure he was fully hard, and found where he needed to be, and shoved it deep. Enjoying the feeling of warmth, the sensation alone nearly making him cum. Then he bucked his hips and thrust in and out of her relentlessly, picking up speed, ramming her roughly, not caring if he was hurting her. He just needed to cum. Eventually, he felt that bubbling in his balls and knew it was time and roared as he finally did to feel the blissful high of release. He was so worked up and hot, his sweat was being flung off as he thrust to land on her face. His cock deflated, had slipped out of her. Tucking it back in, he went back in, needing a drink.

He didn't notice the woman silently sliding down to the floor, not caring about the brick wall scratching her bare back. He didn't care if she felt broken or if she was in pain. He didn't know that she was angry, so angry she'd allowed this to happen. She felt as if she was someone else looking down on this poor distraught woman crumpled in a heap on the floor.

He was now back inside while she sat and wept, not knowing that someone had heard her and came to see what was wrong. He would find this out later. They were shocked by the girl's dishevelled appearance and the red mark on her face. He didn't know they could see blood running down her bare legs. This good Samaritan told the woman she needed to get to the hospital. He didn't know that despite resistance, the young woman eventually gave in and went.

He was lucky she decided not to take it further; he wasn't to know she'd been invaded before, too many times before in her young life. She didn't want samples to be taken, she just wanted her minor injuries treated and to go home.

# 28

After chucking Daniel out, Cora immediately rang the station and told the night staff to start looking into old rape cases that hadn't made it to court. Unable to give them a year, they were to start their investigation when Peter Markham was at university.

Now thinking about it, Cora found it strange there had been no photos of Peter's graduation anywhere in the house. Both children's graduations were proudly displayed with their parents standing proudly on either side of their young offspring. Each child with cap and gown and their certificates clutched tightly.

Peter must have had a graduation ceremony; she couldn't imagine he'd graduated as recently as twenty-twenty when the world stood still because of the pandemic. Why wouldn't he go? Was it because, once he'd sobered up, he realised what he'd done, and could not face his classmates? How quickly the police would have questioned him. Rumours would have spread like wildfire as well. Perhaps he wasn't welcomed, although Cora was sure the incidences of rape at drunken university parties were a lot higher than reported.

A heavy weight settled on Cora's chest. The chances that the young woman hadn't bothered reporting it either were high, which means it wouldn't be on their systems anywhere. So tempted to return tonight to get working, but it had already been a long day, and she knew she'd need to be at her best after a good night's sleep. Tomorrow, things were going to heat up, especially if they didn't find at least one suspect soon. So far, they'd drawn a blank. She needed people to talk. This was a murder case, and all she had succeeded with was more questions.

In her double bed, the duvet bunched up around her where she'd been tossing and turning since she'd put the phone down. Laying on her back, staring at the ceiling, that damp patch had been there since she moved in. Was it her responsibility? Not like she could call anyone to help. The unwanted image of the very handsome DCI briefly flashed in her mind's eye. Just because he's tall, she thought to herself and laughed, and then Daniel entered her mind. He was married now with a child. My God, how did that happen? At thirty-nine, was she ever going to settle down and have children? Her mind drifted back to Felix until she finally fell asleep.

---

After the party at university, the woman left to lick her wounds. She wasn't normally cowed, but the rape had ripped away everything she'd built up in her short life; she couldn't face her rapist again. Already alone in the world, she stayed with her grandmother until she decided what next to do. Her big dream was to be an air hostess, but that seemed out of the question now. It didn't take her long to realise she'd missed her period. Being so slim and having an eating disorder was always hit and miss, but after two months, and struggling to do up her favourite jeans, she suspected the worst.

A quick test confirmed it. Her grandma was understanding and practical. Eve knew her granddaughter wouldn't abort but wouldn't keep it, either. She found out about surrendering the child. They went through the options together. The paperwork was put in place in time for her labour.

Life moved on in gentleness. Eve wondered if her granddaughter would change her mind about keeping the child. One night, it all poured out, her fears of the birth, and anger at her weakness. She couldn't love this child if she tried to. Listening, Eve held her, stroked her hair, and let her talk, and cry the outrage. She knew there was nothing she could say. After that day, the subject was never raised again.

Eventually, the day arrived. The birth was mercifully quick and uneventful. The child arrived six weeks early, a bonny little thing, already a thatch of dark hair covering his head. Such a sweetheart, but her granddaughter refused to even look at him. One photograph was all Eve permitted herself. Her first and possibly only grandchild, so she'd treasure it. He was only four pounds and needed to spend a little time in special care.

For Eve, this was her great-grandson. Couldn't her granddaughter reconsider?

'I want nothing to do with him,' she screamed to her grandmother. 'Don't you understand Peter Markham raped me?'

Recovering from the birth, she rested at her grandmother's for a month and then resolved that she would not let that arsehole ruin her life, so she left. She didn't say where she was going, or what she intended to do, but she had a plan. Eve was concerned so soon after birthing a child, especially a life-changing event that her granddaughter could change her mind, but she had always been strong-willed and independent, so she gave her some money to tide her over and bid her good luck, reminding her she would always be there if she needed a bed for the night.

Often, Eve wondered about the child's father, whether he had a right to know if he was now a dad. She couldn't betray her granddaughter by doing that, so instead she sent a copy of the photo taken on the day of his birth anonymously to his home. She'd just written "your son" on a piece of paper. What he did with it was up to him. She thought about the child and whether his life would be happy. How he'd cope, and if he'd grow up to be a credit to society, or another broken child from a long line of broken families. She hoped he would be given all the opportunities, which meant nurture and would be stronger for it, but she was worried.

The granddaughter had thought about none of this when she left the house that chilly February day. A new purpose had been born in life—revenge.

# 29

When the young woman left her grandmother's house, she wasn't exactly sure what she would do next except to get her revenge on the man who had ruined her life; this would take careful planning. It might take months, years, but she would get what she hungered for; the only thing that kept her going.

After she had sobered up from the ordeal, she knew she couldn't face the rape kit and everything else that went with it. She'd do what she'd always done, take it into her own hands.

Needing to become anonymous, her long dark hair was the first thing to go. A blonde bob took its place. She liked it. It accentuated her sharp cheekbones. Some contact lenses to hide her striking eye colour came next.

Next, a new name. She had read about Erinyes: three women from Greek mythology, who exacted revenge against men who had defied them. Therefore, she chose Erin for her identity. How much more evil could you be than violating a woman? He had used her vulnerability as consent to plant his vile seed. The ordeal had been enough to destroy her sense of worth.

Stoke-on-Trent was her destination, central and safe. No one knew her there, so she could go about her business unchecked. She got a boring office job in a call centre, enough to pay the bills and find a small flat. She settled in, got to know people, and then began asking questions. Gradually, she built up a picture of the murkier element, and who to ask for when needed.

The dark web was also an excellent source of information. Providing her with hints and tips and the materials she would need to both practice and use for real. It enabled her to create the best maximum effects. It also provided sources on how to purchase such items when the time was right for what she wanted wasn't exactly available on the high street.

To kill time and try to stop her from returning to the night of the rape, or the birth of the spawn, she took some evening classes at the local college. The most useful of these was forensics. Fascinating. She could ask those questions which didn't drop naturally into everyday conversations and not be thought of as strange. The tutor thought she was a keen student and Erin came out with top marks. The tutor tried to encourage her to take it further, but this was brushed off. The most enthusiastic of her students, but this student had a different goal in mind.

Another class Erin attended was self-defence. Never again would she be in a position where a man could overpower her. She needed to know she could fight; nothing like fear and lack of control inspired her to practice. Lifting weights was a must. She needed greater upper body strength than she currently did. The new muscles looked strange on her slim frame; Erin was changing into the person she needed to be. Despite money being tight, for the first time in her life, Erin began eating properly. Her body filled out, making her look healthier than she had been since her early teens. The slight pouch she'd gained after carrying the child had tightened. Unfortunately, though, the stretch marks remained a permanent reminder.

Time to move on from Stoke, which was why Erin didn't want to make ties. As friends were unnecessary to her plans —acquaintances and contacts—but not friends. Her only tie was her grandmother, who was getting old now. Struggling alone in her home might mean having to go into assisted living or even a care home. Erin couldn't contemplate that because her grandmother had been her central point, and the place she could always return to no matter what. Health and strength had hardened her, caring was a weakness, and emotionally she couldn't afford to care for her grandmother. Her grandmother would understand if she knew her plans.

Necessary to keep focused and move to London for the next stage.

# 30

Another restless night. This case was becoming a nightmare. They still had nothing on this horrendous murder except speculation from a source which could be said to be unreliable, her ex-boyfriend's story.

Looking up, Darcey shuffled in dishevelled and knackered, checking the clock. It was just after eight and clutching a cup of Costa coffee like her life depended on it. Cora had to laugh, trying to think back to the times when she'd walked into work looking like that, but couldn't recall a single one. Too much pride in her appearance and in her image, she supposed. God forbid, she let her image slip, even once.

It was time to brief the team to share the important information she'd been given by Daniel as she always told herself. Anything was better than nothing, but was it? Chasing dead-ends. Holding up her arm for quiet wasn't necessary, for they all were subdued. When you are getting nowhere, frustration is evident. With Daniel, it was always a hope related with no proof, but if it were true, then they had something to work at.

'Before I catch up on what happened yesterday, I have a

major development that occurred overnight. Someone visited my flat and informed me he was a lorry driver for Peter Markham. They became friendly and went out together for a few nights. During one of those nights out, Peter let slip he'd raped someone at a university leavers party. My source could not provide any more details than that, so I rang it in immediately. I am expecting the night staff to have something for us.'

A low ripple of noise spread around the room upon hearing this. For the first time, there was a clue and something to investigate.

'Boss,' called out Luke. 'Can you say who your informer is, just for the record?'

'That's private to me, Detective Constable Marshall, and under my protection.'

A murmur of interest again flowed around the room. While Dave was quietly sitting at his computer. Did he ever go home? Whenever she wanted him, he was there waiting at his computer, fingers ready to fly over the keys.

'Dave, I need your input. Have you found anything?'

'Don't I always come up with something?' His eyes disappeared from the thickness of his lenses. 'Peter Markham was at Northampton University, studying Business Management. He graduated with a first in 2007. I'm compiling a list of his alumni from that year. Many of the other students have gone on to get married and changed their names, so it's a case of cross-referencing and bringing it all together. Give me another hour or two and I should have it ready.'

This man was a wizard.

After going around the room and catching up on what little had been learnt since the last briefing, Cora gave Darcey the signal to get ready to leave. She didn't miss the dark look passing over Luke's face.

---

At 11 am on the dot, Cora rang the bell of the luxurious manor house located about a mile back off the road. The house was in the country and exuded wealth. A large gate opened; they passed a gardener collecting the last of the autumn leaves. He tipped his head at them. Large hedges ran around the periphery and cameras followed their every move until they stepped inside.

Despite the decadence and wealth present, a small, white-haired gentleman answered the door. Cora and Darcey both held their badges without being asked. Mr Montgomery narrowed his eyes at their intrusion, even though he should have been expecting them.

'Good morning, Mr Montgomery. May we come in?'

'Morning detectives, very prompt, good. I do hate my time being wasted. As I have said before, I have one hour, no more, so you had better come in as time is ticking.'

Cora watched as he walked in front at a brisk pace, belying his age. Darcey looked at her boss and raised her eyebrows. Cora laughed. She didn't say I told you so, but she was certainly thinking about it.

They followed as Mr Montgomery took a sharp left to find themselves in the library. Why the game of Cluedo popped into her head, Cora was clueless. They weren't offered a seat, while Mr Montgomery sat in a high-backed armchair and poured himself a drink. Again, the two women were not offered anything.

'Time is ticking detectives, I thought you had some questions for me?'

It amused Cora to see a flustered Darcey taking her trusted notebook out of her pocket, to do something with her hands.

'Mr Montgomery, what can you tell us about Peter

Markham? How long has he worked for you? Was he competent? Did you have any concerns about his work? Anything else you could expand on?'

Watching the old man closely in that instant, she didn't like him. Too self-assured and smug, too... He held qualities she disliked in anyone, especially when questioning.

'Ah yes, Mr Markham. I believe he's been with us for about twenty, twenty-five years; I'm not sure exactly. Very inconvenient he's gone, most inconvenient indeed, but these things happen even to the young.'

'What do you mean by that sir?' asked Darcey.

'He could be difficult.'

Darcey couldn't see her boss' face. Cora decided that pacing the room suited her mood better, but this was the sort of attitude that would normally blow her gasket.

'I understand you have a son?'

'A son that would rather be a girl,' jeered Mr Montgomery. 'I have no time for fads and affectations. He is a complete waste of time.'

'And what about Peter Markham? Did you see him as your next successor?'

'A greedy little man who thought too well of himself and was too eager.'

Cora and Darcey exchanged looks.

'So, Peter Markham was out of the running.'

'Out of the running? Yes, he was. I've always intended my son to have it. He's blood. Anyhow, what has this to do with his murder?'

'Do you have any idea why Mr Markham would have been murdered, sir? Did he have any issues at work?'

'No, detective. I told him what needed to be done, and he did it. No questions asked, no arguments. He went away and got on with it,' and then Mr Montgomery grinned. 'Everyone wants what I have, and he was no different. People like him can be handled.' That grin again.

'Can I ask you what you mean by that?'

'The answer to all mankind's problems is money.'

'I see,' said Cora. No, she absolutely didn't like this man. 'What about problems at home? Was he likely to share his home life with you? Did he ever let anything slip?'

'No, absolutely not. I didn't want to hear what people did in their own time, and thankfully, he didn't want to share details of his private life. Except, he was very pally with the staff. I think he was trying to plot some business coup, but I am the one paying the wages.'

Cora had stopped pacing to look at a display of photos with Mr Montgomery shaking hands with various dignitaries and royals.

'Boss, is there anything else you would like to ask Mr Montgomery?' asked Darcey a few more questions later.

'Not for the moment, except I need to know where you are, Mr Montgomery, in case of more questions. Thank you very much for your time today.'

Montgomery didn't rise. He stayed sitting and rang a bell by his side. An older matronly woman in a black skirt, white blouse and black apron appeared from a door that neither Cora nor Darcey had spotted before. She looked pinched with sallow and pale skin. She didn't show herself to be a fan of the man when she answered the call. There was a story there if they cared to look deeper, but they were on a murder case.

'Lucyna, show these women out, will you? I'll take my coffee now.'

Bowing slightly, Lucyna quickly took them to the door with a sad, tragic look before closing the door.

'God, I'm glad that's over and done with,' said Darcey as they belted up.

Cora waited until they were some distance out of the gates before speaking.

'He was reluctant to say anything decent about his late employee. Do you know, I am inclined to believe that he had an involvement with Peter Markham's murder? I don't know,' sighed Cora. 'It might have more to do with how much I dislike him.'

'Do you think he could be evil enough to have had Mr Markam topped? Using him and then when he had enough —Do you know what boss—I think Peter Markham was blackmailing him?'

'That's the trouble when there is no tangible evidence. Everyone starts to jump to impossible conclusions.'

'Where to now, boss?'

'Back to the station, to update everyone on what we've found.' Cora's eyes were on the road, but her mind was elsewhere. Where had Peter Markham's income come from? What had Peter been up to? Well, for certain, if Lisa Riley was in the running to take over, it had to be her that was angry and thirsty enough for success.

Both returned in silence as they went over everything in their minds. A light drizzle had started to fall, and a low fog was rolling across the hills, reaching out its icy fingers to caress the car as it drove. Cora hated this time of year when the sun was low. Her mood was especially low after this awful interview.

This was the last moment of peace either of the women would have for some time.

# 31

The drive back from the country manor to the station took a surprisingly short time, something Cora was grateful for as the driving conditions were getting worse. As the light faded, the fog became thicker. It was going to be a grotty night.

'Miserable night, boss. One to be resting with your feet up, in front of the fire in your PJs.'

'I thought that myself. I'll be glad to get back to the station. Let's hope nothing has broken while we have been out, so we don't get stuck there all night.'

'I'll drink to that,' said Darcey. 'There are some strange characters in the world.'

The station was a huge modern red brick building. When the three forces combined to form major crimes, they constructed a brand new hub with plenty of parking spaces. Slotting the pool car easily into a space, a few cars were missing. 'What on earth is going on?' Cora muttered to herself, looking at the empty spaces.

Already out of the car by the time Cora had untangled herself from her seatbelt, grabbing everything she needed was Darcey.

'Hey Lorraine, don't you ever go home?' Cora called out when they passed.

'Ha, ha. Don't feel like it, ma'am. I'm picking up some overtime this week, so the kids are with their dad. God knows what I will have to sort out when I get home. I love my husband Cora, but there are certain skills he lacks. With Christmas coming up, every extra pound helps.'

'True enough, don't work yourself to death, though, Lorraine. Who knows what this station would do without you—'

Seeing Lorraine happy at the unexpected compliment, Cora walked to scan herself into the inner sanctum.

'Is it true that being married is like having another child?' Darcey asked, trotting alongside Cora.

'You have much to learn, young lady. Why do you think I'm still single? Men are too much trouble. Don't rush into marriage. Have your fun first.'

Going across to Dave to get a quick update on what had been added to HOLMES2, he had one of those marvellous photographic memories and could recite everything with no hesitation. The details of the postmortem were up there, but still awaiting tox results.

'Cause of death was officially given as shock from the result of blood loss of a slash to the abdomen,' said Dave. 'His heart eventually gave out. The knife was likely an eight-inch non-serrated knife, taken from measurements of the cuts on the body.'

*A standard kitchen knife,* thought Cora.

At that moment, the DCI popped his head out of his office. 'You got a minute, Cora?'

A blush crept up her neck at the sound of his voice. What was wrong with her? She wasn't a teenager. She should be able to control her emotions better than this. She hoped no one else had noticed.

'Be right there, sir.' Cora took her notebook. She needed something in her hands to fiddle with, so she didn't look as incompetent as she felt.

'How are you getting on?' Felix asked, sitting comfortably. 'What's the latest update with the Markham case?'

'Not so good, sir,' Cora opened her notebook to give herself a moment. 'We've spoken to the owner of the company. Mr Montgomery, such a cold fellow. He didn't show any distress about the death of one of his workers. For some reason, I had the impression that their relationship was close.'

'Nice man.'

'Yes, that's the general consensus. While we've been out, contact has been made with a Ms Lisa Riley. She's due in tomorrow morning.'

'She's coming here willingly?' Cora laughed at the intonation in Felix's voice.

'Yes Sir, we told her it wasn't necessary, but she insisted; she will be here at 9 am tomorrow. I shall ask her about Mr Montgomery. He has not been complimentary about her. I got the feeling he doesn't like anyone. The assumption is there's no love lost between the pair of them.'

'Thanks, Cora. As you can imagine, the big boss is on my case while the press is a nightmare. We are trying to keep a lid on certain details for now, but we will need to put out a statement in the next hour or so. Hopefully, it won't break before then. Dave filled me in with the update. While I think about it, where are we with tracing his phone and car? Has ANPR been able to locate any movements after he left the hotel?'

'His phone last pinged at the hotel. There was no trace of it being used after that. Calls to it rang out, so we assume his mobile was left in his room dead or turned off. ANPR caught his car near the hotel heading out of town, but it disappeared quickly. We can't trace it after that, but that's our biggest lead so far. No one seems to know why he would go in that direction. We are still trying to collate his movements and have submitted all the relevant paperwork to the mobile companies. We're still waiting for them to come back to us.'

'Probably best I don't voice my feelings on that particular minefield. So, we have absolutely no hints as to who would want to do this yet. From what I've seen, his halo is slipping, but not enough for someone to want to kill him, especially horrifically.'

'I want to go back to the hotel and speak to them again, I keep on getting the feeling that they haven't been quite honest, and yet, alternately, I can't imagine they will have anything groundbreaking which will crack open the case.'

Cora told Felix about her ex turning up and about the rumour of Peter raping someone at university. It could be true, but it also could have been one of those drunken boasts. Anyhow, it was being looked into as they spoke, but the database had thrown up nothing.

'Okay, thanks Cora, I'll leave you to it. Keep me updated.'

'I will, sir. It has my full attention.'

'Whoever committed this murder had no intentions of being caught. That said—we will not give up. I feel very positive about our team. Every time I look in, I can feel the enthusiasm, and it's all down to you, Cora. You are the inspiration. You're doing well.'

'Gather round everyone,' clapped Cora, returning to the centre feeling much brighter and happier after hearing her boss's confidence in her and the team. 'Updates for where we're at. I'll begin.'

And always a boost when she asked for her teams' attention, to watch them go quiet and listen. It meant that she must have earned their respect. Commanding a room full of drunk punters at a comedy gig was no problem, but a room full of coppers. Terrifying.

'We interviewed Mr Montgomery, who was reluctant to go into any detail about Peter Markham. Reading between the lines; there is some sort of corruption going on, either fraud or blackmail. A man like Markham doesn't go from zero to gold in fifteen years. But would this be enough for a man like Mr Montgomery to murder his employee? Or would he get someone else to do it for him? "People will do anything for money." These were Mr Montgomery's own words—Mark, Luke, ANPR, mobile trace?'

Mark stood. 'ANPR traced the car leaving the hotel car park and checked for CCTV around the area. The hotel had CCTV at the entrance, but because of the location, there wasn't much around. It was caught on one more camera heading out of town, but there have been no more sightings.'

'Thanks, Mark. And you, Luke?'

Luke stood. 'Mobile was pinged at the hotel and then at another mast heading out of town. There have been no more pings since. We have recovered phone calls and going through the social media will take longer. So far, nothing stands out. Mainly messages to his wife and children and one friend. Little or no contact with anyone else. A lot of phone calls from staff and business contacts. A busy man.'

'Thank you, Luke. That's great. If you dig anything else up, then let me know straight away?' It was hard to tell if they were making progress. The feeling kept on occurring that the murderer was laughing at them. Whoever it was had covered themselves well. 'Have the children of the dead man been interviewed yet?'

'I called and spoke with both of them.' Beverlee raised her hand. 'Neither had any idea about their father's indiscretions, and both loved him dearly; they were shocked and in denial and are taking his death hard, so I didn't push too much.'

'Thanks, Beverlee. Maybe worth another chat later, but it doesn't seem like there's more to be gained there. Okay team, carry on. I haven't had the impression yet that this is a serial killer. This feels personal to me. So far, whoever it is has been clever. What we need is one tiny clue and a motive. Quick debrief at 5 pm before we knock off for the day. I don't want you all tiring yourselves out.'

No one responded. They knew there was no need as they returned to their desks and phones or whatever they were doing before they were interrupted. The buzz of noise slowly increased. Everyone wanted to find that tiny piece of evidence. As with everything else, the best-kept secrets were staring them in the face. They just didn't know it yet.

---

Finally, a break came. The phone rang, and it was Luke who answered the call.

'*Hello, are you the police officer investigating the Peter Markham murder?*'

'Hello, yes, I am one of the team. Can I ask who is calling, please?'

*'That's not important, but I have some information. Do you have a pen?'*

Luke scrabbled around for a pen and a notebook, then pressed the record button.

'I'm ready.'

*'Okay, are you aware that Lisa is skimming money through wages from the company?'*

'No, carry on.'

*'Well, they have a private bank account where they move the*

*money and split it fifty-fifty. I can tell you how I found this out, but I won't tell you who I am. But I assure you, it's all true.'*

At that, the ringtone sounded in Luke's ear as someone hung up. He shouted for Cora. The wheels of this investigation were now moving.

'It looks like we might have a killer,' Cora muttered to herself. Somehow, Peter Markham must have found out and was holding this over Lisa Riley's head. Serious blackmail. There was no love lost between them.

They had a prime suspect. Could there be others?

# 32

Harrison Drew snuck out again; his foster parents didn't have a clue. They had given him an early curfew. What nearly sixteen-year-old kid had to be home by nine and in bed by ten? Most of his mates were often out until midnight. Their parents didn't give them grief. Some parents didn't even notice or had given up trying to enforce rules on their children. Yeah, he knew his foster parents cared about him, but come on, they were being unreasonable.

Being a foster child to Harrison meant not testing his foster parents too much. He didn't give them cheek or backchat and tried to be good at school. He wasn't particularly smart, but he did enough not to attract the attention of the teachers and not enough to be teased for being a nerd. He was beginning to understand cooperation, to give and take. But a curfew, nah.

In return, his foster parents let him have a television in his bedroom, and his own laptop for homework. He was allowed a mobile phone if he stayed in contact when he was out. The penalties for not doing so were severe, as he found out to his cost. Thinking it was stupid to keep checking in, Harrison didn't bother. When two police turned up to take him home, Harrison realised his foster parents weren't messing around. His mates still teased him about that.

The only rule they enforced was the curfew. He'd never asked why, mostly because he didn't care, knowing it was their house rules and not his place to question. But tonight, he was going to meet his mates, have a laugh or two, and see how Kit Domino was. She joined the gang along with Landon Young, Andrew Houchin and Jaden Campbell.

They'd all been friends since Harrison had moved to this foster home from his previous one in Bristol. He'd been kicked out of that one for being too much trouble and was arrested after setting too many fires and getting caught. Rebecca Stevens, his previous foster mother, was a patient woman, but even she had eventually flipped. He felt bad about her, for she was good to him, but he just couldn't control the urges. He was told in no uncertain terms this was his last chance and if he messed up again, it would be a remand home until he was released into the world on his own. That was three years ago. Since then, he hadn't been in any trouble.

Not that Harrison had committed no crimes; it was just that the police hadn't caught up with him yet. Discovering weed was wonderful, he moved onto shoplifting to pay for it. There was also the thrill of the deed. There wasn't much his foster parents stopped him from having, but all teenagers shoplifted, *didn't they?* Sometimes he sold the stolen stuff to buy weed, sometimes he just kept it. Andrew, his friend, who was also in the foster system, had warned him against this, as it could be used as evidence.

It was just after 10pm when Harrison left. Knowing already his foster parents would be fast asleep. That was part of the reason for their early curfew. They went to bed at ten and expected him to do the same. They didn't want to be disturbed by him coming in late or making noise on his laptop. The funny thing was they were heavy sleepers who would sleep through a bomb going off.

Creeping down the stairs, knowing which steps to avoid, especially the squeaky ones, he didn't want to risk being caught if one of them went to the bathroom. Tonight, he would exit by the backdoor and leave it unlocked. It was a good area and probably safe. Besides; he wasn't planning on being out too long, he just wanted to have a joint or two, ready to face the end-of-year tests. Failure was something he couldn't face. He needed something to calm him down. Also, he was still having nightmares about that body he and Kit found; easier to sleep with the weed.

Landon and Jaden were brothers and had been labelled trouble from primary school. It was often assumed they were twins, but there was a nine-month age gap between them, which meant they ended up in the same school year. They'd also had a rough time at home. Absent father, a mother who couldn't care less, and tried to drink her troubles away. Instead of succumbing to bullying, the young lads went on the attack with a reputation that followed them from primary school to now. Harrison was allowed to be part of their gang after he flipped and knocked out the kid who'd been tormenting him for months. And then there was Andrew; he was far from violent and was known as the thinker of the group. Harrison had been taken under his wing when he first arrived, and they'd remained close friends ever since.

He loved Kit, probably because she was the wild child and wasn't ruled by anyone. Odd because she had a happy, stable upbringing, and loving parents, yet for some unknown reason, she rebelled at everything. Rainbow-coloured hair, piercings all up her ears, through her tongue, both eyebrows and nose, and in some places Harrison wanted to investigate further when they were alone; she was a nutcase, but an intelligent one. Always wore a full face of make-up. Her specialised uniform of black and red comprised the shortest skirt and the biggest boots. She was a confusion of her own principles. No one understood her, least of all the school.

The teachers had given up trying to get her to wear the school uniform. Lots of people thought school bored her, that's why she acted up. Yet, if Harrison was struggling with maths or science, he knew he could turn to her, another reason to love her.

Unfortunately for Harrison's friends, that night wasn't going to plan at all, and the consequences of which would affect them for the rest of their lives.

# 33

Lisa Riley arrived at the station as promised at 9 am and was promptly cautioned. An investigation into the Company's books had shown up embezzlement. A lot of secrets get spilt when a murder is being investigated.

Cora didn't want to comment on anything at the moment. Everything was possible; a murder was a strange and unusual crime. People wanted to help, so sometimes they would make up something to stick on others. How many people had gone to prison because of someone else's denouncement?

'You will find, Luke, that things that have been contained for years will emerge. You'll discover a lot about life when someone is murdered. Go with it and see what you can come up with. A little bit of digging into the accounts of those in the upper echelons of the business can certainly uncover some discrepancies.'

They were now sitting in a room with a large screen and watching the interview of Lisa

Riley currently taking place. A reward for Luke. He would take the interview with Lisa Riley while a constable sat in. Sitting back with interest, Cora watched.

---

If Lisa was surprised by this turn of events, she didn't show it, except to request her solicitor. While they waited, she was placed in one of the small uncomfortable interview rooms with a dodgy coffee from the station machines. She sat still without fidgeting with her hands, nor did she smooth her hair, straighten her smart skirt, or adjust her blouse. She did nothing but sit and wait. Beverlee stood with Cora and Luke and watched as the solicitor entered the room.

'Morning Lisa. You had coffee?' Beverlee said as she took her seat.

Lisa looked up and with a slight smile. 'Can we get on with this, please?'

Nicola had shown her solicitor in, one the station was familiar with. They had just finished their private consultation while Guy had read Lisa her rights.

'Lisa, you understand why you are here and why you are being questioned under caution?' asked Felix Blackwell.

'Yes.'

'And your solicitor has explained everything that is going to happen and you're happy to continue.'

'Yes. Can we just get on with it, please? I'd like to get this over and done with so I can go home.'

The solicitor reached over and put a gentle but firm hand on her arm, warning her not to lose her temper. Lisa took a deep breath to calm herself.

'I'm sorry it's been a long wait to get here,' began Felix. 'But unfortunately, that's been out of our hands. I'm sure you're aware we are investigating the murder of Peter Markham.'

Lisa flinched.

'I would just like to begin by asking you how you knew

Peter Markham. When you first met? First impressions. How you became partners in the business. Stuff like that.'

'Well, we were thrown together by accident. Peter was a nobody then, but he soon ingratiated himself into the business, making himself indispensable. Suddenly, everything had to be channelled through him. My father had been an investor until Montgomery decided he didn't need my father's money. It was understood that I was to take over after Montgomery passed over until Peter came along.'

'Can I ask in what way this was understood?'

She flinched again and looked offended. 'It was a gentleman's agreement.'

'I see, nothing concrete.'

'Excuse me,' interrupted the solicitor. 'My client has come to the station voluntarily not to be accused.'

'You're correct,' nodded Blackwell. 'So, it's safe to say you weren't a big fan of Mr Markham?'

Taking a deep breath, then looking at her solicitor, she gave a slight nod to continue. 'No, not really. I know we shouldn't speak ill of the dead, but he was a sly, underhanded man. Nice to your face, but all the while stabbing you in the back. I know for certain he had been spinning lies about me.'

'What sort of things do you think he'd been saying about you?' interrupted Felix.

'I can't say for sure except that while he was going up in the world, I was coming down.'

'And this made you bitter?'

'Of course it did. I didn't trust him, and yes, I hated him —' Lisa paused. 'Ah, I see where this is going. No, I didn't murder him, if that's what you're trying to get me to say.'

'Thank you. You've been helpful.' Felix didn't move a muscle. If she wasn't giving anything away, then neither would he. 'Would you be able to give us a list of those he didn't favour, it would be useful to talk to them? When we spoke to the staff, no one had a bad word to say about him.'

Lisa nodded but didn't comment. Her solicitor shifted in her seat and pulled at the collar of her blouse.

'Okay, Miss Riley, I just have a couple more questions for you and then we can get out of here for some air; it gets a bit stuffy in here.'

Opening a folder, Guy took out the two sheets of paper, turned them around, and slid them across to Lisa.

'For the benefit of the tape, I am showing Miss Riley exhibit number JC01. Your bank statement, JC02. Ms Wendy Ellis's bank statement, an LM05.'

'Why is this only being brought to light now?' asked the solicitor. 'This should have been disclosed before the interview unless my client is under arrest.'

'Now, Ms Chaudhuri, you know we can introduce more evidence when we need to.'

Her professional anger prevented her from noticing all the colour draining from her client. Guy had, however. The game was up as both Ms Chaudhuri and Lisa took time to have a quick look through the paperwork.

'I am going to need to have a consultation with my client,' said Ms Chaudhuri.

Guy leant over to turn the recorder off, and they all stood, holding the door open as Ms Chaudhuri led her client out of the room; Guy followed.

Walking back into the thrum of the incident room. The phones were ringing, keyboards clicking, voices shouting and printers spurting out reams and reams of paper.

'I better see what's going on,' said Cora, leaving the room.

'You heard what was said,' said Guy. He had been waiting for her outside.

'Yes. That was a surprise.'

'Last minute information from your Dave. What did you think about Lisa and how she received it?'

'A turn up for the books, but I have to give it to her. She was cool and open. She didn't seem too worried about slagging him off, but is she a killer? No, I don't think so,' Cora sighed. 'It would make our work much easier if she said it was me who murdered Peter Markham. Her revenge was to hit the business where it hurt financially. It has just occurred to me; do you think he found out and threatened to go to the big man about her?'

'It did pass my mind. What was done to Peter Markham was pure rage. I can't see her getting angry enough.' Guy was thoughtful, and then he smiled. 'I was warned once to never underestimate a woman. To get to that level of rage and inflict those injuries requires a whole different type of anger and detachment. And that lady sitting in there doesn't have it, nor the strength. Her cheeks didn't flush with anger, her pupils didn't change. She's not our killer.'

'I'd have to agree with you there. Whoever murdered Peter Markham had been planning this for months, even years. This had become a way of life for whoever, because it can equally be a man dressing it up in a woman's fury.' Cora looked at Guy and then away. 'It was something that Luke said about being a one-off murder and now that he or she had done it, they could get on with their lives. But back to Lisa. What I saw when she was shown the bank statements was more of acceptance than shock. Luke, what's your gut telling you?'

'I agree with you both that Lisa is a thief, but not a murderer.'

'Why is that, Luke?'

'Too calm, too open. She didn't like the questions or the implications, but there again, who does? But she was truthful in her answers. Her body language has been open throughout. Maintaining eye contact, no fidgeting, wringing of hands, tapping her foot, or any of the other signs we're told to look for as signs of nervousness. I know these are only guides to go by, but usually guilty people show something. Yet, I have to agree that she is a strange person, but we might, you never know, have it wrong. A very cool customer playing the game. I wouldn't like to discount her completely.'

'Thanks, Luke, very observant of you. It's what I too concluded. She hardly moves and is remarkably calm considering the situation she's in. Some might argue that's a sign of a psycho. Oh, I don't know. We might have to consult a profiler, I know. It's always the budget.'

---

They filed back into the interview room, Guy with the constable while Cora, Luke and Beverlee took their places in the surveillance room. Once everyone was seated, Lisa and her solicitor exchanged looks, but neither said anything. The constable restarted the recording and did all the technical and legal bits. Leaning back in his chair, Guy appeared as he always did at ease with the world.

'Do you have any comment about those bank statements Lisa? I know what I think, seeing it, but I may be reading it completely wrong.'

Looking at her solicitor, almost for reassurance rather than permission, Lisa began.

'No detective. I was just taking what should rightfully be mine.'

'But it wasn't just the wages.'

'No, it wasn't. I wanted more, a lot more. I was ranting on the phone to my partner and Wendy overheard me about how unfair it had become. Come on. I ended up working for him when it was me who should have been taking over the business. I am not going to be so graceless as to pass all the blame onto Wendy, but she suggested it was possible to do something about this.'

'Yes, I understand. But why did Wendy want to get one over Peter? When DCI Snitton interviewed her, she was indifferent to his death.' Guy glanced at his notes.

'Peter was sleeping with Wendy, and when she'd had enough and wanted to break it off, he wouldn't take no for an answer. She told me he raped her, detective. He forced himself on her. Of course, he apologised and told her he'd leave her alone, then he said that if she ever mentioned it to anyone, it was her who could go down, and he would make sure of it. He told her that people would believe him over her, a happily married man. She wanted to destroy him, and I don't blame her. In my opinion, he deserved what he got.'

A story they were now hearing repeatedly. How could Markham's wife be so oblivious to this side of his character? Or maybe she wasn't.

'Why didn't she report it to the police?' Guy asked calmly.

Lisa suddenly became exasperated. 'Really, detective? The man was devious. Who would believe her over the golden boy?' This was the first time Lisa had shown any genuine emotions. 'From the whispers of her colleagues, some would believe she led him on, and never consider that she was innocent or a victim. That's how Peter played it. Two sides of a coin; he was a delightful man when he got what he wanted, and when he didn't...' Lisa grinned. 'I played him at his own game.'

'And what game would that be?'

'Getting even. At the time, I had an enormous mortgage, and I wasn't prepared to lose my house. Don't you understand, my father was an investor, but Montgomery managed to find some dirt on him when there wasn't any, and that's what killed my father and his career. Wendy said we could get away with it, and I believed her. That money Peter was filtering into his bank account should have been mine?'

'You should have taken Peter Markham to court.'

'Look detective, you and I know I wouldn't have won, not with Peter.'

'So why be open today? You were both were obviously onto a good thing. There could have been an explanation for the transfer into your account. Why confess so easily?'

'But I didn't get away with it, did I? Anyhow, it doesn't matter. In many ways, I wish I had never agreed to Wendy's proposal. I began distrusting everyone, fearing they had found out. I believe in karma. Since the money has been pouring into my account, I've never had peace. So, there you have it.'

'Well, thank you for your honesty. You realise you'll be charged for this?'

'Of course, detective, when we had a break, I instructed my solicitor to begin to put my affairs in order, I have been prepared for this day, so it won't take long, luckily, I never married or had children, so there's no one left behind because of my actions. However, this will hit Wendy hard. I don't feel bad for her. Greed gets us all in the end.'

Inside the comfort of the surveillance room, Cora smiled. She couldn't help but like this woman, despite everything she'd done. It could be her honesty or the fact that was getting back at Peter Markham in the only way she knew how. Peter was not the man he had made himself out to be.

'Thank you, Lisa,' said Guy. 'You have certainly made our job a lot easier today, but we haven't got to the actual matter we rang you about, the murder of Mr Peter Markham. So can I ask you, did you murder him?'

Cora, Luke, and everyone waited, each holding their breath because if she was the murderer. Would she confess? The slightest twitch may make this woman a liar.

'No detective, I did not. I may be a thief, but I am not a killer.'

# 34

Harrison walked along the back streets. They had those stupid new LED streetlamps which only lit the small bit of floor underneath them and left the rest of the pavement dark. He could walk along the edge of the curb and remain hidden. Wearing all black as he always did, he was going to catch up with his mates at the park at the end of the street. He felt fed up with the beginnings of those black moods coming on.

The gang was already there; Kit, as usual, was bouncing along the pavement, walking to her own beat. Harrison was bewitched by her, but did she care about him? He didn't think so.

Skulking now, head down, kicking everything that crossed his path, he was annoyed about something.

'Hey Harrison, what's up, bud?' Jaden asked.

'Nothing,' he shrugged.

'C'mon bud, I don't think I've ever known you to be so quiet,' said Andrew. 'Usually, you're telling us what mad scheme we are up for tonight or moaning at us for something or other. We barely get in your eyeline before you're bellowing something rude at us down the street.'

Landon joined in. 'Yeah, Harrison, Andrew's right. Usually, we can't get a word in once you get going. What's up?'

Even Kit stopped dancing and Jaden looked intensely at Harrison 'Something's defo up. You look miserable as sin mate, I mean you ain't no happy normally, but yer proper down in da dumps, init?'

Kit put her arms around him, not because she wanted the human contact, but because she was nosy, and thought it would work to get the information out of him. It did.

Stopping, Harrison turned around and faced the four of them.

'The fucking rents found the weed, and they found something else, too. So that's it, I'm out, and back to the home where I'll rot 'til then.'

'Shit bruv, that's really shit. How'd they find it? You're usually so careful. What else did they find?' asked Jaden, the question they all wanted to know.

'Coke, man, they found coke.' Harrison looked down; a slight blush rose as he mumbled quietly. 'They didn't know what it was, but I took some and was wasted. I passed out on my bed, didn't I? They came to tell me my dinner was ready and saw it and flipped their fucking lid.'

'Coke? Harrison, you fucking idiot. What were you thinking? I didn't think you were ever gonna try the hard stuff. You knew this would happen. Kids like us don't stand a chance,' shouted Andrew.

Andrew was shaking, trying to contain his anger. He knew he weirdly cared about what happened to him as they'd both been in the system and knew what happened once you'd screwed up one too many times. *Cut off, ignored, cast aside.*

He also knew Andrew had been rebellious once. Compared to him, Harrison had a fairly easy ride through the system. Not knowing why his mother gave him up, he liked to think it was because she was a young single mum who simply couldn't cope with a baby. Yeah, he was cute and had the bluest eyes, except they were brown. As a baby, he was taken on quickly. Who would have thought his adoptive parents would have died in a car crash while he survived?

His first foster home didn't go well, though. The woman was taking on as many kids as she could to get the money, but didn't bother passing that down. The kids had to scrabble around for scraps of food and slept three to a bed. It took a long time for social services to realise what was going on. The children were all split up and sent off to emergency foster homes. Although Harrison didn't remember, this was where Andrew first encountered him. He wasn't there long enough to make a connection, but when he showed up again at his school, he knew he needed a friend and made sure he would be there for him.

Without responding, Harrison marched around waving his arms. He didn't need another lecture when he'd already heard it from his foster parents. They were livid when they found the drugs. They had a younger daughter in the house and had made it clear the first day he came to live with them that drugs were a big no. They would not tolerate them in their house, and if they found the slightest hint, then he would be straight out, no second chances.

Harrison could see Andrew watching him, trying to cuff away the tears, but it didn't work. He saw his face soften, knowing it wasn't anger but fear his friend was feeling. The other two didn't have a clue; Jaden and Landen's parents weren't the best, but at least they had some. They'd never been through the system, yet he could see how dumbstruck they were. They'd never taken drugs, not even weed. Their reputation didn't allow it. But what they didn't want anyone else to know is they'd seen the havoc drugs caused and didn't want that for themselves. They were thugs, but they weren't junkie losers.

'C'mon mate, I reckon we can find a way around this.' Harrison flinched when Andrew put his arm around his friend's shoulder. 'Please don't tell me you admitted it was coke. If they've never seen it before, can't you tell them it's for a science project for school?'

Laughing, Harrison seemed to brighten briefly, then deflated again.

'No, they would ring the bloody school and check. I'm done for, man. What am I gonna do? I can't go back, man, I can't.'

It wasn't good when Andrew looked scared, and he did. He looked terrified. He could see Andrew thought he should say something else. When he was in trouble, Andrew suffered alongside him. If Harrison was honest, he knew that if he said he was gay to Andrew, then there would have been one of those relationships. Yeah, he loved Andrew, but only as a brother; they had shared a lot of grief.

Looking up, Harrison could see Landen and Jaden were bored knowing this wasn't what they'd signed up for when they snuck out of their house. When they walked straight out the front door, no one was there to question them. Just as he was about to tell them they could go if they wanted, Landon announced. 'We're outta here. I don't wanna dealings with this shit. If Andrew wants to be a pussy, let him deal.'

Jaden nodded, and without asking, Kit just followed them both, skipping along behind, still dancing to her own beat; she had not uttered a word, but no one found it odd. All three took a side road to go somewhere else to cause mayhem. Kit hadn't even said goodbye. This was the last straw for Harrison. Stressed out about the exam tomorrow; he had been looking forward to speaking to her; he wanted to know if she was having nightmares about the body like he had.

Unable to deal with the disappointment, Harrison started lashing out, kicking doorways and shop fronts as they walked along the high street, taking Andrew by surprise at the sudden bout of madness. Andrew was worried about Harrison. If he didn't calm down, he could see him smashing a window, and then there would be more trouble to deal with.

However, it happened the sound of glass shattering was quickly followed by the cracking spits of disintegrating glass, a spider work of cracks spread quickly from a central point, the window was broken. His anger, though, hadn't burnt out. Taking off his coat, he wrapped it around his hand and began knocking out the rest of the window until every shard lay on the floor.

'Man, have you finished?' screamed Andrew. 'What's the matter with you?'

Harrison just looked at Andrew like he wasn't there.

'What the fuck did you do that for, you idiot? You could have got away with a slap on the wrist if you'd just left it smashed. Now the cops are gonna be after you on top of everything else.'

Either Harrison hadn't heard or was deliberately ignoring him. He began stamping on the glass.

'Oi, bud,' Andrew poked him on the arm. 'I was talking to you, probably the only real friend you have in the world, apart from your foster parents. That gives a shit what happens to you. Don't you think I deserve better than to be ignored?'

Harrison's expression was odd, as if nothing was registering. 'You don't really care about me. No one does. Not even my foster parents. Why would you care about a loser like me?' This was punctuated by kicks to whatever happened to be in his way. He then pulled out a bottle from his coat. Andrew couldn't figure out what he was doing until the smell hit him as Harrison started spreading it around. *Petrol, fuck.*

'Harrison, you dick, what are you doing?'

'I ain't going back to the home man, I'd rather go to jail. I can't go back to those homes. Them kids are fucked up, man. Some of the shit they do, or make you do. I can't anymore.'

'Bud don't do this. Shit man, you are already in enough trouble, and you've broken in. Put everything into the past. That side of your life is over and done with. You and I have a future; we've been given a second chance because these people think we're worth it. Walk away from this.'

'I need to do this, man, don't you understand? Now you gonna help me or what?'

'No, I'm not helping you set fire to this shop, man. What's got into you? I know you don't wanna go back to the home, but this is extreme even for you, isn't it? You actually think jail is gonna be better? Where do you think loads of those kids from the homes grow up and end up? You think the stuff they do in the homes is bad? You've not heard what it's like in jail. You're a real prick sometimes, you know.'

Harrison was in a kind of trance, swinging the bottle from side to side in wide arcs. It was only a small bottle, so he was obviously trying to get a fine spray across a wide area. He didn't respond to the question; there was going to be no reasoning with him.

Stepping forward, touching Harrison's arm, Andrew went to speak, but before he had a chance, Harrison had turned and punched him on the nose, probably breaking it. It started bleeding and hurt like hell.

'Oi, you fucking prick, what the fuck did you do that for?'

'Shit, sorry man, I don't know what came over me.' Harrison looked horrified. 'I was somewhere else. You made me jump, and I just hit out.'

'This fucking hurts man, I think you've broken my nose. C'mon, enough of this now. You've made your point, haven't you?'

'Sorry mate, I really am, but I have to do this. You landed on your feet with your foster family, but I have really screwed up with mine. If it takes jail to straighten me out, that's what I will do.' He then tossed a lighter onto the puddle of petrol.

There was a whoomph as the petrol ignited. It crackled immediately; the flammable dry materials of the shop caught. In no time, the fire was raging. Andrew was just in time to pull Harrison from the flames.

'Where are you going? What you gonna do now? Have you not heard a word I said? If you don't wanna go home but go to jail instead of the children's home, why don't you stick around and wait for the cops to arrive?'

'I got some shit to sort out first, mate, okay? I'd appreciate it if you didn't ask too many questions. I don't wanna lie to you or implicate you in anything else, so just go home. Go to bed like the good little boy those foster parents think you are, and forget about me, all right? If the police come calling, tell them what you like. I don't care.'

'Harrison, it doesn't have to be like this. I can ask my foster family for you to come and stay with us. What if your parents don't want to kick you out? They might have been bluffing.'

'It's too late, man, and those two little pricks that fucked off will probably already be calling the police anyway. I just have something to do, then I am ready to hand myself in. I just need to do this, and do it alone, okay?'

He didn't want to hang around to find out if Jaden and

Landon had called the fire brigade. He wanted to stay out of trouble as well and to stay with his foster family as long as he could until he could go off to uni. *Fuck it, I'm going home. There's no helping Harrison now anyway.*

Harrison had already gone when Andrew looked up. Harrison was completely alone now.

# 35

The clock slowly crawled its way to 10 pm. Amanda was looking forward to going home and picking up DI Bliss to find out what mischief the hero had got into. At least reading would take her mind off the day. Being good at the dead-end job didn't mean she enjoyed it. How much longer she could keep doing it was the problem. It either meant her snapping at someone on the other end of the phone or being fired as a result of throwing it across the room in disgust; only a matter of time before she walked out. A fine line each day and it didn't feel like it would take much to push her over. She needed to look for something else before she quit. That was why she was meeting Helen after work for a drink to compare horror stories.

Walking through the town centre, smoke was rising from one of the small shops just off the main thoroughfare. It could be the newsagents, where she often got a lottery ticket when there was a big jackpot. No one else seemed to have noticed the smoke. It might be an idea to find out what was happening. A young teenager nearly collided with her, trying to dance both ways to get away. Dark hair, skinny, he was running away from something. Kids, Amanda thought and nearly shouted out to him to be careful, but he carried on running. Oh well, it was his life.

Reaching the pathway, a smashed shop front was pouring out flames; a blazing furnace was building, eating everything its angry flames could find. This was no accident. Judging it too ferocious for her to tackle, it would be foolish to even try. Her face began burning from the concentrated heat. Taking out her mobile while keeping an eye on the fire, Amanda gave the emergency services the situation and location as succinctly as she could. She said she would wait until they arrived, as it wasn't immediately obvious from the main road.

There was nothing more she could do but stand back and wait for them. It surprised her how calm she was in the situation. Some of it must come from dealing with fiddling clients. This must have given her a certain hardness.

'Such a waste,' Amanda muttered to herself. Bored kids, no doubt. There had been a spate of small fires, but mostly in skips and parks where no one could be harmed. But this was bigger and more dramatic. What were they hoping to achieve?

Rubbing her arms trying to keep warm for despite the flames licking their way along the building's edges, the chill outside the envelope of heat was cold. Shock probably upon coming across this, but there again, her thin frame and stylish coat weren't much to fight off the winter chill. Pausing for a moment, she stood stock still and waited; had she heard a noise like a person coughing? Straining her ears, she could only hear the fierce roar of the fire increasing in intensity and the crack and bangs of objects breaking and falling. It must have been her imagination on top of the strain of the day. How long was it since she had made the 999 call?

Then she heard it again. A cough and what sounded like

someone calling for help made her spine tingle. Someone was in that furnace.

'Hello, is someone there?' She shouted into the smoky darkness. 'I thought I heard someone cry out. Can you shout again, so I can try to locate where you are in this smoke—if anyone is there?'

The voice, so faint, but audible, croaked again.

'Okay, wait there. I'm coming. Don't move. Help is on the way.'

Was it foolish to look for this person, as this could become two fatalities? Yet if the person injured could not move, how could she leave them to burn or choke to death? This would lie on her conscience forever.

Stepping carefully towards the burning shop now fully ablaze, flames reached out the front and were making their way upwards, meaning she had to be very careful. Pulling her scarf around her face and keeping low to the edge of the cloud of smoke, Amanda, now terrified, edged her way to the alley that was at the side of the shops.

Picking her way past empty beer cans, cigarette butts and who knew what else left by mindless, lazy people. Her eyes streaming from the corrosive smoke, yet in this haze, she thought she saw a figure a yard further along. He was half sitting up as if he had been struggling to remain conscious. Visibility was poor because of the high walls on either side. No artificial light leaked from buildings and no streetlights penetrated the gloom. Grabbing her phone again, she turned on the torch.

'Hello, I heard your calls.'

For a moment, she thought he was dead until he softly said yes.

'Are you okay? Can you walk?'

It was the homeless man, the one she sometimes saw begging by the main parade of shops. He used to be a soldier and now was down on his luck. Sometimes, when she had the money, she would buy him coffee and a pastry. 'What happened? Was it the fire?'

The man tried to sit up but started coughing. He must have been caught close to the fire to be this affected by the smoke.

'Don't worry, the emergency services are on their way. I will call 999 again and request an ambulance. I didn't realise you were here when I first called.'

The man was becoming increasingly agitated, so she bent down again to get close to his face, even though he smelt awful.

'Kids, it was kids,' he whispered. 'I heard them.'

He started coughing again in earnest, making Amanda more concerned about him.

'Look, you don't have to tell me, save your breath. I was only passing. I'm not the police.'

'Make sure you get them. The kids were angry.' He grabbed her arm. 'Drugs...foster mum... but I don't... deserve...to die.'

Amanda was really worried now; she didn't have a clue what to do in this situation. Turning her phone around, she dialled 999 again. What was taking the fire brigade so long?

'I didn't realise there is a man in the alleyway who has inhaled a lot of smoke; he's struggling to breathe. I can't move him.'

'Don't even try to,' said the voice at the end of the line. 'An ambulance is on its way.'

After what felt like an hour, she saw blue lights flashing in the distance. The man had fallen silent. She was uncertain if he was still alive. His eyes were closed. She hadn't left him.

On seeing the lights, she ran out to the road waving her arms. Many people were awoken by the light from the fire and the smoke. Fire had caught the frontages of their houses. The firefighters ran around their truck, pulling out hosepipes.

Standing awestruck at the power of the fire, Amanda had seen nothing like it or the damage the fire was capable of. The speed and efficiency of the firefighters surprised her as well. Everyone had their role to play, and each carried them out quickly and effectively. No communication was necessary; they worked as a team.

Minutes later, when the fire was under control, the head firefighter came across and introduced himself.

'Hi, I'm Graham Bartlett. I assume you're the lady who rung this in?'

'Yes, I smelt burning and followed my nose and thought I'd check it out. It caught quickly and there was nothing I could do but call it in and wait.'

'We found the man you talked about. He's in the ambulance and has been given oxygen. Everything we can do is being done for him. I need to ask you if you inhaled any smoke or were burnt at all?'

'No. I put my scarf over my mouth to go along the alley, but once I was there, the smoke cleared a little and I could breathe easily.'

'You, young lady, are very brave. Thanks for sticking around, and for trying to help the homeless man. Whatever his outcome, you did your best under the worst possible circumstances. You need to be checked over, though, just in case. And I am afraid we need a statement.'

More blue lights flashed in her peripheral vision. This time, it was the police.

Coming across, Cora and Felix looked at the scene.

'What are you two doing here? It's a bit late for you,' said Graham.

'We were just about to leave when the call come in.

What's going on here?' asked Cora, looking around the scene and holding her hand up to her nose.

'Foul play is my guess,' said Graham. 'This was no accident. I suspect kids, but it's too soon to give a verdict. There might be other things going on. The glass frontage of the shop was smashed inwards, so it was definitely arson. It could be an insurance job or someone out to attack the owner.'

'What's happening to people? Why are we trying to destroy one another? Something is going wrong with the judicial service. What is this sudden outbreak of hatred all about?'

'There's a witness over there,' Graham pointed to a woman in the crowd of interested on-lookers. 'She saw the smoke and called it in. Unfortunately, a homeless man was discovered down the alley. We've got him out, but he's not in a good way. This could be more than just arson.'

'Bloody hell. Really? Where is she? We better speak to her?' replied Cora.

'I told her to get checked out by the paramedics. She might have inhaled smoke. She seemed very calm and unemotional. Probably just shock. Who can tell?'

In the direction where Graham had pointed, Cora and Felix saw a tall, slim woman, her dark hair styled in a neat plait at the back, standing with obvious grace that one couldn't help wondering if she was regal, yet her arms crossed over her chest in a protective stance was contrary to her confidence.

Advancing, Cora touched the woman's arm gently, trying not to startle her. Yet she must have heard their approach because she had already turned in their direction. If she was surprised to see two police officers, she didn't show any emotion. Seeing the police, people automatically feel guilty about something, for her eyes were wary.

'Hi, I'm DI Cora Snitton, this is DCI Felix Blackwell. What's your name?'

The woman tore her eyes from the alleyway to look properly at who was speaking. 'Amanda Kelly.'

'Hi Amanda,' replied Cora, 'I know this has been a terrible shock, and the fire officer said you've been incredibly brave, we'd like to ask you a couple of questions before you get checked out by the paramedics, is that okay?'

'Yes, of course, officer. Ask away.'

Felix kept quiet, knowing Cora had managed to form some sort of rapport with the woman. He scrutinised them carefully.

'Can you tell us, in your own words, what happened here this evening?'

Amanda relayed the story of seeing the smoke and the fire taking hold. Then she heard coughing and realised someone was in the alley. It was a shock to find that she knew him already.

'Thanks, Amanda.' Cora tapped her pencil on her pocketbook. 'I can see how this has been scary for you. We will need you for further questions and to make an official statement, especially if this turns out to be a crime scene. Is that okay? I just need to get your contact details, please?'

Amanda reeled off her contact details without thinking. 'He's dead, isn't he?'

'I don't know, I can't say. The paramedics are doing everything they can for him, but I'm no doctor.'

'I know he's dead, and it's my fault. I didn't get to him in time,' she was starting to hyperventilate clutching at her chest.

Confused, Cora and Felix looked at each other; no one blames themselves for someone else's death.

'It's okay, Amanda,' Cora tried to catch her eye,

wondering what on earth was happening. 'There's a chance he will pull through.'

This was the time for the paramedics to come out of their ambulance; the news didn't look good when they spoke to Graham. Cora and Felix noticed, as had Amanda.

It must have been the shock, because Amanda began sobbing. She didn't know why she cared; she didn't even know the man's name, but he was dead when there was no reason for him to die.

One of the paramedics crossed over to Amanda, grabbed her strongly by the arm, bringing her upright, then helped her over to the ambulance. He sat her on the steps and checked her eyes, skin and then lungs, examining for shock, surprising what shock can do. So far, she looked fine, but if there were any changes, he'd like her to visit the hospital. Any signs of a cough or if she felt at all unwell, otherwise, he was happy to let her go. Like all heroes, her modesty exceeded her deeds as she hurried to get away, embarrassed, too nervous and shy that she declined Cora and Felix offered to drive her home, saying she only lived two minutes away. Some people are like that. What can you say?

# 36

'What do you make of that?' asked Cora, still puzzled to Felix in the car. Earlier fatigue had gone. Now there was another case of murder to investigate. 'A bit over the top her reactions, don't you think?'

'Death affects everyone differently.'

'I guess you're right. A dead homeless man wouldn't usually cause a stir, but when he dies at the hands of someone else, everything is different. Another murder scene, an accidental death, but no less a murder.'

Walking into the building, trying unsuccessfully to shake off the cold seeping through their clothes, they passed the currently deserted reception desk and scanned their cards to gain entry. Using the stairs to climb to the first floor. Cora wanted to get down everything she'd seen and heard while still fresh in her mind. This could be vital somewhere down the line when it came to justifying decisions, even if it never went to court. A good habit to get into, and Felix obviously had the same idea.

'That was one hell of fire,' began Cora. 'I've seen nothing burn that quickly. It was as if it had been started by the devil.'

'Helped on by some propellant, that's my guess. You sound like you were spooked,' said Felix.

'Well, you have to admit, it was scary. I was surprised when Amanda broke down. A bit over the top, didn't you think?'

'Yes, I was going to ask you about that. The way she stared at the fire, I thought she started it. A bit weird, especially dropping to the ground.' Felix frowned.

'I wasn't sure what to make of her at first. She seemed more worried about the homeless guy than I would have expected of someone she didn't know. Invisible people—sometimes it makes me think more and more about how people are turning their backs on each other. But she wasn't like this. She truly cared about this forgotten man.'

Cora waited as Felix went back to scribbling for a moment, but couldn't let it go.

'Why was she so, I don't know, emotionless until she saw that nod from the paramedic? If she knew him or something, I would understand. Collapsing, I have never seen that before, even when a relative died. Odd. Okay, so I know she sometimes bought him a coffee.'

'I have no idea, but she was strange. It would be interesting to see what the fire investigators come back with. Without any doubt, it was arson. But I don't know why someone would target a newsagent. As far as we know, nothing was stolen. Cigarette cabinets weren't touched, no alcohol was missing from what they could gather on their first sweep. Why set fire to it?'

Cora held her pen over the piece of paper on which she was writing as if her mind and hand couldn't work independently of each other while thinking about the question Felix had posed.

'I agree about it being arson. The window being smashed inwards. We might have to agree that it was pointless vandalism except for the unexpected death. Will we catch whoever it is? We don't appear to be doing very well.'

'You're right,' said Felix suddenly. 'We all have troubled pasts.'

'You Felix, having a troubled past? Sometimes, you're so laid back, you're almost horizontal.' Cora smiled indulgently as Felix added an extra strong and heavy full stop to whatever he was writing.

'Go home and to bed. There's nothing more we can achieve tonight. We'll update the team in the morning,' said Felix. 'The PM won't be carried out until tomorrow. Unfortunately, a homeless man will not garner the same amount of interest as the lovely Mr Markham. You know that as well as I do.'

'You're right. It's just so sad. The more I learn about Mr Markham, the more of a sleaze ball he seems, and yet everyone seems to be heartbroken over his death. This world is a messed-up place. That homeless man would have been someone's son at some point, grandson, maybe even brother, uncle, dad, or husband. You know, sometimes I wonder who would miss me, or how long it would take for my absence to be noticed. Would it be just because I didn't turn up for work? My family doesn't bother with me, or me with them. I don't have any friends, really. I sometimes wonder what it's all about. I have my dog, and the old lady from across the way keeps an eye out, but is that it? Is that what life is? It feels like I'm not too many steps away from being like that man in the alley.'

For God's sake, she was crying, keeping her head down while trying surreptitiously to wipe away the free-falling tears from her cheeks. She didn't want Felix to see her, he would be shocked by her outburst. So unlike her. She always kept her cards close to her chest. She didn't think he knew she had family, having never mentioned them before.

Didn't talk about anything that wasn't work-related. It wasn't even that she had anything to hide; it was just how she was.

Eventually, she looked up and interpreted Felix's surprise as being uncomfortable.

'Oh my gosh, I'm sorry. I don't know where that came from. Forget I said anything. I'm so embarrassed. I was just feeling maudlin. I didn't know that was in there waiting to pour out.'

When Felix reached out to touch her arm, she flinched, considering herself unlovable and uncared for except by Nibbles.

'Cora, you never have to apologise. This is the first time I have known you to show any genuine feelings. You have always been the tough guy. It's good to know that you are in touch with your humanity. I know I'm your boss, and I know we have to keep a professional distance, but you are still a human being, and you may be affected by what you see on the job, so you never need to apologise for that, okay?'

'Thanks, boss, it can be shit at times, can't it?'

'Yes, it can, and if you ever want to offload, don't hesitate. I like you Cora, I know you are professional with the team, but I can see you have a soft spot in there. You seem to let your guard down with Darcey, and that's great. I'm glad you have someone to confide in. I am always here too.'

'Thanks, boss, let's get off, shall we? I would quite like to get some sleep before we start this all over again tomorrow.'

Still ashamed, Cora didn't know what to make of what Felix had just said and wanted to get away before she grabbed him and sobbed on his shoulders.

---

Driving home, Felix wondered what had just happened in the office between him and Cora. For him, there had been an electric reaction of what? Comradeship. He respected her, but she didn't make it easy to like her. Cora was often cold and standoffish most of the time. Never had she lost her cool demeanour except to Darcey. He'd even suspected her of being gay; such was her attitude towards the men of the team, especially poor Luke, who at times was like a little puppy trying to please its master.

But there was an unmistakable heat between them, though. When he'd reached out and touched her arm, he thought he detected a slight flinch and a blush. He didn't even know how he felt about it. He'd never looked at Cora that way and hadn't even considered her a desirable woman. Too busy trying to negotiate his new job to find out that he was more of an administrator than a cop.

Pushing those thoughts to the side for now, Felix went back to the events of the evening. This was a strange one. A dead homeless man was, sadly, not uncommon. A shop fire, because of arson, is also not uncommon. The woman who'd witnessed it, he thought, was odd. Sometimes when you work so hard, you can't see the forest for the trees.

Slowing to stop at a red light, progress meant more rules. There were so many traffic lights through the centre of town, and now made worse by roadworks that seemed to go on forever.

Peter Markham was a man with a definite past. A *Jekyll and Hyde* character. The perfect husband at home, while away a rapist who treated his victims with contempt. In this case, Markham had upset the wrong person this time. The image of his decaying body returned in that instance. That was some vicious killing. But had it been done by a woman? Surely impossible. Even knowing what gender the person was, had become a guessing game. The clipping off of Markham's fingers to conceal his identity—pointless, as the man was a pool of DNA. This murder could have been done either by a woman or a man to look like a woman. It's possible to drive yourself around in circles. What they needed now was evidence. It was turning into a mocking game.

The long road into his estate was quiet tonight, everyone sleeping as they should be at this late hour. This part of town wasn't particularly affluent. The new builds had been built on the land of an old petrol station, jarring against the houses that had been there for decades. The road he drove along dissected new and old. The view from here was just fencing and back windows. A cat strolled along the pavement, barely acknowledging his presence as he drove slowly past. No lights were on in the windows.

A nice area of town for young couples trying to get started on the property ladder. A few families from all over the world, such a variety of sounds and smells in the summer. It was wonderful to witness all the different religious celebrations, some more raucous than others. Eid was always great, as they liked to set off fireworks into the night sky.

Felix sighed. This case had taken too much time already, and they weren't making much progress. Lisa Riley was going to spend a considerable amount of time at his majesty's pleasure, along with her accomplice, for fraud.

Strangely, none of the women Peter had slept with so far had hated him enough to do what had been done to him. On the surface, that is. Only one alleged incident until now of Peter going too far during sex—an avenue to explore further, possibly starting with the call girls. He must ask Cora to continue following up on that angle tomorrow, but knowing her, she probably already was. Was there something they were missing? So frustrating. They had lots of information, but no answers.

His team were a good bunch, a few new yet eager

members; they were just missing a wizened old detective who had been in the force for years and had developed that true copper's nose. Cora was brilliant at what she did, keeping emotion and drama out of the running, pushing all the members equally and trying to find their strengths and weaknesses. He also liked Darcey. She was a lot of fun, infectiously happy, never without a smile. A compliment and a good word to say for everyone. A happy soul, always a pleasure to be around. She would go far and hoped they got to see her progress before she spread her wings and went elsewhere.

What about Cora? Attractive. Perhaps when she's off duty and relaxed, that's if she lets her hair down and the barriers she erected around herself. He wondered what her story was, why she was cold and standoffish. How did Darcey break through those barriers? Darcey had that special something about her. He'd seen how Cora was around the young woman. Curious.

Pulling up to the block of flats, he entered the archway leading to the parking area around the back. Reversing his car disturbed the dry leaves left from autumn. It was too cold to hang around. That was the trouble working the hours he did.

Setting his alarm for the morning, bright and early so he could be first in, to update HOLMES2, and try to get everything together for a briefing on the dead homeless man. A text from Cora, *thanks for the support tonight boss, see you in the morning.*

Not sure what to make of that, but he didn't have long to ponder it. As he drifted off, his tea sat untouched on his bedside table.

# 37

Harrison ran and kept on running until he was out of breath. He couldn't go home now, and losing the drugs was a loss. Ironically, they weren't even for him. *Idiot.* The guy wanted him to just 'hold on to' them for a bit. The oldest trick in the book. How did he not see it? Had his foster parents already called the police? His head was pumping with thoughts.

Feeling tired and out of breath, Harrison stopped to regain composure. Heart thumping, lungs desperate for air, he bent over. Across from him were some large communal bins where he could hide. Looking around like a fugitive, he didn't even know where he was in a part of town he'd never explored. The blocks of flats were new. His breathing was slowing down now as peace was regained. Quiet enough here, he could probably stay for a while, set up a home of a sort, but as with everything, he just hoped no one wanted to come out and use the bins.

The wall surrounding the small courtyard must have been about six feet tall and heavily graffitied, with tags of rival gangs and random crude words. This was a brick-built store for the large wheelie bins. Huddled between them kept him shielded from the wind. Still freezing, and he wasn't dressed appropriately for the weather conditions. *Why couldn't I have done this in the summer?*

Leaning up against the wall, he listened to the distant sirens going mad. Would any of those sirens be looking for him? Some must be. He hoped they would get the fire under control before trying to find out who did it.

Had Andrew gone home as he'd said, or gone to the police to dob him in? A fellow foster kid wouldn't do that, but he couldn't be sure, and yet he would understand if he did because he could lose his home. Kids their age, especially boys, had no chance if they couldn't stay with a family.

The world had gone to sleep. Oh, the mess he was in.

Boys weren't supposed to cry according to his friends. But he was alone, and everything had gone to shit. Jaden was right, he should have talked himself out of the situation. He could have said it was anything, or said he was holding them for someone else, and realised it was a stupid thing to do. Would his foster parents really kick him out, or was that a threat to make him understand how serious they were about having drugs in their home? Adults lied all the time, didn't they? He'd been lied to his whole life by the adults he had come across. Even teachers. Why did they think kids didn't know they were being lied to? How he wished he had an adult he could trust. He was truly alone. His only real friend had abandoned him at the first sign of trouble. Let me ask you if there was really someone up there; was he such a bad kid? He didn't think so, no worse than some boys at school who weren't there much and spent their time in detention. He tried to learn, although it was hard. The words swam on the page sometimes, and his mind wandered when a teacher droned on.

One thing he would not do was risk going back, though. Would he be tough enough to last on the streets, or maybe he would go to London? *That's what everyone does when they are homeless, isn't it?*

Making his way to the local train station at Leagrave, Harrison was going to sneak onto a train. He knew they went directly to the city; his foster parents had often taken them on trips to London like trips to the Aquarium, and also treated him to a day in the London Dungeon for his birthday; that was what he'd wanted, even though they were petrified throughout. But he'd loved it. Esther and Graeme had been great to him. That was a great day. Swiping his face, to stop the tears escaping, he went to the front to watch the guard to see if he had any pattern to his patrol.

The guard was returning his way, so he ducked behind the bin by the front entrance. When Harrison dared to peek over, he saw a container with the free Metro newspaper issued at all train stations. Looking again for the guard, he spotted the headline.

'Fire at local newsagents kills one. Local homeless man dies.'

Harrison's blood ran cold. Snatching a copy of the paper, he hid in the bushes to read the article.

*A local man, Reg Webb, died of smoke inhalation after the newsagents on High Street North was set alight. The fire was said to be arson, and investigations were ongoing to find the culprit.*

*Mr Walker had recently found his children, and contacted his ex-wife, and was working to get help for his addictions that had led to him to living on the streets. When questioned, his ex-wife was distressed. She was said to still loved her husband, and only agreed to the divorce to make him see that his behaviour was damaging their family; she urged him to get the help he needed.*

*She hadn't realised he'd become homeless and was heart-*

*broken that things had turned out as they had and angry that he'd died unnecessarily and alone. She was keen for anyone with any information about who started the fire to get in touch with the police.*

*If you have any information, please contact the Bedfordshire Police, or Crimestoppers anonymously.*

The monster people were talking about and warning of was him.

---

At the accountant's office, all was quiet. Beverlee had been sent to question Amanda Kelly to get her official statement on the fire.

The main office to the accountant firm was empty. Then Beverlee noticed the small office tucked in the corner; the door was ajar. Uncomfortable just standing there, it was so quiet. Where was the ambient sound, or muzak to make the guests feel less uncomfortable? It wasn't the doctors or dentists.

After no one appeared, she peeped around the door and saw a striking young woman, very slim, sitting with her long dark hair left loose. It was hard to place an age. She could have been anywhere between thirty and forty-five.

'Sorry, no one was at the reception,' Beverlee surprised the woman. 'I waited a while.'

'That's all right, love, Deb's on her lunch break right now. I'm Amanda,' she smiled. 'Come in and take a seat. Sorry, who are you?'

'I am DC Beverlee Swayzee, from the Major Crime Unit. I've come to take your statement regarding the fire you witnessed on the second of December twenty- twenty-two.' She held out her hand for Amanda to shake.

'Oh yes, pet; I made a fool of myself, poor man.'

'Can I just ask you, your accent—Newcastle?'

'Close pet, Sunderland. I get that a lot. I'm far from home.'

'Yes, you are. What brought you so far south?'

'I went to Uni in Northampton and never left is the short version.'

Beverlee took out her pocketbook. 'Do you mind if I ask you some questions? You weren't here when I came the other day.'

'Of course, detective, ask away.'

Beverlee ran through all the questions she needed to fill in the prepared statement for the investigation. Amanda had never expected to find a fire raging away. Something wicked had propelled it. Neither had she seen anyone running away or hovering. *What about the boy?* She looked up and smiled. The interview was over.

'While I'm here, can you tell me what it was like as a company working for Mr Markham?'

'To be honest, pet, I didn't see a lot of him. He went straight through to the boss's office when he visited. I don't interfere in other people's lives. It was a shock, though, to hear of his death.'

'How about his relationship with the other staff? Were there ever any problems?'

Leaning back in her chair, Amanda seemed to drift through the filing cabinet of her memories.

'Honestly, pet, I don't think so. I'm just an admin person. Who would want to talk to me? I'm a nobody who just gets on with my job. But it makes you think, though, doesn't it? Whatever we do, every one of us has enemies. Some it seems more than others.'

Beverlee considered Amanda. There was no reason to disbelieve her. She had no nervous tics, and her answers were clear and willingly given. She was too nice. So why did she have a feeling she was hiding something? A slight clouding of her eyes when Peter's name was mentioned, though this didn't make her a suspect. The police were desperate, but not as incautious as that.

'I'll be off then. Thank you for your time. I need to get this statement typed up.'

'Have a good day, pet.'

When Beverlee smiled, Amanda's smile didn't reach her eyes. A strange encounter, thought Beverlee, returning to the station. She found her too familiar, and why that was, she did not know.

# 38

As Philip scrolled through the endless hours of CCTV footage from the last couple of days, he felt himself about to nod off. His new baby had been screaming all night, and he was exhausted. The first few months with a new baby he was told were tough, but he did not realise it would be this hard.

Just as he was losing all hope, a car looking remarkably like the description he'd been given came into view. The registration wasn't visible, but that was no matter. He watched now with renewed energy.

A young woman stepped out from the car, slim, fairly tall, with long dark hair tied back in a sleek ponytail. Not what Philip was expecting. Now wide awake, he looked closer as the woman walked round to the boot to remove a bottle and something else.

Slowly walking around the perimeter of the car, Philip could see that she was chuckling, her shoulders were shaking. Opening all the doors, she began soaking the seats with what he assumed could only be petrol.

This was confirmed when he saw the other item. Fiddling with it, this produced a small flame. *A box of matches, of course.* The woman threw the match on the back seat and jumped back, swiping her hand across her eyebrows. She must have caught some of the heat.

In that second, it looked like the film had frozen as the woman stood transfixed, unable to move as the car caught and burned. It was only the trim falling, and the decreasing size of the bodywork that showed it was still going. Eventually, the woman, taking up a backpack and hooking the straps over her shoulders, walked away. Not once did she look back.

Philip watched her as far as the camera would allow. He couldn't tell if she had a car parked, or an accomplice waiting to pick her up. However, now they had one of the biggest clues so far. Nearly jumping up and down in his seat, he couldn't wait to let the boss know.

'Boss, boss, I've got something. I have it,' Philip was grinning, cheerful, waving his arms.

Looking up at the call of her name, Cora saw one of the team waving her over.

'What is it, Philip? We are just going to the morning briefing.'

'You'll want to see this, boss. It may be the break we needed.'

Curious, she walked over.

'Well, go on then. I'm listening. Especially if it's the break we're looking for. I'm all ears.'

'I've been viewing the video footage from the camera the farmer had installed where the burnt-out car was found, and losing the will to live when there she was. The woman.'

'A woman? What woman?'

'The woman,' flushed Philip excitedly ready to burst. 'On the third of November at seven fourteen am a car arrives and parks right in front of the camera. The registration isn't visible, but it's clearly a BMW, the same colour as Mr Markham's car.'

'Philip, stay still, I can't see the film,' but Cora's eyes brightened.

'A young woman stepped out, slim build, Caucasian, long dark hair, about five foot eight, I would say.'

'A woman, really?'

'Yes, boss, no question. You can see she's a woman. Her assets are very clear.'

'Thank you, Philip. I'm assuming there's more, so if you could hurry and get to the point.'

'Well, this woman gets a bottle and a box of matches out of the boot,' Philip became more animated, almost unable to contain himself. 'And after thoroughly dousing it around and in the car, she sets it alight. Then she stands back and watches for a while, then gets her backpack and walks away. This is the killer, and she doesn't know she is being recorded.'

Releasing a long breath, the discovery of this was huge. Could it be possible that it was a woman who was Peter Markham's murderer?

'Thanks, detective,' this was too much. Cora had to maintain some sense and composure. 'I'm sure you know how helpful this information is, but we don't know the relevance yet. Can you get an enlarged image of her, and then see if you can identify her from social media, etc? Once I'm done here, I'll chat with the DCI and see if it's worth going to the media. Good job, really good job.'

Grinning, Philip got straight to work on the usual social media websites to locate the mysterious woman.

---

Trying not to earwig was difficult in a small office, Guy heard the excitement. Guy and Philip knew of each other but hadn't got to know each other yet. There had been a lot of change in the team lately, with a bunch of new people joining as others more experienced officers left.

DI Snitton had made it back to the front of the room, calling for attention. She had with her the most exciting piece of news yet and this needed to be presented calmly. Everyone was quiet and attentive in less than a minute. This was the first time she was excited about the case. She wanted to yell out that we've got the murderer, but nothing was ever done and dusted until the guilty were behind bars. Her eyes were beaming.

'Okay, come on then, you ready? I will do most of the speaking, but if you think there is something obvious, I am not asking, don't be afraid to speak up. I am not too proud or confident in my ability. I value any input from my team. I'd rather you stuck your hand up and waited to be addressed. First round at the pub for anyone sitting on something, okay?'

Cora smiled as the team laughed, some of them remembering the harsher punishments in the form of post-mortems attended and hours of CCTV viewing when they dared overstep the mark.

'Thanks, everyone. Right, to get you all up to date. Last night we were called to a fire on High Street North, thought to be arson by the attending Fire Investigation officer. The window of the newsagents was smashed, and the glass had fallen inside the shop. And there were signs of accelerant usage. The fire was quick and fierce and burned out relatively quickly once it had consumed all the incendiary products in its way. But of course, the damage was devastating.'

Cora scanned the room, looking for any reaction.

'Sadly, that wasn't the end of the story. The witness who called it in, Miss Amanda Kelly, made us aware of a homeless man who had been overcome by smoke in the alleyway at the side of the building. He succumbed to his injuries and passed away at the scene. This has therefore become a murder inquiry.'

There were a couple of gasps around the room, but otherwise, you could hear a pin drop. The police rarely had the same opinions towards the homeless population as the public, having a lot of dealings with them, and moving them on meant trying to help them with things they weren't credited for.

We already have an ID on the man, a Reg Webb, sixty-two years old, homeless for eight years, and had just reconnected with his family. So, you know what to do, CCTV, forensics, contact the owner of the newsagent to find out if they had any enemies. I'll try to drag in some more uniforms to help; I know we're snowed under. Any questions or comments on that?

A hand rose, Cora spotted it and nodded for him to go ahead.

'The witness, boss. Any chance it was her who lit the fire?'

'Great question,' smiled Cora. 'Sorry, I'm still learning names. But no, she wasn't responsible. She was totally clean and had just walked past on her way home. She lives about two minutes away. She heard the man in the alley and went to help.'

'It's Guy, ma'am, Guy Gardner, and thank you.'

'Thanks, Guy, great question, and as I said, there are no silly questions. Now onto Peter Markham's case. Just before calling this meeting, Philip spotted a woman on video from a nature camera setting a light to Peter's car in a farmer's field. We need to find out who she is. I believe that when we find her, we are close to solving this murder case. Well spotted, Philip. Jobs are on HOLMES2. Keep in touch and let's go. Grab your coat, Luke, you're with me today.'

# 39

Cora used her seniority to make sure she was the driver, and Luke wasn't brave enough to argue; he was pleased as punch to be going with her. The weather, though, had dropped significantly.

Waiting patiently while Luke buckled himself in, she wasn't in any rush to get going today and needed to wait for the windscreen to clear a little, anyway.

'Where we off to, boss?' Luke broke the silence.

'To see Mrs Markham again, since some of her husband's extracurricular activities have come to light, I'd like to speak to her about it face to face and see what her reaction is. Do you know why that is?'

'So, you can tell if she knew from her body language and tone of voice whether she is lying in answer to your questions.'

'Well done, Luke,' a sly smile lifted the corners of her lips. 'I'm not very good with emotional women, so I will let you lead the questions; the FLO will be there as well. Some of the news may be a shock to her if she truly isn't aware of what her husband gets up to when he's away, so I know you don't need to be reminded to be gentle and sensitive.'

'Of course, boss. Do you know exactly what we need to ask her about?'

A car cutting in front of her made her swear while swerving to get clear of it. Trying to memorise the registration, knowing it wouldn't do any good. Lucky day for that idiot, and luckily for her, she wasn't in a marked car as well. Bet he wouldn't have done it if he knew she was the police.

'Bloody arrogant drivers, one day they'll cross my path, I'm sure of it, then they'll be sorry.'

'I don't doubt that, boss,' Luke said, laughing. 'I wouldn't like to be in their shoes when they do. '

'No, you wouldn't. One thing I can't abide is people driving dangerously. It's never them who pay the price, usually some poor innocent family or youngster with their whole life ahead of them. It really pisses me off, you know?'

Glancing across, Cora saw Luke look surprised. She must stop with her random curses; it was putting her colleagues in an awkward position.

'Anyway, where were we? Oh yes, Mrs Markham. Just think of what you want to know from her and gear the questions around the best way of getting that information. I think instinct is best.'

They arrived in front of the large house in no time. The gates were still closed and locked against intrusions. It was also handy for keeping out the press, although it wasn't deterring them. Camped out front, cameras poised for the slightest flicker of movement; it was offensive. Microphones were ready, and when they saw the car slowing near the house, the entire bunch of them moved as one to face them. Hair ruffled, skirts smoothed, lips plumped, in case this was their moment.

'Not a word to these parasites, *no comments* or anything, okay? We have a media liaison officer for that; these journalists will jump on anything to sell their papers. Head down, move quickly, and firmly.'

A mute nod as Luke opened his door. Taking a deep breath, Cora quickly followed. As they approached the gates, one automatically opened. It had been worth texting the FLO before they left to let her know they were on their way. The door was opened, and they were in. Yvonne was sitting on the sofa, calm and patiently waiting.

'Hello again Yvonne, sorry to disturb you.' Yvonne said nothing. She just sat looking upset with hunched shoulders and legs tightly knitted together. Cora, though, wasn't playing that game anymore. The feeling was growing that this lady was a tough cookie. 'There have been certain elements of your husband's past that have come to light, and I wanted to ask you a few questions, if that's okay?'

The FLO was sitting holding her hand while Yvonne looked worriedly at Sharon. Sometimes, to get to the truth, you're going to upset people.

According to Sharon, the woman had barely slept since she had been informed of her husband's death. The bags under her eyes and a general gaunt and dishevelled appearance attested to that.

In her text to Sharon before they arrived, Cora told her what she needed to discuss, and asked her to watch the woman's body language closely. The more people they questioned, the more the Saint Peter image was being destroyed. It was becoming increasingly impossible to believe this woman was entirely blind to what her husband had got up to.

Knowing exactly what Cora was after, Sharon was ready. Allowing Luke to lead also meant Cora could watch and observe closely.

Luke sat in front of the distraught woman, trying to

catch her eye, but Yvonne showed she was oblivious to his attempts. So, he began anyway.

'As you know, we've been investigating your husband's murder; one bit of evidence which has come to light, and could be vital in discovering who was responsible...' He paused for a couple of seconds. 'There's no easy way of saying this, so I will just tell you that your husband was accused of raping a young woman at university. The case never made it to court, but we need to learn more about this woman, and whether it was motive enough for her to kill your husband.'

At the word rape, Yvonne raised her head, her body stiffened slightly, but she didn't recoil in shock. Neither did her breathing quicken nor were there any outward signs of this being new to Yvonne. *Interesting.*

'In 2007, your husband completed his degree at the University of Northampton.'

Another barely imperceptible nod, so Luke continued.

'Were you aware that during a party thrown to celebrate the end of exams, a young woman was raped? The man accused of raping her was your husband. The woman wanted to take the case to court but didn't go through with it. Had Peter told you about this, Yvonne? Did you know?'

There was a pause as Yvonne slowly straightened to look Luke straight in the eye. 'Yes, detective, I was aware. Peter and I were husband and wife, and we had young children at home. He told me all about it. He was drunk, and not eaten much. The alcohol hit him badly. He said he was convinced she was coming onto him and that he did everything he could to spurn her advances, but she wouldn't stop. I had no reason to disbelieve him.'

The transformation was sudden and drastic. Yvonne became angry and indignant. She was no shrinking violet.

'Peter thought no more of it. Everyone went their separate ways, moving back home and trying to find jobs; Peter also came home. When the police knocked on his door, he was genuinely confused why they were there. He is—was a very law-abiding man, detective.'

Cora, Luke, and Sharon never moved a muscle. All eyes were on Yvonne. There was fury in Yvonne's eyes that had never been there before.

'He wasn't arrested. I found out later the woman had been to hospital. I think it was her friend who took her and persuaded her to tell the police about how distressed she was. But a lot of that was put on. They found bruising, of course, they would, down there, a sure sign of rape, apparently.'

'There were no witnesses, and they were both drunk. Peter was so relieved when the case didn't go anywhere and thought no more of it; we got on with our lives. I couldn't even tell you the woman's name who accused him. But you can bet that it was all down to money.' She rubbed her thumb against her fingers.

Cora was taken aback by the woman's frankness. She thought she'd have to explain about the rape and further upset this woman, but that plainly wasn't the case because she already knew.

'As we are looking for people that may hold a grudge against your husband, Mrs Markham, I'm sure you can imagine she'd have a convincing argument for wanting revenge.'

The woman stiffened. 'No detective, I don't. That was sorted years ago. My husband was released because there was nothing to convict him with. That was the end of the matter. How can she hold a grudge? Men and women have been getting together at parties for ever. I don't understand how a woman can cry rape and a man must suffer for the rest of his life, especially when it was her who chased after him. There are lots of women calling rape over nothing.'

Cora looked at Sharon and raised her eyebrow, taken aback by the cold and dismissive attitude of the woman sitting in front of her.

'It's possible, Mrs Markham, that this woman felt aggrieved. Maybe she believes it was your husband who came onto her and feels violated.'

Now Cora was getting annoyed with this woman and her cold attitude towards victims of sexual assaults, Cora had sat with too many sobbing women in too many hospital cubicles, refusing to be subjected to the invasive and humiliating tests that would be needed to take it further. She knew even if they didn't, the chances of the case getting to court would be slim to non-existent. Taking a breath, trying to tamp it down, she continued.

'At the moment, it's just an avenue we are looking into. I wanted to find out if you knew of the allegation, and to make you aware before the press gets hold of it.'

Yvonne smiled and withdrew her hand from the grip of the FLO. Her tears had stopped; she had complete composure. Here sat a different woman from the broken shell when Cora walked in.

'Well, if that's all, detective, I need to be getting on to my children to inform them of the situation. You'll see yourself out?'

Bewildered, Cora stood waiting for Luke to lead the way to the door. Walking quickly back to the pool car, Cora sat heavily in the seat. After a moment, she started the engine.

'Who would have thought she knew—' said Cora, staring out through the window.

'Never mind that,' began Luke. 'Who would have thought she would have forgiven her husband?'

Both detectives sat in contemplative silence as they returned to the station.

---

When Cora got back to the station, she went straight for a coffee, holding it to warm up her senses. The heating in the pool car was best described as temperamental, a wheezy asthmatic after a marathon.

There weren't many of her team about. Darcey and Guy were both out. She was hoping to bounce ideas off one of them. Something about the encounter with the grieving widow had unsettled her, especially the change in attitude when speaking about the rape. Without doubt, Yvonne knew more than she was letting on. Love is blind or stupid while Mrs Markham lived a very comfortable life, and Peter had provided it for her. Why would she want to destroy the golden goose when there was nothing to gain from it? Something like that would only ruin her wonderful life when all she needed to do was to turn a blind eye.

From their investigations, it was clear the saintly Mr Markham had a few skeletons in his closet, but that was a big one. What else was he hiding, and how much did his wife know?

With no one to bounce her ideas off, she decided to get back to her office and check out the list she'd made to see if there was anything she had missed.

Looking back through her notebook, she found a few questions that needed answering. Firstly, who was the victim? Well, they knew that now, and were gathering a lot of information by the day about him. The only bonus was him being such a high-profile figure, with a lot of secrets that were now coming to light.

Next up, why the shopping centre? It was an out-of-town

location with privacy, but the actual answer to that wouldn't come until they found the killer.

Was Markham supposed to be found? That was a hard one to answer. Cora suspected the killer wanted him to be found, that he/she, and it was looking more likely that it was a woman wanted everyone to know what this man had done. This is the reason they exhorted such harsh payment from him. And yet there was the alternate idea of wanting to put the murder behind them, not get caught and get on with their lives. It seemed impossible given the horror of the injuries that Markham's murderer had been a woman. But why not? Women can hate just as well as men, some would say even worse.

Next question, what on earth had Peter Markham done for someone to exact this revenge? Was the rape enough? Lots of women got raped, very few got prosecuted, and even fewer men ended up dead and tortured in a disused shopping centre. Could there be more to the story?

It was clear now that Mr Markham would fuck anything moving. As far as she knew, he was sleeping with the hotel manager, as well as one of the senior women from the business, and the accountant. He had a couple of nights with the cleaner and regularly got the hotel receptionist to call escort services for him. Yet his wife and children wouldn't have a bad word said against him. Did they know about this other predatory Peter? Was there any way to get the family to talk? She wondered if sending Guy to talk to the son would work, man to man. The daughter seemed to be fiercely loyal to her dad from the brief conversation she'd had over the phone with Olivia. There didn't seem any point going there, positive that she wouldn't get any more out of her. Might have another try at the wife, though. She'd made it a point to ring the FLO later to see if she'd let anything slip after they'd left. Families rarely realise that although a FLO was there to help them, they were still police officers and there to gain intel.

Looking at the other options she'd written as a potential motive for his killing, business problems were something she hadn't investigated. She'd get one of the team to look into that. Newbie Katy Baldwin seemed to be good with the tech stuff. Could Peter have gambling problems? Cora couldn't see any evidence of that so far, and his bank accounts revealed he was solvent. The only other thing left was jealousy. The potential inclusion in the King's Honours was grounds for hate, but would that be enough? Yes, jealousy is a powerful force.

Sitting back, Cora threw her pen down, combed her hands through her hair, and rested her head on the desk. There was fraud, rape, the hotel manager and unrequited love, the woman torching his car. Lots of random pieces that didn't seem to fit together. What was she missing? There was something so obvious staring her in the face, she was sure of it.

# 40

Yvonne was furious. What right did that stupid cow have to call her husband a rapist? Peter wasn't a rapist. The woman was all over him, wearing next to nothing. He said she was pushing him against the wall, took him outside and pulled down his trousers. Peter could have stopped her, of course he could, but he was drunk. They were the bad days. They argued about it, massive shouting matches where items were thrown, and doors slammed. In the end, they'd come to a truce for the sake of their children. One particularly vicious row had awoken their son, which made them realise they couldn't carry on as they were.

It was all forgotten until that photo came through the door. Some woman claiming to be the grandmother of the girl who'd been raped. The letter explained why she'd never progressed with the medical examinations with details that Peter had told her, so she believed the authenticity and the bombshell. The woman had a baby boy, and it was Peter's. Yvonne had torn the letter into the tiniest pieces she could, then burnt it for good measure, but strangely, she'd kept the photo hidden in her bible against a verse about revenge. If Peter were ever to come across it... but she doubted it. He wasn't religious at all. This was her grenade to throw down if Peter dared stray again. Yet, she secretly wondered what the boy was like, whether he would have completed their family. After Olivia, she could not have any more children.

Yvonne noticed the FLO, Sharon sitting quietly watching her pacing and muttering to herself while wringing her hands. She knew Sharon would step in eventually to stop her by getting her to sit down, but she needed to move, to walk, to scream, anything.

Seeing how restless Yvonne was, Sharon came to her, placing her hand gently on her shoulder, applying a little pressure, but Yvonne shrugged it off, none too gently. She didn't want to be mothered or patronised. But Sharon wasn't put off. She put her hand around her upper arm and guided her towards the sofa.

Allowing herself to be led, her adrenalin had dissipated, and she was suddenly exhausted.

Then the tears came. Yvonne hated this about herself. She wasn't upset—she was angry, furious, and seething—but this always led to tears. It made her look weak when she wasn't; she was not a weak woman and refused to allow anyone to think that. The FLO slid her hand gently up and down Yvonne's arm, annoying her, but she was too tired to fight. Just sitting and letting the tears come until she could compose herself enough to stop them.

Eventually, Sharon spoke, 'You want to tell me what's going on, why you're so upset?'

Yvonne didn't want to open up, but she'd kept this in for fifteen years. Maybe it would be good to get it off her chest. Taking a deep breath, resting her hands in her lap, she lifted her tear-stained face and looked the middle-aged woman in the eyes. Motherly, kind, gentle, she wouldn't judge her, would she?

'When Peter came home, he looked genuinely

confused,' started Yvonne, exhausted. 'There was no guilt there, you know. He immediately admitted he'd had sex at the party, but it was all her fault. Of course, it all came out over the next few days, and Peter told me about the party, as much of it as he could remember about feeling old and left out. I felt for him. It had been a hard decision to go back and study with people so much younger than him. I was proud of him for that. A married man with children: I understood when he tried to fit in with everyone else. To be young again, how could I hate him for that? Every dog has its day. He tried his hardest to catch up with everyone else there, drinking. He remembered about nodding off and when he came to, this young woman was coming on to him. He doesn't remember much of what happened next. It was jumbled and confused, and then he thought no more of it.'

Yvonne gathered herself. She had buried it so deep; it had been so long since she'd even thought about Peter's betrayal.

'What happened next?' Sharon asked.

'We just carried on. As far as I was concerned, there was nothing else we could do.'

'Very admirable. I'm not sure I couldn't do that if my husband admitted cheating on me.'

'Do you think it was her who killed my Peter?'

'We just don't know at this point; we have a lot of information, and we are working our way through it. You'd be surprised how much time it takes; I know on television it looks like it's all wrapped up in a day or two.'

'There is one more thing I need to tell you. That wasn't the end of the story, and this is something I have kept hidden for fifteen years. There was a child, a baby boy.'

'A child? She had a child?'

'Oh, you didn't know. About six years after the threat of a court case, I got a letter through the door from the grandmother; she was dying and didn't want to go to her grave without telling someone that Peter had a son. The child was given up for adoption, but it didn't mean Peter couldn't get in touch if he wanted to. She needed to get it off her chest so she could die in peace. She included the only photo that had ever been taken of the child before it was whisked away by social services.'

'Do you still have that photo, by any chance?' Sharon was trembling.

Silently, Yvonne jogged upstairs and got the Bible. Removing the picture, she cradled it gently, as she returned and handed it over.

'I don't know why I kept it, really. It just seemed a shame to erase the only history of this child. He didn't ask to be born that way. Can I get you a drink, Sharon, tea, something stronger—you're looking pale?'

'No, thank you, I just need to make a phone call.'

---

Sharon sat in her car; she needed a moment to compose herself before she rang DI Snitton. This was huge. How could no one have known this woman had a child because of the rape? Surely there were records even if the baby had been given up. But that wasn't for her to worry about now. She'd just pass it on and let the team do their thing. Finally, she called Cora, who picked up almost immediately.

'Hey Sharon, everything okay? I was going to call you later to see if Yvonne had said anything after we'd left. That was a strange chat we had.'

'Yes. She was fuming when you'd gone, pacing up and down, and muttering to herself. She must have got tired because when I asked her what was going on, it seemed like she decided the other part of the story needed telling.'

'Don't keep me hanging on Sharon, this might be the break we need.'

'Sorry, just thinking of the best way to word it and keep it short. She completely believed her husband was innocent of any rape, that much was clear. At no point did she suggest he might not have had sex with the woman, despite being drunk. It was the woman who came onto him and that's all there was to it.'

'Carry on,' said Cora after the moment of shock passed.

'Everything was quiet until nine years ago when she got a letter through the door from the grandmother of the victim. She was dying and needing to relieve her conscience before she died.'

Sharon paused, sensing Cora's excitement and astonishment despite not being in the same room. She didn't wait for the DI to admonish her this time, she just came out with it.

'Subsequently, there was a child, because of the rape, a baby boy, which she gave up.'

'That's it?'

This wasn't the reaction that Sharon was expecting. 'The grandmother sent a photo, and Yvonne kept it.'

'In a Bible by the bedside?' Cora cut in.

'Yes, how did you know?'

'I saw it when I was having a look around after he went missing. There was something odd about the photo. The pages opened directly to a passage about revenge. It's been bugging me since the very beginning, now I understand. Thank you, Sharon. I'll get the team together and let them know. You're a diamond.'

# 41

Cora, Darcey, Luke, and the rest of the team were gathered in the incident room for the late team briefing. By the power of social media, Luke found a photo of the victim at the university party. And now he was trying to find other guests at the party to add and get a broader picture of that night.

'Everyone,' Cora stood with almost quiet serenity. 'Over here. We have a lot to get through.' Cora's excitement was shining in her eyes. 'A lot of information has come in during the last 24 hours; I feel we are finally making progress on this case.'

'To summarise where we are, Peter Markham was accused of rape in his final year of university. It was at a party to celebrate the end of final exams. It was reported, and nothing more was heard about it.'

'When Luke and I went to speak to Mrs Markham about the news of the rape before it broke in the papers, her reaction was odd. She was angry and dismissive. The FLO, Sharon, called not long after, saying Yvonne had spoken after we'd left. The rape victim gave birth to a son because of the rape.'

Cora waited for the ripple of surprise to run around the

room and wasn't disappointed. A few gasps before they settled down. It was possible to hear a pin drop. She had their full attention now.

'Yes, exactly, this could be huge and could be the break we need, or a vital clue, at least. Being raped and impregnated with your rapist's child could be a motive for murder. The child would be around fifteen or sixteen by now, so we are looking at him as well. The child was a boy and was given up for adoption. Luke investigated this for me. Over to you, Luke.'

'Thanks, boss.' Luke was nervous, standing in front of everyone. 'I was asked to search birth and adoption records for around nine months after the party, give or take a month on either side. There was a baby boy born four weeks premature at a Sunderland hospital. As soon as he was born, he was passed over to the authorities. It was remarked that the mother didn't even want to hold him.'

'Thanks, Luke. What happened to him after that? Did you manage to find anything?'

'I was just coming to that, boss. He was named Harrison Drew and passed over to the adoptive parents: the mother hadn't even had her pre-birth checks. She turned up at the hospital in advanced labour. Less than a year later, the adoptive parents died in a car crash while the child survived. He was then passed around various foster homes and given up a couple of times for bad behaviour but nothing too horrendous, only boy stuff. He's landed with one of the best foster families who have an impressive record for turning out well-behaved children who were once a bit wild.'

'Graeme and Esther Chilton. We've met them,' stepped in Darcey. 'You'd be surprised to know that we have also met Harrison Drew. He was one of the kids who found the body.'

This was extraordinary. No one spoke. What they were hearing was surreal?

'Thanks, Luke. Anyone else got anything, any information from searching social media? What about the image from the video near the burnt-out car? Anything back from forensics for the car?'

'Still waiting, boss,' said Hayley Bibby, one of the new DCs.

'Thanks, Hayley, okay, can you get onto them? I know they will say they're busy, and that everyone wants everything yesterday. But this could be important; it feels like we are making progress. Darcey and I will go to see the Chilton's and find out if they can tell us any more about Harrison. Thanks everyone for the good work. I know this case has been frustrating, but thanks to your perseverance, we've narrowed down our suspects. There's Wendy Ellis, who rejected Markham's advances, but she's in her mid to late fifties. Marge Smith at the hotel, but she's also older, and there is Tracy Littlechild, who tried to sue for unfair dismissal. I want to know if there is more to her story. However, none of them have mentioned being at Northampton University. Are we missing someone else?' Cora lifted her head to look around.

No one spoke. The coincidences were startling.

'Darcey, go grab the keys to a pool car, and I'll go get my coat. It's Baltic out there; I'm not getting caught out again.'

# 42

Stopping outside the modest semi-detached on the edges of Dunstable; the street was long, and there was a wide variety of housing types. A park close by which Cora knew hosted Saturday football games, and a boules court hidden towards the back. It was a popular dog walking area, a small child's playground at the bottom. She could hear the excited squeals and giggles of young children, and mums sitting and chatting, clutching their coffees close to them, just a normal day in a life that everyone took for granted.

The house was plain. The garden had been block paved the same as the majority to fit on the increasing number of cars each home owned. The front door was white PVC. A bronze letterbox in the centre. There were no plants or anything decorative around the front, no window boxes, or fragrant-smelling flowers.

Ringing the bell, the door was opened almost immediately, and the woman standing in front of them looked agitated. Greasy straggly hair, red puffy eyes like she'd been crying. Concerned, Cora and Darcey stepped in and closed the door behind them.

'Is it Harrison? Have you found him? It's bad news, isn't

it? It must be, you wouldn't be here otherwise. I can't believe it. I'm such an idiot. I was angry. I didn't mean to shout at him like that, but he's gone, he's gone, isn't he?'

Cora gently took the woman's arm and directed her to the next room and guided her over to the sofa to sit her down. By instinct, Darcey sat next to her.

'What do you mean, he's gone?' asked Cora. 'We came here to talk to you about Harrison. He's come up in another investigation we are currently involved with. But you said he's missing. How long has he been missing? Have you reported it to the police?'

A small sob escaped, a deep breath, and then Esther spoke.

'As you know, Harrison is my foster son. We've had him for around three years now. He's not the most difficult kid we've had, but he's had his issues. He settled in quickly. We gave him his own room and a little space, and most of all, our love. I think that's what he needed, and he calmed down. He tried hard at school; we had a couple of phone calls but that was just boy stuff. I told him the only rule for living under this roof was no drugs. We have another foster child, a young girl who was living in a drug den. He'd smoked some weed. I let that pass. I'm sure most of us did that when we were teens. But the night before last I found a bag of white powder in his room. I shouted, and we argued, and he ran away, and I've not seen or heard from him since. I haven't reported it. I keep expecting him to get cold and hungry and come home, but he hasn't.'

Esther's great strength broke. There was no doubt she loved this boy. She cried until she had enough. What next? Her pink eyes waited.

'A cup of tea would be nice,' suggested Darcey. 'Yes?'

'Yes. Tea is the password in our house.'

'Good, I'll make it.'

Photographs tell you a lot about people's lives, the one with him covered in mud, holding a trophy. Another with them in front of the Alton Towers amusement park.

Darcey handed the tea to Esther and sat back beside her.

'I'm sorry to hear that Harrison is missing, Mrs Chilton. I had no idea. Has he shown any signs of distress after finding the body or said anything to you about it? Darcey will put the wheels in motion to make it an official missing persons investigation.'

'No,' frowning, Esther shook her head, 'He's a teenage boy, detective. It's anathema to them to speak to their parents. I've heard him tossing and turning some nights; he has nightmares. That's all I can say.'

Darcey left the room, her phone already to her ear.

'We came here about another matter, so if you don't mind,' carried on Cora. 'I just wanted to ask you a couple of questions, then we'll take down all the information we need to locate Harrison and bring him home.'

'I didn't want to involve the police,' said an emotional Esther, gripping her cup tight.

'Yes, I understand. As you know, we are currently investigating the murder of Peter Markham. I'm not sure if you've seen it on the news. Anyway, it turns out that because of an incident at university, Peter Markham's fathered a son. We don't know if he was aware of it before he was murdered. We believe the child was Harrison.'

Esther's hand flew to her mouth. 'My Harrison was the son of that man. Oh my God. The dead man he stumbled on was his father.'

'All the evidence points to that being the case. We wondered if you were aware of his parentage when you took him on. I know nothing about how the fostering system works, or how much you are told.'

'We weren't told his parentage; I don't believe the social

services knew either when he came into our care. I didn't have a clue. I can't believe his father was alive and well, and wealthy, yet wanted nothing to do with his son.'

'It seems likely, Mrs Chilton, that Peter was entirely unaware of Harrison's existence. The mother gave him up as soon as she gave birth. I hate to say this, but she was raped, and Harrison was the result.'

The tears glistened, this time from reproach. Darcey, who had been hovering at the door listening, saw her opportunity to comfort Esther. She sat by her and took her hand again.

'That poor boy and I shouted at him, and he's gone. I'm such a terrible person. I love him like my own child.'

'Where is your husband, Mrs Chilton?' They would not get nothing more from Esther. 'He should be here with you. Would you like me to call him for you, or anyone else?'

'He's out searching for Harrison. Graeme hasn't been home since yesterday morning. My husband has spoken to his friends. They said Harrison was upset and in a weird mood when they last saw him on that night.'

'Okay. We need to get back to the station, but we'll be in touch as soon as we have any news. If Harrison turns up, or you hear from him in the meantime, please let us know straight away. Here's my number,' Cora passed her card. 'Any time. Don't worry, call me.'

'Thank you,' whispered Esther.

# 43

Things were ramping up now. They had the image of the woman on video whose identity they were trying to confirm, as well as locating anyone who was in the area. Like a train heading to its destination, slowly but surely everything was coming together and pointing in one direction.

Lisa and Wendy had been prosecuted for fraud, which left Marge. Did she have the profile for murder? The woman in the video footage was tall, so it is possible it could be her. What they needed was something concrete to link the cases. Time to chase up forensics to find out if they had anything from what they'd sent over.

'Heya Selphie, did you get anything off the fabric Felix found?'

'Hi Cora, glad you called. I was just about to call you. Was just double-checking something. It's odd. Very odd.'

'Well, don't keep me in suspense. I badly need some evidence in this case.'

In the background, Cora could hear rustling. Selphie was searching through pieces of paper.

'You ready? That was a fantastic find by Felix. We didn't find any trace evidence on the body, or anywhere surrounding it. The piece of fabric clothing was from a pair of female pants. We were fortunate the fire hadn't destroyed everything; there were secretions on them; and we have extracted and run DNA analysis.'

'Yes, and?'

'Well,' Selphie said, infuriating Cora further. 'There was no direct DNA match. However, it did flag up a familial match with another case I believe you have, the death of the homeless man in the fire. There is a link to whoever set that fire.'

Cora fell silent as the potential implications sunk in.

'Oh my God,' Cora broke the silence. 'That's huge. So, we have two members of the same family, both responsible for deaths. That is incredible. We just need to find one, and that should connect us to both. Thank you so much, Selphie. I owe you a drink or two.'

Selphie laughed down the phone.

'Just doing my job, Cora, before you go, I am interested in the outcome of this case. It's an unusual development, so please keep me in the loop.'

'I'll do my best. You still coming to watch me at the open mic night on Saturday?'

'Wouldn't miss it, you know that, and not because you die on stage. You're getting very good. I reckon you're gonna smash that competition out of the park.'

Laughing, Cora blew a raspberry before hanging up.

# 44

Arriving back at the station, Beverlee was keen to update the team on what she'd discovered.

Opening the double doors to the incident room, Beverlee entered a hive of activity, ringing phones, clacking keyboards, the buzz.

'Hi, Beverlee, where are you off to in such a hurry?' smiled Darcey, surprised.

'Just got back from getting the statement from Amandy Kelly, the one who witnessed the fire in the newsagent. She let slip she went to Northampton Uni, the same place where Peter Markham went.'

'Someone just rang in, refusing to give her name.' Guy held up his hand, shaking it with excitement. 'She said she worked at Warleggan Foods and was raped but like all Peter Markam's victims, she also said she was threatened.'

'Seems to be a pattern here. I wonder how many other women have reported or unreported rapes in their backgrounds. This silent crime makes me so angry. It shouldn't be like this.' Standing at the front, Cora drew everyone's attention. The anticipation and buzz had become a virus.

'Okay, everyone, quieten down. Thanks, this is important. I've just come off the phone to Selphie Ho, our forensic scientist, and she has some results back. The piece of fabric the DCI spotted in the drum yielded some DNA.'

A round of applause ran around the officers. The excitement was dense for the hunt. Cora waited for them to settle before continuing.

'Unfortunately, the profile didn't match anyone on record, but it produced a familial match to a profile from another case we are working on, the arson in the newsagent. Not to the man that died, but to whoever started the fire.'

Another murmur, and a few mutterings between fellow cops.

'So,' started Cora. 'Thoughts, comments, questions?'

'Do we have any idea who these two might be, boss?' asked Guy, getting right to the matter.

'Not yet, but I am getting some ideas. Shall we go over where we are at? Then I will ask for anything else that's cropped up since we last met.'

Sitting up straighter, more eager now, some with their pocketbooks ready to take any notes, were keen people.

'Right, we have our murdered man, Peter Markham, found on the service road of the old shopping centre. Tortured, penis removed, abdomen slit until he bled out. As you know, he was found by two young adults, obviously no chance of them being guilty. Peter Markham stays in a hotel, had an affair with the manager, and regularly had call girls sent to his room.' Cora's scanned their avid eyes. 'Then you have the workplace, Lisa and Wendy defrauding the company. Wendy had to rebuff his advances strongly. While Lisa Riley believed herself wronged, assuming that Mr Montgomery's enterprise should go to her instead of Peter Markham. But it wouldn't go to Markham if he was dead.'

'I don't know how far we've got with our updates, but we visited Yvonne Markham. She was aware of the rape accusation and became angry when asked about it. What she told us was the woman had come on to Peter. She didn't accept at any point that he could have stopped what happened. However, after we left, Mrs Markham broke down and said that Peter had a child as a result of that rape. The grandmother of the raped woman sent her a letter and a picture of a newborn baby. The baby was Harrison Drew.'

Several breaths inhaled.

'We spoke to Harrison's foster parents, who told us he had gone missing. Esther's husband, Graeme, was out searching for him. There had been a huge argument about drugs. Now the foster mother is frantic. She didn't know about Harrison's parentage. I think that's all I have. So, first things first, where are we with finding Harrison?'

'Not well boss,' a voice from the back shouted out. 'We are trying to track mobile pings, but he's on foot, so it's making it more difficult. We don't know what happened after he left his friends, although they all said he wasn't in a good place in his head that night. None of them would elaborate. He was later spotted on CCTV heading towards the town centre. But we lost sight of him again. Too many cameras are broken. It's been an arduous task.'

'Okay, thanks. Keep at it, don't forget about dash cam footage. Any private CCTV? There are some private residences down the high street. Anything else?'

'Marge Stevens reported a rape years ago,' Darcey stuck up her hand. 'But nothing came of it; something else to keep in mind.'

'Great, thanks, Darcey. Interesting. Can't see Marge being our murderer, but there are a few things going against her at the moment. Anything else?'

This time, Beverlee stuck up her hand.

'I just got back from getting the statement from Amanda Kelly, the woman who called 999 after she spotted the fire.

She disclosed she was at Northampton university at the same time as our victim, Peter Markham.'

'Yes, excellent, well-done Beverlee, Luke, are we any closer to identifying the woman seen on the video in relationship to anything we have so far? I'm sure once we have this connection, the rest will start falling into place.'

'Not yet, boss, but we are close. Dave is helping, as master of the keyboard.'

Dave tightened but made no comment, barely slowing down his fingers as they flew across the keys, even with the slight distraction. Cora smiled and wished again she could share that level of competency with technology.

'Okay everyone, you're doing great. I feel like we are really closing in now. The break will come. You all know what you're doing. If you don't, the list is available.'

# 45

Amanda was looking forward to her night out with her friend Helen. It surprised her they had clicked so easily, seeing they'd only known each other from her brief visits to the coffee shop. Friends were something that was missing from her life and the gossip which went with it. Following the blossoming romance between Helen and Jack, as well as the comings and goings of the regular customers brought her those special rewards of sisterhood. Even hearing about Ethel, the old woman who for her own reasons didn't like her, well that's all right because she didn't like her either.

During her latest visit, Helen suggested a proper night out, as it was getting close to Christmas, and neither was having a works Christmas party; it was something to look forward to.

They had agreed to go to the local *Sugar Loaf,* as it had recently had a makeover. Have a drink, and if they felt like it, get drunk. As the evening progressed, the venue became more of a nightclub, they could dance the night away. This crowd was slightly older tonight, as the younger ones went off to the local nightclub, leaving the over-thirties to dance to their eighty's classics.

When Amanda arrived, she was surprised to see Helen waiting outside for her.

'Closed early,' said Helen. 'It was dead anyway.'

'That rarely stops you,' laughed Amanda. 'I think this is the first time you've ever been on time. Why do I suspect Jack may have something to do with your early closing? It had nothing to do with meeting me at all.'

A flash of annoyance passed rapidly for a smile. Helen had a fun afternoon with Jack, finally consummating their relationship, a secret she didn't want to share.

Slapping Helen teasingly on the arm, Amanda giggled before slipping her arm through Helen's and guiding her into the warmth of the pub.

'I want to know everything, but first, what would you like to drink? I'll go to the bar while you can find us a quiet corner, where we can discuss all the gory details.'

Helen's blushes were covered with confusion. This was a very special moment for both of them. She felt something big was happening. It was the first time she'd felt something like this for a man, especially after witnessing the sexual assault of a friend when she was at university, the friend she was with now.

A question she had never asked Amanda—she must have remembered the assault—it was so ugly. Helen was always waiting for Amanda to bring it up, but then their friendship took over. A lot of alcohol was involved. Neither was she sure if her friend remembered her from back then. Over the years, Helen had changed a lot from morbidly obese to someone quite shapely. No man would have looked at her twice at university. Definitely not in that way. She was everyone's fun friend; the one they would laugh with and tell all their secrets to because they trusted her. Each time a guy spoke to her about something private and asked for advice, her heart swelled with hope. Then she would see him snuggle up to the pretty girls. So for her, Jack was special.

Amanda, though, had always been stunningly pretty, and skinny, thanks to an eating disorder which had followed her into adulthood, judging by her still slender frame. Helen had lost weight to a healthy level; she'd had a lot of help from various professionals and let's not forget the hard work. Yet, she still had to be careful, but now she didn't feel as bad about herself as she used to and could dress in clothes she had admired on her friends. Quickly being brought back from her reminiscence, Amanda had returned from the bar with their drinks.

'You okay there? You looked miles away.'

'Yeah, just thinking back to uni. Do you remember those days? Much less stressful than now, right?'

Amanda smiled, but it was a tight smile. She didn't remember her university days with any fondness. That's when her life had gone from shit to the cesspool. It had taken her a long time and a lot of therapy to even go out for a drink with a friend.

'I was glad to see the back of them, to be honest. My university days didn't end well.'

Helen, sipping her drink, put the glass on the coaster. 'You really don't remember me from uni, do you? I was in your class. We weren't friends exactly. I didn't have friends back then, but we worked on one project together.'

Bunching her eyebrows, Amanda frowned. Thinking back to a time she had tried to forget wasn't easy, especially trying to place the woman in front of her from then. She couldn't create a mental picture because of the aphantasia, so this was a lot harder.

'I'm so sorry, but no, I don't. I'm mortified. No wonder you were so friendly to me the first time I came into the coffee shop. That friendly face from the past, and I didn't know. What must you think of me?'

'I figured you didn't recognise me, and hoped over time you might, but I have changed a lot physically. Back then, I was enormous. I was the fat friend everyone was okay to offload to, but never invited to the cinema or parties.' Helen half-laughed.

'Oh my gosh, you must think me so shallow not to remember you. I have a condition called aphantasia, which means I'm unable to create mental pictures in my mind, but that's not an excuse. What an awful time you must have had! You didn't have any friends back then?'

'Yes, I did, you. You were the only person who didn't treat me like crap, like someone who was getting in the way. You included me in group discussions and asked me to sit with you in lectures if I was sitting alone. Do you remember, just after exams? You seemed to get quite close to that older guy in our class. Cosying up to him on the sofa and running your hand up his leg.'

Amanda inhaled a deep breath as several memories rushed back that she'd tried to suppress, unwelcome now as they were back then.

'Oh pet, I'm so sorry. I feel awful. I didn't realise you'd felt so alone. Of course, I remember you. I always tried to get you to join in, but you seemed reticent, always holding back. You're right. I remember that party and that man I made the mistake of flirting with that led to the incident which ruined my life' Amanda looked at Helen. 'As we are being open here.' Amanda stared at Helen as if she was waiting for permission. 'I may as well tell you, he ended up raping me. It never got to court. It would have been difficult with my word against his. Everyone had been drinking that night.'

'I was there, I saw it, I saw what that man did to you.' Helen lowered her voice. 'It was awful, bestial.'

Standing so quickly that Amanda's chair toppled backwards.

'YOU WHAT? You saw, and you did nothing, said nothing? Do you know the impact it had on my life? I tried to commit suicide. I was sectioned. I spent time in a psychiatric hospital. I had a child, a son, that had HIS face. I couldn't bear to look at it after it was born. I gave it away. Just as I was getting over it, he won an award. Photographs of the golden boy with his fucking family. Every time I tried to forget him, his smug face appeared everywhere. And you saw, and you said nothing. I don't believe this.'

Amanda left while Helen sat there stunned, wishing she'd said nothing, but also wishing she'd spoken up all those years ago.

# 46

Yanking on her coat, Amanda was nearly screaming with frustration and kept putting her arm in her hood. The weather had closed in whilst she'd been in the pub and a cold mist had dropped, covering everything with its icy tendrils. Pavements were slick with the sudden freeze. Helen's apologies meant nothing to her.

Upset and furious, the few people brave enough to go out in this chill were giving her a wide berth. Stamping the ground with her boots, she remembered the first time she'd seen Helen's face when entering that coffee shop and wondered why Helen hurried to see her as if she was meeting a long-lost friend, so that was the reason. She had known who she was since the first time they'd met; it was only now had she chosen to explain who she was.

Now, there was a problem. As far as she was aware, no one else knew she'd been raped at that party. She thought she was safe, but Helen had been a witness to that night. How stupid she had been because she had let slip that she'd had a kid. Put one and one together—it wouldn't be long before the police began piecing things together and knocking on her door. She had been so careful, doing lots of research beforehand, but if Helen realised that the Peter Markham, who had been murdered was the same Peter Markham in their class at university, would she add these things together and go to the police?

Walking past a Christmas display, Amanda punched an inflatable snowman. She kept punching and kicking until it deflated. It shrunk, folding into itself. Its once smiley face had been no protection against her angry fists. Had someone seen this crazy woman hitting a helpless balloon and called the police? Amanda walked swiftly on.

---

Going straight home, Helen didn't even bother to finish her drink after the humiliating incident in the pub. Ignoring all the friendly, well-meaning strangers asking if she was okay; tears streamed down her cheeks and her hands trembled as she tried to tie her scarf around her neck. Eventually giving up, she left the pub in a wave of flapping coat and trailing scarf.

As the pub was in the town centre, there were always taxis outside; Helen hailed one and instructed the driver where she wanted to go. Giving the driver a *'don't bother asking'* look when it looked like he was going to ask if she was okay. He closed his mouth and turned back to his seat.

The journey passed in silence, allowing Helen to reflect on what had happened that evening and where it had all gone so wrong.

This aphantasia thing was a better excuse than amnesia. She had never heard of it, and when she got back, she would Google it. Her mind had flustered all over the place, for honestly, Amanda's rage had shocked and unsettled her.

They'd been chatting for a few years now in the coffee shop and neither of them had made any mention of university. In fact, thinking back over their conversations, Amanda had revealed little about herself at all. Giving short answers, she always returned the conversation to Helen and what she was doing.

That night all those years ago, the party was supposed to be a celebration of the end of three years of hard work. Everyone went a little crazy drinking and then quickly on to kissing while she watched from a distance later, then from her bedroom window, envying them. All inhibitions dissolved. It suited students to believe they would never see each other again.

The sound of fire doors bursting open had attracted her attention back to the window and to leave her packing. Looking down across the courtyard, her friend emerged, entangled with the man she'd been flirting with on the sofa. Unable to take her eyes off the drama, Helen watched him pushing her up against the wall while Amanda was trying to resist, slapping his hands and saying no. Then he became angry and forced himself on her. Gripped in fear and fascination, Helen watched as Amanda struggled, then gave up. Helen knew she was witnessing a rape. She had seen it and said and did nothing to stop it. She had intended to call the police, but then someone else found her friend slumped on the floor and took her away.

---

Back in her small flat, there had been only two places that Amanda regarded as her sanctuary. Now all that was ruined. She broke her own rule by confiding in someone else after doing everything she could to make sure they didn't catch her. All that research into forensics, CCTV cameras, mobile phone tracking, using the dark web for searches and everything else could all come crumbling down if her former friend blabbed.

Could she do it again? Kill. This time, though, to protect her secret and keep her freedom. That's all she wanted, to close her door to the world and feel safe. Wanting revenge for so long from the man who'd caused her all that pain, and now this man was at last dead. It had been a relief, but now she had another problem, Helen.

Walking to the kitchen, Amanda opened the fridge; and found the half bottle of wine she'd left after last night's dinner. She'd needed something to calm her before she did something stupid. If she was going to sort Helen out, she needed to be sensible and plan.

---

Walking into her cold flat, Helen was greeted by her cat, fussing around her legs, and purring as she rubbed behind the ears. Taking off her shoes, she hung her coat on the hooks just inside the door. Placing her shoes on the rack to go to the kitchen and look for a drink but she flicked the button down on the kettle for tea instead. The wine glasses were still in the sink. She'd made her speciality, lasagne, and salad, but that remained untouched in the fridge, as they'd became distracted. Discarding their clothes right there on the floor, and hurried upstairs to the bedroom.

Smiling slightly before her heart sank as she remembered the argument with her friend. Absent-mindedly, Helen opened cupboards, collected a mug and tea bag, and then took a tin of food for the cat. Taking the milk from the fridge, Helen opened the tin of food into the cat bowl.

Eventually, tea made, and cat happy, she went into her living room to sit on the sofa. Placing her cup of tea down on the coffee table, she switched on the TV. The late-night news had just started; the leading story was the murdered businessman. Helen was still shocked at the level of Amanda's anger as she listened to the newsreader confirming again the violence that had been inflicted on the man. The net was closing in; the police believed the murderer was a woman.

As the news anchor gave the latest updates of the story, which wasn't much, they put up a picture of the man when he was younger. When the image appeared on the screen, Helen stood, hand to her mouth. The cat who had crept up to paddle her legs before settling down to sleep had been upset. She knocked the coffee table and in the ensuing chaos; the tea went everywhere.

It was his face, Peter Markham, the man who'd raped Amanda all those years ago. Could Amanda, her friend, be the murderer? Surely not? Her friend was gentle, calm, and placid until tonight. *Listen to me, don't you remember how she blew up tonight? I've never seen her like that before...*

---

Peter Markham was very weak now. It was time to finish this. Grabbing his chin to shake him awake, he came to and looked at her. Still no hint of recognition.

'I've waited a long time for this, Peter, after you ruined my life all those years ago. I swore no one would make me feel that small or helpless ever again. I had endured years of abuse at the hands of my father, you see. Not my real father, of course. I have no idea who he is, and I doubt if my druggie mother does, either. She dumped me when I was barely a day old and didn't look back. I had to be weaned off the drugs in my system. Think of it, Peter—a day-old—can you even imagine that? You see, I'd never known having a family, Peter. My foster father started creeping into my room when I was ten years old. Can you imagine someone doing that to your little girl when she was ten? Olivia, isn't it? How's her pregnancy going? She must be due soon?'

Angrily wiping away a tear, she continued.

'So where was I? Oh yes, my foster father creeping his way into my room in the early hours, when everyone else was dead to the world. Do you have any idea what it's like to lie there, wide awake, dreading the sound of the floorboard creaking, the one that he can't avoid just outside your bedroom door? Silly me, of course you don't. Well, let me fill you in. You lay as still as a statue, daring not to breathe. You hoped when his heavy tobacco and alcohol stinking breath gets nearer, he'll think you're asleep and leave. I learnt quickly that it didn't bother him, not in the least. Can you even imagine the agony when he shoves his dick up you that first time, tearing your hymen? The sustained pain as he keeps going until he's got what he needed and leaves you bleeding and crying, silently. This is something that haunts me to this day. And I'm a big girl now. He tells you that calling the police won't matter because they won't believe you. And then comes the threats that if I did, he would hurt my pets, my foster mum, and my grandma, the only things I cared about.'

'Each time after that is no less painful, but at least there isn't the feeling of internal tearing. You learn to just go out of yourself and think of something else. Sometimes it's like you're floating above watching a scene you don't recognise. He leaves and you curl up in the foetal position until the pain eases and you can fall asleep. Do you know how long this carried on for Peter? Three years. Almost every night for three years? What stopped him, you might wonder? And I'll tell you. Getting my period. He didn't want to take the chance of knocking up his foster child. That wouldn't look good to the authorities in case they wanted to foster more kids. Where was my foster mother in all this, you might ask? Well, she worked nights at the local children's hospital. She had no clue. A good woman, but a dumb one. When I was old enough to leave, the day I turned sixteen, he tried to have sex with her, and she turned him down. She'd had a stressful day at the hospital, and she was tired. And you know what he did, Peter? He killed her. Saw red and beat her to death. He was jailed and was dead inside within six weeks. Murdered with a shiv by an inmate. Even fellow criminals don't like people that rape kids, Peter. I wish my story ended there, but it doesn't, and I swear to you, every word of this is true. You'll wonder how anyone can endure all this and carry on, but here we are. So, I left home at sixteen. But bad luck of all the bad luck. I landed in a house owned by men who thought I could sell myself for sex to earn my disgusting room in their house. So, I went from being raped by my foster father to being raped by these three dirty men and all their disgusting friends. Finally, I managed to escape them at eighteen when they were caught and jailed for grooming children.'

She paused in reflection.

'When I went to uni, I was just getting my life back again. I was beginning to feel normal, as normal as anyone can be. I shrugged off my childhood and tried not to let it beat me. I start afresh. I hadn't experimented with boys at school, or during my time at university. At that point. I hadn't ever drunk alcohol, I never wanted to lose control. Or be in a situation where someone could take advantage of me. It was impossible to tell at that party what was alcohol and what wasn't. And I was tipsy, not fully drunk, but never having had a drink before, I let my guard down. Then when you started groping me, I sobered up quickly and knew I didn't want this. I tried to stop you. Tears streamed down my face. Not that you noticed. I even said no. But you were like an animal, pawing and bucking at me. There was no way you were going to stop, so eventually I stopped fighting. Do you realise how angry and humiliated I felt, but I let that girl take me to hospital. I soon realised I didn't want to be touched again. To have my private areas inspected by strangers, so I refused all their tests. They knew I'd been raped. They begged me for ages, but in the end, I slipped out when they got called away. I was furious that I had to rebuild my life once again. Not from the very bottom this time, though. Then Peter, I found out I was pregnant. You weren't worried, unlike my foster father, about the possibility of impregnating me. I don't believe in abortion, Peter. Never have. I gave birth to a son and immediately gave him up for adoption. I didn't even name him. I couldn't imagine raising a child with your face and watching him grow into you—'

She laughed and looked at him with a smile.

'But do you know what, Peter, nurturing and birthing gives you an unknown strength? I can't explain it to you. You simply wouldn't understand. But once I'd given away that demon spawn, I vowed revenge on the man who had put me in that situation. I've been very patient, I've done an awful lot of research, Peter. You would be surprised. Painful torture methods, how to keep someone alive whilst being tortured. So now you know who I am, and why I am doing this. Do you have anything to say before I end this?'

Peter nodded, tears streaming. It was too late to say sorry. He hung his head; he didn't know; he didn't remember. He'd blocked that period from his life, but he never expected it to come back to haunt him after hearing nothing for all those years. *I have a son; my kids have a half-brother.*

This was Peter's final thought, as the knife was rammed into his stomach, almost deep enough to come out the other side. He didn't feel it as it was wrenched up, opening his abdomen, guts spilling out from the gash, the blood loss causing his heart to stop beating once and for all.

# 47

Back at Luton Police station, the late afternoon briefing had caused a lot of chatter, as a great deal had happened since the morning.

Coming from her corner desk, Cora went to the front, and as usual, clapped: the meeting had begun.

'Sorry it's a late one everyone, but as I'm sure you're aware, we released the victim's image on TV today. I believe we have our prime suspect.'

'Is she our only suspect, boss?'

'Great question Luke, everyone is a suspect until they can be eliminated. We are slowly checking alibis, and with the help of science we are keeping an open mind—and you should too. It doesn't hurt being unbiased in the investigation. Go where the evidence takes you.'

Luke smiled, pleased with the praise.

'I believe our primary suspect is Amanda Kelly, and the reason I believe her to be the person we are looking for is down to some intensive trawling of photo archives from the records of the University of Northampton. Piecing together what we can, Luke and Dave have managed to find a change of name by deed poll in 2020, by one Erin Cartwright, to

Amanda Kelly. Previous to that, the suspect went under the name of Maryann Dunn. I don't know the significance of the name changes, except that she must have been going through a personality transformation to get herself ready for the kill. People who change their names, I find particularly fascinating. For those who don't know, the derivation of Amanda is beloved. Yes, I can see you also feel beloved is a joke since what her intentions were. As is Kelly, which means war, lively, and bright.' But we are looking at a complex and highly intelligent person whose entire goal in life is to put an end to Peter Markham's life. She gave us nothing to go on except chances and luck.

She paused and looked around at her eager detectives.

'From these previous name changes, it was easy to go back and match up Maryann Dunn as being in the same class as Peter Markham at university. Dave managed to contact some of the other students who might have been at the party to see if they had any photos for identification. As a result, I am as certain as I can be, that Maryann Dunn, who later became Erin Cartwright, then Amanda Kelly, is the one who set fire to Peter Markham's car. This was captured on a nature camera set by a farmer. An appeal has gone out in the news tonight, so we are confident that we'll get more information about her whereabouts, as she is mostly off the radar. There's no doubt about it she's been clever concealing herself. No car is registered with the DVLA, and neither can I find any records of where she lives. She's had two name changes for two good reasons. She wanted to bury Maryann Dunn and then Erin Cartwright.'

'Hang on,' Beverlee sprung up. 'I've spoken to her, Amanda; in fact, I questioned her. She worked at Peter Markham's company's accountancy firm. She's the one who let slip about going to the same university. Very strong accent. I thought Newcastle, but she was from Sunderland.

She's our killer? Even then, where she was working, she was keeping tabs on him.'

'Yes,' stared Cora. 'This had been her plan from day one after she gave up her son for adoption,'

'So why aren't we arresting her? What are we waiting for?' Luke was frustrated that nothing was being done.

'Evidence, solid evidence. We have a lot of circumstantial evidence, but it's not enough. You know the CPS, they want a rock-solid case, and we just don't have that yet, even with the car-burning footage, but we will, I assure you, we will. I don't want to get it wrong this time. A good lawyer can take the case to pieces.'

'Any news on the boy, Harrison, boss?' Darcey asked from the front.

'No sightings at all. We mustn't forget him. He's vulnerable, a frightened young man, who must be hungry and cold. He must have been spotted somewhere, keep at it.'

Cora was grateful for the question; she was guilty of pushing Harrison to the back of her mind to get this murder solved.

'Anything else before we leave?'

The silence was followed by shakes of the head.

'Okay. Let's get home. 7 am tomorrow, please.'

Although the mood had been subdued, there was a renewed energy. Having a solid suspect gave them something to grasp hold of and run with. Quietly putting on their coats and gathering their belongings, thoughtful now as they left, there wasn't much chatter between them. They had their killer. All they needed now was the qualifying evidence. A bitterly cold December night was waiting.

# 48

Stepping into the quiet flat, Cora hung her coat on the hook and carried her handbag through into the living come dining room. She was gasping for something stronger, but the night she'd been building up to for a long time was tonight, so sobriety was essential.

Approaching her fortieth birthday was one of those salient ages which needed to be celebrated by doing something special, also out of her comfort zone, and to test herself. Why on earth she chose stand-up comedy was a mystery even to herself, but she went for it. Anyhow, it was too late to back out now. She'd paid for her three-minute spot and only needed to get through it. Previously, it had been necessary to pull out from a couple of spots because of work commitments, but the ones she had done, she'd loved. Tonight, there was no excuse and despite being nervous, she was sure she'd get through it.

Making the shower as hot as she could to cleanse her body, but not her thoughts. Her mind, though, was still on the case: who was Peter Markham's murderer? The answer was within sight of them; she felt it. A couple of more clues and they would be home. Her talented team worked together brilliantly; she didn't even need to push them, nor was there one lazy failing team member there. Motivated, eager, and forward-looking, and she was proud of them.

Peter Markham's murder was one of the most violent Cora had ever seen and committed by a woman added to the horror. She struggled to marry that level of violence with the size of the woman on the video. Yet she knew women were just as capable of strength and intolerable brutality.

It was a funny old life. Cora grinned, clearing the images out of her mind. Law and humour, there had to be a link there. Turning down the temperature to as cold as she could bear, she let it run for a minute and that was enough. The towel was placed ready from this morning. Everything she did was ordered and controlled.

Scooping up her discarded clothes to chuck into the washing basket. With some dismay, the basket was overflowing. One of the first signs of Cora's depression was showing its ugly head in the household chores. However, she was in the middle of a busy case, so it was simply that she hadn't had time to do it. The fortnightly call with her therapist was due soon. It was a toss-up if she could keep the appointment, this time though she needed to keep it. Five years ago, when it happened, the walk to the bridge, the cold wind beating her face and then the voice telling her to jump while another voice said no made her realise how close she'd come to taking that leap that it had scared her enough to seek help. Subconsciously, Cora rubbed the small semicolon tattooed on her wrist, a symbol that her story wasn't over.

What was she trying to do to herself tonight? Was she mad? Welcome, my old friend. Insecurity leads to self-sabotage.

'You silly sod. Look at you. You're stark naked and still thinking about the case.'

Under her bed was a plain purple cardboard box. A small white label declaring its contents. Insurance documents and the other boring paraphernalia necessary for being an adult these days. Here was her journal of her days after her suicidal thoughts and the coping mechanisms she was taught. There had been no need to look in this box for a long time. What did it mean to look again? The job? Or was it thoughts of her mother, or perhaps it was letting people in at work and breaching her self-imposed barriers?

After reading through, Cora brightened. She knew there was something she needed to sort out, something subconsciously bugging her. But right now, there was even less time to get ready for the spot she worked hard for.

The outfit had been chosen months ago. Simple jeans and a shirt. Boots with a flat heel, she didn't want to start by going arse over tit walking in heels. The top was purple, her favourite colour, with a smart blazer.

Finally dressed, Cora admired herself in the mirror. She looked okay, no, more than okay, great. So, very well, there were parts of her which needed some toning and working on, but the chosen outfit hid the worst of them. Come on, Cora, you look fantastic.

Letting down her damp hair to dry naturally. The greys were kept at bay to some extent. Frequently, she was told she looked a lot younger than her almost forty years. Not big on make-up. Tonight was no different, *au naturelle* was better for the skin, anyway.

Taking a deep breath, Cora collected her small bag that she'd readied last night, containing a few things, a purse, comedy material and mobile. Tapping her special knock on her neighbour's door to warn her she was going. Nibbles was spending the night with her, so she didn't have to disturb her in the early hours.

Thoughtfully walking to her car, Cora slung the bag onto the passenger's seat, taking a deep breath, before igniting the engine.

'Las Vegas, here I come.'

Cora put the car into gear.

'To the train station, James,' she revved up the engine. 'And London, if you please.'

This was the life, her life.

# 49

Reaching the tiny pub where Cora was due to do her set piece, she met Selphie. Where on earth did she have to go? Deciding to get some Dutch courage; Cora ordered a small G&T for herself and a wine for Selphie, then asked the barman where the open mic night was.

He pointed to a small door tucked away in the far corner. And then it hit her; she was here; this was the night. A million questions came to mind, desperately needing to be answered. Was it busy? Had others showed up? Had he ever done it and if he did, did he have any tips? But this was a busy pub in central London, and he was busy serving a bunch of young, rowdy, and already tipsy young women.

Downing her drink, Cora left Selphie went toward the grimy door, paint peeling off it. She noticed everything, especially the dirt and grime. What did it matter? Nerves. *Who me? Heading a murder investigation and suffering from nerves? What do you think I am? A coward*. Pushing the door to embrace the atmosphere, the door crashed behind her and made Cora grin. *Well, we need to make an entrance.*

Signing in, the man she'd been communicating with by email was by the desk.

'Cora, is it?' He could see she was nervous. 'There are ten on tonight, and you are number five.'

Taking her number pleased that she was not first or last. At least she could get the feel of the room and listen to the others for comparison. Life is all about competition. If it didn't stack up, she could up and run and never return.

As it was, she found herself enjoying the night, laughing, and commenting with the others. There was another woman who did her bit on mothers, which made Cora roar with laughter. So many types of jokes, and the crowd was extremely supportive.

Then she heard her name being called. Her legs quickly turned to jelly.

'Good luck,' shouted Selphie.

Everyone was watching Cora as she trudged onto the stage. She walked like she was walking to the gallows. All her previous joviality and good humour sobered. Stepping up to the mic, she introduced herself. After her first bit, she was away.

In no time, the crowd whooped, whistled, and clapped until she finished. Taking a bow, Cora stepped down and went back to her seat, grinning. It had gone well, and the crowd laughed where she'd hoped they would. Taking a deep breath, and a gulp of the ice-cold water that had been placed there in her absence.

Selphie handed back her bag with a nod and a huge smile.

'Well done. That was great. You were hilarious.'

'Thank you,' blushed Cora. 'You should give it a go sometime?'

Selphie smiled, 'no chance, Mrs.'

'I'm last up. I'm sure that guy has it in for me. Every time I've done this pub, I've either been first or last. He must have taken a shine to you. Very rare for a newcomer to get the middle spot.' A woman at the table said.

Cora and Selphie laughed.

'Well, you'll bring the house down, I have no doubt. I can't wait to hear it.' Cora grinned.

Neither woman had more time to discuss the issue as the other woman, Laura, heard her name called. Making her way to the stage, she took the mic. Laura launched straight in and had the crowd in her palm in seconds. Cora was impressed. She still had a lot to learn.

'Wow, that was amazing! You had them eating out of your hands straight away. How'd you do that?'

'Practice, my dear, just practice. You girls fancy a drink, a proper drink? Not some water with a hint of gin in it?'

'I'd love one, thanks.' They said in unison, then laughed.

Enjoying sitting back and going over every word, line, and laugh with this stranger, Cora finally relaxed as her tension slowly evaporated.

# 50

Early morning, the team bundled in still rubbing the sleep from their eyes. The coffee machine was being worked hard. The more money-conscious or organised clutched travel mugs in their hands.

It was one of those early morning starts when officers questioned why they were there until they remembered. For the love of justice and to put these bastards behind bars. They had her run through their mines. She was going down. This was what they had been working for.

Waiting for her team to settle and quieten, Cora read back what she had, and what she wanted to tell the team this morning when the phone rang.

'Morning Mrs, how's it going this bright and beautiful winter morning?'

'Selphie,' Cora groaned. 'How can you be so happy at this time of day? It's not even seven yet, and still dark. You're weird; you know that, don't you?'

'Still, not a morning person I see, and here was me with some good news for you. Your hunch paid off.'

'Don't keep me hanging, woman, out with it.'

'Well, I had to extract the DNA from the toothbrush that you sent Beverlee to collect.'

'Selphie, just the short version, please.'

'And not tell you about how amazing I am, and about how hard it was to get this information, and what I had to put to the side.'

'SELPHIE,' Cora shouted into the receiver, becoming frustrated. She hadn't had enough coffee throbbing through her veins for these games.

'Okay, keep yah knickers on, will yah? Jeez, haven't you had your fill of coffee yet?'

Cora kept quiet, waiting.

'Before you shout again, you were right, Harrison Drew is Amanda Kelly's son. I sent it over to the forensic scientists. They came back with confirmation just now. They found a match on the NDNAD. I asked if I could be the one to give you the good news, especially if you were gonna be as grumpy to them as you were with me.'

'You absolute beauty. Have I told you what a diamond you are? You're a legend.'

'You were getting annoyed with me not two minutes ago.'

'Aww, you know I don't mean it. You know I love you, really. Right. I'd better go tell the team. Thank you. You're the best. So, did you enjoy last night?'

'Yes, I think you will win this competition. You were by far the best. I can't wait till the next one.'

'Thanks, Selphie. See you later.'

---

Walking into the main room, the hubbub immediately died down. She didn't need to clap for their attention. The sight of all those faces looking in her direction expectantly never failed to amuse yet intimidate her.

'Okay, everyone. Morning. I said today would be the day that things came to a head. Already I've had some good news. I've just had a phone call from Selphie. Previous to that, I sent Beverlee to Amanda's to get her to sign a missed page on her statement and collect DNA for elimination purposes. She touched the homeless man before he died, so we have some more vital evidence. Selphie sent the buccal swab off to the forensic scientists, who checked it against the NDNAD and it's a match. The full report will be emailed over shortly.'

No sound, nothing. A pin dropping was a bomb going off. Watching silently from the back was Felix.

'First, the DNA that matched that of the suspect in the newsagent fire case was a mitochondrial DNA match. For those not aware of what that means, mitochondrial DNA runs down the mother's line.'

A ripple ran around the room for those who understood the implications. Feeling in a good mood, Cora thought she'd let someone else have the moment.

'Luke, you want to tell us why there was a reaction to that news for those that haven't got there yet?'

Smiling, Luke stood grinning with excitement.

'Yes boss, it means that Harrison Drew, the suspect in the newsagent's arson attack, is the son of Amanda Kelly.'

'Well done, Luke. Yes, that's exactly right. Thank you. The DNA is also a match for that on the small piece of fabric the DCI found at the crime scene. It seems there is little question that Amanda Kelly is responsible for murdering Peter Markham. We will now arrest her and bring her in. Any questions?'

'Are we going to tell her about Harrison being wanted for a crime?'

'Thanks, Guy, brilliant question, and at the moment, I don't think so. I think it's going to be too much for her to deal with, and we need to focus on the murder. Don't forget innocent until proven guilty.'

Giggles erupted around the room. With a positive DNA match and video showing her torching a car, it was unlikely she was innocent, but stranger things have happened, especially with lawyers.

'Before we go, any news on Harrison, any sightings?'

'A couple, boss, but he's never anywhere long enough to bring him in,' began Beverlee. 'He was caught on CCTV at Leagrave railway station, but there are a lot of fields and a bit of woodland around that area, so he may be lying low.'

'Okay. Jobs, usual place. Great teamwork. Let's get this sorted by the end of the day, and drinks are on me.'

A collective cheer erupted around the room. The noise level gradually increased as everyone started collecting belongings for trawling door to door. They were to speak to shops and residents.

Cora looked up and spotted Felix, still standing at the back. He nodded. She smiled to show she understood. Holding up her finger to say she'd be a minute when she turned back, he'd gone.

# 51

Amanda had staked out Helen's flat. Her mind was set on what she was going to do as she crossed town to the posher area. Crouching down in the bushes, she looked up at the building, but couldn't work out which flat was Helen's. There were no outward indicators of flat numbers. The buzzers were video-activated, so that wasn't an option either.

Frustrated and trying to keep warm, Amanda waited, her eyes looking for signs of life from the windows. The coldness bothered her only because it made her numb; her thinking instincts had reverted into a killer again.

Her confidence had been in thinking she could go straight in and confront Helen and hadn't foreseen a building as secure as this. Was she capable of killing Helen, her friend? It wasn't a simple question to answer. But it might have something to do with being unable to trust Helen. Okay, then, she would give Helen a chance and hear what she had to say. Would Helen give her a good reason not to kill her? Amanda couldn't decide what to do with her. She needed to get in and see her first.

Just like that, the solution came to her. She would pose

as an off-duty cop to one of the other flats, and say she'd seen someone prowling around. *They'd let her in for that, wouldn't they?*

Checking the sharp kitchen knife was still in place up her sleeve, she quietly stepped up to the buzzers, starting with flat 1.

———

Harrison was tired, cold, and hungry, so hungry. The nights were freezing, and the woods weren't the ideal place for hiding out and keeping warm. There was a little burrow where he curled up and put his coat over him, but he shivered the whole time. He wasn't stupid and knew he could be caught on CCTV, so the main shopping areas were a no-go.

After seeing the newspaper at the train station, Harrison knew the police would be looking for him after killing a man. What an idiot. His stupid temper again. Why had he set the fire? Why hadn't he checked first to see if there was anyone there? Because you just wanted to create a scene, didn't you? To break stuff and release anger, that's why. He couldn't last much longer, though. scavenging scraps of food from discarded takeaway wrappers near the bins was okay, but it wasn't enough. It was gross too, and once there was something else in the bag that he'd rather not remember.

By now, Harrison knew his foster parents hated him and were glad he was gone because if they cared, they would have texted or called him; they hadn't even tried to look for him. Mind you, his phone was dead now anyway. There isn't an available plug socket when you're slumming on the streets.

Leaning up against a tree, Harrison allowed the tears to fall. What was the point? Why carry on, he was screwed whatever he did. Neither was he cut out for living on the run. He was so cold. He wanted a hot shower and some of his foster mum's chilli followed by apple crumble and custard. Never again was he going to get that. A prison cell where he'd be someone's new best friend, or beaten black and blue, or he'd be found out here frozen to death.

Standing now with defiance, he would not end up like that. He may have been abandoned many times, but he would end it on his terms by creating a scene to make sure everyone knew why. Setting off, he headed towards the M1.

---

A couple of miles away from her home, Helen stared at her mobile phone. Nervously, she placed it on the table and stepped back like it might explode. She'd done the right thing; she knew she had. Last night, she had seen another side of Amanda. In all the years she'd known her, both at university and now, she had never seen her lose her temper or raise her voice. But last night, Amanda was furious, and this anger was something different. The word evil came to Helen's mind.

Could she be in any danger? If Amanda had killed Peter, which now she was convinced she had, then she could kill her. After everything Amanda had done, could she afford to leave a witness alive? Helen had never been so scared.

Confident that Amanda didn't know where she lived as she had never been there, but come to think of it, she hadn't been to Amanda's place either. In fact, she couldn't remember if Amanda had mentioned where she lived. The few times they went out, it was to a pub or restaurant. Thinking back over the many hundreds of conversations they'd had. Did she really know anything about her friend? A shiver ran down Helen's spine.

Doing the only sensible thing she could think of. Helen

picked up her phone and called Jack to ask him if she could stay with him for a while. She knew it was probably too soon in their relationship, but she couldn't worry about that now. She wanted to be held and feel safe.

# 52

In Felix's office, Cora went over the plan to bring Amanda Kelly in.

'So far, she does not know she's under suspicion, so it should be easy. I don't consider her a risk; she's already had her revenge. So, there is no need to go in with all guns blazing in the early hours of the morning.'

A quiet approach was better for the budget too, although Felix didn't say it, yet Cora knew.

Once the plan was in place, and everything was agreed upon, Cora went to speak to her small team. They had been working long hard hours and were ready to bring this case to a close, so all listened intently to what she and Felix had discussed. Cora looked around the room again.

'Anyone seen Darcey?'

'Got a call while you were in with the DCI, boss. Harrison Drew has been seen hanging off a motorway bridge looking like he is building up the courage ready to jump. Darcey leaped up straight away and said she'd go. We tried to talk her out of it and to leave it to the professionals, but it was mostly to her back as she was out the door in a shot.'

'Okay, thanks Luke, well great news on Harrison, I guess. Will try to send some uniforms to back her up, but I don't want to spook the kid. I don't know if he's truly suicidal or just trying to get attention.'

A hand shot in the air. 'Yes, Dave?'

'Probably not important now, but we gleaned information from Peter Markham's phone which confirms his various affairs, but there was no mention of Amanda Kelly or rape. He er laughs with Montgomery about getting rid of *troublemaker* Tracy Littlechild, so her dismissal was unfair and spot on. Definitely a different tone with the guys and gals, he messages and emails, but nothing damning. Pings give us a rough idea of the route Amanda would have taken, which we can't confirm because there were no CCTV cameras. She's been very clever indeed.'

'You sound impressed, Dave?'

'Not er impressed, boss, just respect that despite the attention to detail she put into this, it took a small piece of fabric and a farmer's nature camera to catch her.'

'Fair point. But there were a few other leads as well. Thanks for that Dave, great work. Right, just gonna let the DCI say a few words.'

Stepping aside, Cora let Felix give the group a rallying talk.

'Thanks for all your hard work, the commitment and long hours given to this case. I imagine your families will be glad to see what you all look like again.' The case was about over. 'I won't insult your intelligence and tell you what needs doing. I've seen how you work, and I'm impressed. When Amanda Kelly is in custody and the CPS have agreed to prosecution, we will celebrate. Until that moment, the work doesn't stop. Thanks all. I'll see you in the pub later.'

A spontaneous cheer and smattering of applause broke out.

Felix had been hanging around the periphery, quietly observing, but putting Cora on edge with feeling like she was being judged. She was grateful he wasn't a hands-on DCI and allowed her to do what she thought was needed and only step in if he had to. Nothing had been mentioned about that special moment after the fire, which was probably best. Work relationships, especially with the police, are never a good idea. She didn't even know if she wanted a relationship, anyway. The pressure was too much for that, and besides, she was fine on her own.

'Right, everyone, don't forget, we need to make sure all the paperwork is in order, all the i's dotted, and t's crossed, so when it goes it to court, they can't pick at anything we've done.'

A murmur ran around the room. Cora knew only too well how damaging a missed signature could be to a case.

# 53

Amanda slammed her front door.

'Not home, not home. Where the fuck is she?' She circled like a dog hunting for its tail. 'Of course, Helen was at Jack's. Shit, shit, shit. Now what am I going to do?'

Flinging herself on the sofa, the first thing that came to hand was the remote. It hit the wall and smashed as batteries flew everywhere. Hardly any damage, but did the trick of blowing out her anger and calming her down. Going to the kitchen, Amanda grabbed a glass of water and downed it.

Fishing her mobile from her pocket, she brought up 192.com. Simple, she thought as long as she kept her cool, she could find out exactly where Jack lived. This would be where Helen would be. She could draw her out, or sit and wait until she left his house for work in the morning. Fortunately, Helen had let slip that Jack's middle name was Rodney, which helped narrow the search down, and in a few clicks, she had his address. He lived in one of the big houses on the edge of town. Lucky Helen.

She didn't want to be shivering outside Helen's flat. In

her bedroom, Amanda threw open her wardrobe doors and searched for every warm item she owned. Including the heat pack she used when her sciatica flared. But she needed a plan to get at her. It would not be easy.

# 54

Darcey had caught the call saying that a young man had been seen waiting on the motorway bridge. A concerned motorist had been worried enough to call it in.

Pulling up close to the bridge without being exposed, Darcey approached as quietly as she could, but it didn't matter; Harrison's sharp ear heard her approach.

'Don't come any closer, copper. I'm not coming back over. I can't do this life anymore.' He was terrified. All the time, he was looking at Darcey and then at the motorway. 'It's all shit. What sort of chance does a kid like me have, especially if you arrest me like I know you're going to do.'

Darcey halted, shocked by the frankness of the young man. He was right, she needed to arrest him. A man had died in that fire, and Harrison had a lot of questions to answer. But even so, he still had something to live for.

'Okay, I'll chat to you from here, Harrison. I won't come any closer, but please, can you come back over the railings? You are so slight. I worry a strong gust of wind may take that decision out of your hands.'

'You think I really care? I'm done for. I got nothing left to live for now. I've really fucked up. I've been in the woods for days. I'm so cold, starving, and filthy. I'm no different from that poor man I killed. My foster mum won't want me back. I saw in the paper that a homeless man had died. His family was back in touch, don't you understand? I took a dad away from his kids. At least someone wanted him. No one wants me. I'll be another failed product of the system.' He took one arm off the railing to prove his point, wobbling, yet he stayed solid on the thin ledge for now.

'You don't know that, Harrison. There're loads of opportunities for everyone these days.'

'Listen here copper, I'm a lost kid, another of those sad ones that are pushed from pillar to post through the system. It was made clear we weren't wanted, first by our birth parents, then by any poor sod that takes us in before they realise we are too much hard work. What chance do I have?'

Darcey sighed. 'Of course, you have a chance, but sometimes you have to make opportunities, and you won't do that by hanging there.'

Harrison twisted slightly.

'Look, even the rich kids have little future as I see it. I'm not thick, no matter how I'm treated. Listen, I've got street smarts. I have two options, and I don't fancy either. To sit on benefits, or probably get drawn into a gang. Drugs, and OD my way outta this life or work my arse off from morning till night, earning enough to sit in a cold shit hole flat. No light or heating coz I can't afford to put it on and I ain't eaten for days. I've seen it with some of the older kids. That's their life now.'

Darcey had taken a couple of steps closer during this speech. Stepping with the utmost care so she didn't attract his attention, her hard gaze on his eyes defying him to see what she was doing.

'That's a very negative opinion you have, Harrison. Have

you ever looked into options? You can go back to school, go on to university and have a career.'

'Really miss? You think that? From where I'm standing right now, this is not the top of my list of priorities. First, you're gonna arrest me; you haven't said you aren't. I ain't thick, you know. So bam, I've got a criminal record; kicked out of me foster mum's house; expelled from school. Then what, no college, no education, poorly paid job coz that's all-ex-cons get.'

Darcey had taken another couple of steps, seeing Harrison wobble as he was getting more passionate and animated was causing her to panic. Occasionally, he removed the same arm he'd been using to make a point. She was scared that if she suddenly appeared behind him, he would be shocked into releasing the fragile grip he had on life.

'You don't know all this, Harrison. I bet you haven't even spoken to your foster mum, who, by the way, is sick with worry. She cares about you, you know. She's a very kind woman. She just wants you home and safe. We went to speak to them, and she said she just wanted you back where you belong. So, you can't assume she will kick you out. I can ring her now; she can tell you herself.'

'No offence copper, I don't believe you. I know you'll say anything to get me to come back over, but I have nothing to live for. I've fucked up; perhaps my birth mother should have aborted me. What good has giving me life done for me? Still messed up my life.'

Darcey opened and closed her mouth but couldn't think of anything to say that wasn't trite to anger him further.

'I can call her. I'm sure she just wants you home,' offered Darcey.

'NO. Don't call her. She doesn't deserve a fuckup like me. I will only bring her hassle. She is a good woman. I've brought the police to her door again. Was bad enough after we found that body. I'd be better if I was gone forever.' Eventually, the tears that had been threatening started trickling. Darcey saw what a scared young man he was. Being sent from home to home meant he had no stability and didn't have the support network he needed, or the unconditional love of family.

'Oh Harrison, that is simply not true. When I got the call that you'd been seen, the first person I called was your mother. She's not slept for days. She loves you, Harrison. She's told me that so many times. She told me she tries not to get attached to her foster kids, as they never seem to hang around for long, but she saw potential in you. She has a real soft spot for you and considers you the closest thing to a son she's ever had.'

'Really?' Harrison was surprised. 'She really said that. Like I was a son?'

'Yes Harrison, I am hardly going to make something like that up, am I? You're too smart. You'd see right through me. It's you who holds the power here. I just want to get you to safety. Will you come back over, and I will take you to your foster mum?'

Harrison shook his head vehemently.

'No. I've proper fucked up. Why would she want a son like me? I ain't got nothing to offer. I can't ever repay her for what she's done. I mean, I'm hanging off a motorway bridge coz the only way I could repay her is to smoke weed and set fire to a shop. I'm an idiot, a worthless waster.'

'Oh Harrison, don't you think we all did stupid stuff as kids? Admittedly, I never set fire to any buildings, but I did plenty of stupid things. Our parents expect it, you know. It's how we learn right from wrong. Now please come over the railing, you're making me nervous.'

The tears ran unchecked down his cheeks, and he said

something so quietly that Darcey had to strain to hear him over the traffic and the wind and everything else, but she was sure he said *I love her too.*

'If you love her, don't do this. It will destroy her.'

Speaking louder now, but barely audible, Harrison continued. 'Look miss, you don't get it. We learn quickly not to get too comfy, too attached, and have no possessions, so it's easier to pack up and move on. This time felt different. I had my own room; I had a wardrobe and clothes that weren't hand-me-downs. I could put stuff on the walls. Have a telly X box and stuff. She trusted me. She trusted me.'

There was nothing Darcey could say. She now realised why this young lad was hanging off a motorway bridge. Pushed from pillar to post all his young life, he'd finally found somewhere he might call home, and he'd messed up. But she was certain his foster mum would understand if she could just get him back over the railing.

She'd edged almost close enough to grab the boy if he decided to jump. Yet Darcey still hoped it wouldn't come to that. But he was listening. He seemed to take in what she was saying. She hoped she'd build a rapport, one of the first rules of these sorts of things, not that it was her speciality. Now her heart was in her throat, and the tension was making her feel sick.

He suddenly spoke again, calmer now.

'You did stupid stuff, really? How come you got to be a cop then, thought you lot had to be squeaky clean.'

Darcey laughed. 'I never said I broke the law, Harrison. I just said I'd done stupid stuff. I was influenced by my friends and got swept along in the excitement of it. Do you know when I was not much younger than you are now? We didn't even have the Internet, so we had to amuse ourselves in different ways.'

Harrison smiled slightly.

'Wow miss, you're old. But I'm still not coming over. I'm a mess. I have thoughts all the time of hurting myself, yah know. My brain has this constant noise, telling me to do stupid things, and reminding me of every stupid thing I ever did. I can't escape it; I'm fucked in the head. My foster mum could see it, she knew. I don't know how she knew, but she knew. She hugged me. I don't think I'd ever been hugged before. So, what do I do to repay her, bring drugs into the house, and set fire to a shop? What a prick. Prick, prick, prick.'

The last of these were punctuated with punches to his forehead, making his grip on the railing even more tenuous.

It gutted Darcey from the inside, not understanding how someone so young could feel that way. She'd had a normal upbringing, part of a two-parent family, loving and generous, not rich, but she didn't go without. Siblings she kept in touch with. She'd never been afflicted with any mental health issues, nor had any of her family, to her knowledge. She was feeling out of her depth, not knowing how to get through to this kid. But she would not let him go over. She had to try.

'That's not the answer Harrison, I promise you, there's medication that can help those thoughts. I've heard they do wonders these days, so please, just climb back over.'

Harrison shook his head but reluctantly turned to face her, eyes streaming down his wan and emaciated face, eyes puffy and haunted.

'You don't get it, do you? You don't understand that I don't wanna live. I can't take this anymore. I want to stop it all, to end the noise and pain.'

It was at this point that Darcey realised she'd failed; she hadn't got through to him at all, and he was getting ready to let go, so she moved as quickly as she was able and managed to grab one arm and his coat hood. She thought for a moment he was trying to remove his coat so he could fall free of her grip. For one horrifying second, she thought he'd succeeded when the pressure on her arm lessened slightly.

What had actually happened was he'd spun round and grabbed onto the railing with both hands. He pulled himself up. Darcey grabbed an arm to help him as he didn't have the strength to do it himself. And then he was over and holding on to her.

'C'mon Harrison, let's go,' she enclosed him with her body heat nearly in tears herself. She would remember this moment forever. 'I'll put the heaters on in the car. I think there's some of my secret chocolate supply in the glove box. Is that a deal?'

He nodded just a little boy really as he allowed Darcey to lead him to the car. She spared him the indignity of arresting him by putting him in the back seat. He'd needed to be checked over at a hospital first.

Making sure he fastened his seatbelt, Darcey breathed out, and relaxed into her seat for a moment. The tension of the exchange had completely drained her. Checking her phone, there were a couple of messages and a missed call. She deliberately left her phone in the car, so it didn't ring and scare the kid. Realising there was nothing urgent to reply to, she buckled her seatbelt and set off.

The boy sat quietly, staring. Darcey wasn't sure if it was at anything in particular, or whether from shock. The car was warm, and she'd found a Wispa tucked away, which he demolished in seconds. They were on the motorway, the quickest route at this time of day. Her phone rang, and without thinking, she answered it hands-free.

'Sarge, what's up?'

'You get the kid?'

'Yeah, he's in the car, safe and sound. Don't think he's

eaten much the last few days, so he needs to be checked out in A and E. He's freezing, too.'

'The big boss wants him brought straight in and processed. Say nothing yet, but we think that kid might be the dead man's son from the woman Peter Markham raped when he was at university; she had a kid. Just waiting for DNA confirmation.'

'Understood, sarge. Think this kid might need checking out at A & E first, though.'

'Boss's orders, I'm afraid. See you soon.'

Harrison had sat up straighter. He'd heard the conversation that had taken place. He had just found out who his father was. Not that his father hadn't wanted him all these years, he didn't know he was alive. He'd raped his mother and then gone on his way. What a bastard. No wonder his mum gave him up. She wouldn't have wanted to see his face, to be reminded of him. He really was a worthless, unwanted, unloved stain on humanity.

The next few moments were a blur. Harrison waited for the opportune moment; they were speeding along at seventy miles an hour in the middle lane. Looking ahead, Harrison saw what he was waiting for, a huge articulated truck travelling on the inside lane. Waiting until they were alongside, he acted quickly. Grabbing the steering wheel with as much strength as he could manage, he yanked it out of Darcey's hands and slammed the car sharply into the side of the lorry. The bonnet caught the wheel arches. The lorry driver didn't notice what was happening behind him. The truck was always bouncing up and down. He just kept going, dragging the stricken car for another hundred yards, until the sparks and other drivers alerted him.

Harrison didn't make a sound, he died immediately, Darcey was too shocked to make a sound at first as they got pulled under, she released the most blood-curdling scream before the car was dragged and her head whacked the side window, knocking her unconscious. Silence fell.

The driver slowed and tried to pull over to the hard shoulder. The car was wedged into the undercarriage of his truck. Confused, he climbed out and went to investigate. What he saw nearly made him lose his mind. A young boy, a teenager, squashed against his seat. Dead with blood everywhere.

The driver, a woman, had fared little better. She was trapped but there was a slight moan as he leaned in. She was still alive. Running back to his cab, he grabbed his mobile and dialled 999.

# 55

Beverlee and Luke were sent to make the arrest. Luke knew she would have sent Darcey, but she was busy. No one had heard from her yet; he hoped she was okay. He was glad Darcey was going to bring Harrison in. She had the special touch needed with desperate and afraid people; he had a feeling Harrison would be both.

---

Luke let Beverlee drive so he could go over the plan again in his mind. He was nervous, but he would not let on. Beverlee was quiet, but she usually was. The low winter sun was reflecting off the frosty roads, making it difficult to see. Luke saw his breath rise as he breathed out; despite the sunshine, there was no warmth behind it.

Their destination, a block of flats appeared on the horizon. It was quiet at this time of day, except for a few walkers going to work. Slowly easing himself out of the car and putting on his hat, Luke waited for Beverlee to unravel herself and do the same. They both had the same expressions.

Without uttering a word, they walked to the flats and took the stairs to the third floor.

Luke knocked loudly with the special police knock, which they apparently all had. Three short, sharp, but loud knocks on the door. Beverlee stood waiting quietly behind him. A door squeaked open further down the corridor, and a head peeped out with a towel around his shoulders; nothing visible other than his chest.

'You looking for the woman in that flat mate? She ain't in. She went out ages ago, so you're outta luck, I'm afraid.'

Seeing where the voice came from, Luke looked up. 'Oh thanks pal, you sure?'

'Well, she ain't answering, is she? I'm sure, mate, her door doesn't half slam. I've complained about it a tonne of times, all the bloody good it's done me. Heard it bang about seven.'

Luke looked up as Beverlee swore, the first words she'd uttered since they'd left the station.

'Okay, thanks pal, can you do us a favour and ring me on this number when she returns?'

'Sure mate, as long as it's before I go to work. Gotta earn enough money to pay for me luxury lodgings init.' A wheezy cough laugh followed, and the man shut the door, not bothering with any further conversation.

'Fuck, where is she?' Luke turned about him. 'I thought the boss said this would be a simple arrest and transport.'

'No idea, but we'd better ring her and let her know the news. I'll leave that to you, young padawan. I'll be too busy driving.'

Luke got his phone out to call the station, but it was already ringing in his hand. It was Cora.

# 56

The house was set back off the road, like all the houses on this road. The residents of this street didn't have high walls or hedges. The driveways were long. It was apparent they felt safe. Amanda stalked low along the driveway of number 486, the home of Jack Rodney French. She was checking for a video doorbell or any other kind of camera or alarm that would alert them to her presence.

A cat jumped down off a wall and hissed at her, something she wasn't expecting. Gently Amanda shooed it away, but it wouldn't stop until she nudged it with her foot and then it got the idea. Not that she would hurt it, but it was getting on her nerves. Apart from the cat, everything was still and silent. There weren't many Christmas lights up here and the early morning dullness was more oppressive as the houses backed onto the Dunstable Downs on one side, and farmland on the other. The occasional owl screech was the only thing that disturbed the peace.

Stalking around the perimeter of the building, she checked all the windows, peering inside to get an idea of the situation. Everything was locked up tight, so Amanda checked under plant pots and doormats. The back door came up with a key which slid in smoothly. Depressing the handle, as quietly as she could, Amanda stepped inside.

Warm inside and the lingering smell of the curry they'd shared spoke of domesticity. Apart from the ticking clock nearby, there was no other sound. Easing around the large farmhouse-style table in the centre of the room, she was searching for something sharp. There must be knives somewhere. The fourth drawer gave her what she needed. Touching her finger to the blade confirmed it was sharp enough.

Softly moving across the tiled kitchen floor which way would lead her upstairs. Two doors, fifty-fifty chance. Damn. A living room and another cat ready to hiss. Close this door, open the other one. Another tiled hallway, and a staircase at the end. Laying her hand on the bannister, she put her foot on the first step and gently lifted her full body weight, testing for creaks. There were none. On to the next.

Reaching the top, she tiptoed looking for the bedroom where the couple would be sleeping. There was only one room where the door was shut tight, so she made for that.

Easing the door open, this was the right room upon seeing two bumpy shapes in a double bed, gentle snores coming from Jack's side. Biting her lip, she didn't want to kill them both, but would it be possible to stab Helen and leave?

As she went to lift the knife, a pair of eyes were staring up at her.

'What the fuck do you think you are doing in my bedroom? Who are you?' yelled a man's voice. 'I'm going to call the police?'

'Who I am doesn't matter; this doesn't concern you; this is about me and Helen, and the lies she might have told the police about me. You see, we knew each other a long time ago, and she saw something she wasn't supposed to. I can't let her reveal my secret, and for that, she must die.'

This woman was talking out of her mind.

Helen had stirred and was now looking up at the knife blade poised directly over her. She didn't look shocked; it was as if she'd been expecting Amanda.

'Amanda? Why are you doing this?'

'I've come for you. You have to die—you do understand—don't you?'

While Amanda was distracted, she hadn't noticed Jack leaving the bed, and hastening to grab hold of the knife. She was so obsessed, Amanda hadn't seen jack. Taking her wrist, he twisted it around, so now it was pointing back at her. She was no match against his strength. In this unprepared moment, all her training left her.

'Kill me then if you're going to, or let me go,' screamed Amanda, struggling against Jack's strength.

'Helen darling, call the police. As you know this woman, and I'm sure you can explain the situation more clearly than me.'

Amanda watched as Helen took her mobile to dial 999.

# 57

'Luke, where are you?'

'Outside Amanda's block of flats, boss, we've just got back in the car. She's not home. A neighbour on the same floor heard her leave in the early hours. He was sure because her door slammed loudly. I've left him my card to let me know if she turns up.'

'Brilliant Luke. We know where Amanda is. We received a 999 call five minutes ago from an agitated woman called Helen Carlisle. Amanda is with her, so can you both get over there and arrest her as planned, and bring her back here? I'll send the details over.'

'Wow. Okay, yes boss, will do.'

Heart palpitating with excitement, Luke turned to Beverlee.

'Change of plan. Amanda Kelly turned up at the house of a Jack French, his girlfriend Helen Carlisle was staying over, and woke up to find Amanda standing over the bed with a knife ready to stab her. Jack subdued her and Helen managed to call 999.'

'Well, fuck me sideways, that's a turn-up. Where we off to then?'

Holding on to his mouth, Luke tried to keep back a snort of laughter.

'What?' said Beverlee.

'I don't think I've heard you speak more than five words since I've met you. I never expected you to come out with that.'

'Well, buckle in cupcake, there's more of that where it came from. Shall we go arrest us a murderer or what?'

Starting the car, Luke stole a sideways glance at Beverlee and wondered why she'd started speaking now.

Arriving at the house, the two detectives were let in by a dishevelled woman in a pyjama short combo and spiky bed hair. She directed them into a sitting room where Jack had led Amanda, using tie wraps to keep her hands bound in front of her. She wasn't making a noise, sitting subdued, as calm as a mouse.

Luke read Amanda her rights, then let Beverlee lead her out to the car.

---

When Cora ended the call to Luke, it immediately rang in her hand; she cursed, before she realised it was a number she didn't recognise.

'Hi, DI Cora Snitton, Bedfordshire Police. Can I help you?'

'Hi DI Snitton, this is DI Faisal from the Collision and Investigation Unit. Earlier this evening, there was a serious collision on the M1. A car crashed into a lorry. The front of the car was squashed under the trailer wheels.'

'Okay, yes, and why are you telling me this? That's yours to deal with.'

'There were two victims in the car. One died at the scene, the other is severely injured. She's in intensive care.

The surviving occupant of the car was Darcey Clarke. We found her police badge and her mother asked that we contact you.'

Cora didn't respond. She just snatched her coat and ran out the door. No, no, no, not Darcey, not sweet Darcey.

# 58

Hayley walked into the room, still laughing at something Dave had told her. Luke raised his eyebrows; laughter wasn't the place which instantly sobered up Hayley. Everything was ready, so she quickly pulled the chair out and opened her notebook.

Leaning over, Luke started the machine. The legal stuff had already been handled and now he sat back. They'd agreed that Hayley would begin woman to woman to see how they got on.

'Good morning, Miss Kelly. We've had quite the run-around getting you here. I see you've chosen Ms St James to represent you. Are you all set?'

Amanda sat stiffly but appeared to be numb yet nervous. In fact, if Hayley were to describe her demeanour right now, she would say it was indifference. Amanda's hands were on the table in front of her. Not even the tiniest tremble was evident. Her knees weren't bouncing. She wasn't relaxed, but she certainly wasn't tense and looked straight at Hayley as she spoke. She was ready to listen and respond like this wasn't a murder charge being levelled against her.

'Yes pet, I've spoken to Ms St James, and explained that I know the seriousness of the charge, but I am going to answer your questions as fully and honestly as I can. This is against my solicitor's advice, but I don't feel it's in my favour to lie or obfuscate at this point.'

Luke saw the solicitor readjust herself in her seat, unhappy about her client's decision, but unable to do anything about it. Crossing her leg, she still had her pen raised over her legal pad. St. James had been a solicitor for many years and was a familiar face around this police station. Luke was surprised that Amanda had chosen such a high-profile legal representative if she was planning to confess, anyway.

'I would ask one favour, if I may?'

'Yes, what is it Ms Kelly, or would you prefer Amanda?'

'Amanda is fine, and my question is, how did you catch me—what did I miss?'

'We'll come onto that in time Amanda, first, I want to hear your story, the version of events in your own words. If we have questions along the way, we may stop you, but please, this is your opportunity.'

Amanda took a deep breath as if she knew this moment would come, it had been one of her fantasies reenacting this scene and seeing their expressions when she told whoever it was what had happened to her, yet she had never suspected that she would ever get caught.

'I imagine that a lot of this won't be new to you. I assume you've picked my life apart by now to the tiniest detail. You'll also know that the dead man raped me at university, that we had a son who I gave up for adoption, and that my rapist got away with it. What you won't know is how that broke me, how my confidence and my future were ripped away. I was already a child of a horrific upbringing, I'm not sure that's something you'd have come across in your investigations, but I was born to a druggie mum, weaned off from birth, abandoned, taken in, and abused by my stepfather. Champion. Does that excuse what I did? No, I suppose not.'

'I'm sorry that you had such terrible experiences, but there is never an excuse for murder.'

'Do you want my story or not, pet?'

'Sorry Amanda, please continue.'

Consequently, Amanda laid it all out for them, how she'd gone off and researched the forensics, using the dark web to research murder weapons, torture methods, practising on pigs and the like until she'd perfected injuring without killing, but causing the most pain. She went on to detail the abduction of Peter and his subsequent torture, almost revelling in the retelling, and even showing how proud she was of herself.

The detective sat back in his chairs, not knowing what to say or think about this woman. That was quite a story, and it filled in a few gaps for them.

'Amanda,' said Luke. 'We believe we know what happened to the child you had as a result of the rape.'

Luke waited patiently as Amanda remained rigid. She didn't comment, just leaned back for a moment, and closed her eyes.

He smiled as Ms St James reached her hand out and asked if her client was okay. 'Do you need a break?'

'No, I'm okay, please do go on, detective.'

Ms St James merely nodded and repositioned her pen over her legal pad, although Luke noticed she'd written little. He wondered if it was the first time she'd heard the story in full to this much detail.

'You asked at the beginning how we caught you? We believe the son you gave up for adoption was responsible for the death of the man in a fire at a newsagent. By some strange fluke, it was the same fire you happened to discover and report to us. We also found a tiny piece of fabric that wasn't burned in the drum at the crime scene. We were able to extract your DNA from that, and it came up as a familial link.'

Amanda tutted, smiled, and shook her head.

'We also found the car you burned out where you had been so careful to conceal off the road and in a field. Unfortunately for you, it was caught on a new nature camera that had been installed by the farmer the previous week, which you weren't aware of. With clever enhancements, we got a clearer picture of your face.'

'When one of our Detective Constables came to get you to sign your witness statement for the newsagent arson, she also requested a sample of DNA. You obviously thought you'd covered all angles, but the tiniest scrap of fabric hadn't burnt, and that was all we needed.'

The room was silent except for the sound of all four people breathing. Eventually, he saw a tear of anger escape Amanda's eye. She had been completely emotionless until then, but that tear broke the dam.

'I don't want to go to jail. All my life I've been wronged and let down, I've been used and abused by men. If your sister, mother, or daughter were sitting here, would you not want some justice done? I was not given justice so, I had to take it myself.'

'We can't take the law into our own hands, Amanda,' Hayley replied. 'We just can't. I know you've been failed; I can't argue that you've been hugely let down, but what you did to that man was extreme. This was more than revenge. This was evil.'

Silence again.

'Are we done here?' asked Amanda. 'I have nothing else to say.'

Luke leaned over and ended the interview officially.

'Do you want any time with your solicitor before you get taken back to the cell?'

'No, I need to be alone.'

# 59

Cora quietly opened the door and stepped into the room. It was dark, the blinds were closed.

The still form of Darcey lay supine, with many tubes and wires snaking from her body, various machines by the side of her bed, constantly monitoring. The sound of the ventilator hissing and purring was hypnotic. The sterile smell of hospitals that Cora so hated was slightly less intense in here. It smelt different, although she wasn't sure what it was.

And yet Darcey looked untouched. Apart from the big bandage around her head and a few grazes on her face, there wasn't much else to show that she'd been in a horrific car accident.

All the damage was internal, though. The doctors had used lots of big words but said simply it was touch and go for the next twenty-four hours. She had swelling, a small bleed on her brain, along with the internal bleeding because of the impact.

Taking a seat by the side of Darcey's bed, Cora picked up her hand as gently as she could and squeezed it.

'Oh Darcey, I'm so sorry. I didn't realise there was so

much risk. I wish you never went up there. I know it was a freak accident, but I can't forgive myself. I feel like I am responsible.'

'It probably doesn't help, but Harrison died in the accident. Amanda killed Peter. And would you believe it? The young lad was Amanda Kelly's son. Although what she did to Peter Markham was horrific, yet I have sympathy for her. Imagine her life of being raped and abused when she was young and having had to give up her child and living her whole life knowing that. She watched her rapist smiling from the TV and snapped. I think the final straw for her was a mixture of the King's Honours list and seeing him standing proud with his family, especially his pregnant daughter. The remarkable thing about her was her honesty, but once she'd got it all out, she clammed up and hasn't uttered another word since. We've not told her that her son, Harrison, is dead.'

'She will do time, of course, but she has lost her son too. We aren't sure if they were aware of each other's existence. That will come out in the trial.'

Cora looked at Darcey's hand; it was still warm; she was still holding on.

'Darcey, I just need you to keep fighting. I don't normally work well with others, but I enjoyed you being alongside me. I've put in a request with the boss to make you a permanent part of my team.'

A tear slid down this tough woman's cheek. She let it fall. Sighing, she stood and patted Darcey's hand. It is strange how everyone looked tiny when lying in a hospital bed. Personality makes people seem larger than life.

Time to go back to the office and make sure all the i's were dotted and t's crossed. Taking one last look at Darcey, lying there, Cora said a silent prayer before opening the door and stepping out.

As Cora reached the double doors to leave the Intensive Care Unit, she wasn't aware of a sudden hive of activity; she didn't realise they were all running to the room she had just left; she didn't hear the monitoring machine announce Darcey's heart flatlining.

Printed in Great Britain
by Amazon